Read

P9-DGX-645

Acknowledgments

This book could not have come together without a great deal of prayer and research. For that reason, there are several people I must thank.

My main character in *Through the Storm* is an attorney. Since I didn't have the first clue what an attorney's day was like, I had to research it. I contacted several attorneys in an effort to obtain this information, but only one took the time to layout the entire process for me. Adrienne D. Brooks, an attorney in my hometown, returned my phone calls and answered all my questions. She also took the time to email me step by step court procedures. Without her, I wouldn't have known the difference between pre-trial and the actual trial process. Thank you Adrienne. And, much success to you in all that you do.

The pastor's commitment to save the lost in *Through the Storm* is inspired by my pastor; Pastor Paul Mitchell of Revival Center Ministries, International. He doesn't just talk about saving the lost; he meets them on their own turf and encourages them to give God a try. I will forever be grateful that God placed me in this ministry.

I have to give some serious thanks to my editor at Urban Christian-Joylynn Jossel. She believed in this project, and has done nothing but encourage me every step of the way. Joylynn, you are one in a million. Thank you for helping me make sure each book is what God has designed them to be. A special thanks also goes out to my publicist, Rhonda Bogan (You go, girl! Do you!) and Seana Reeves for taking the time to proof *Through the Storm* and provide invaluable feedback.

I am humbled by the number of bookstores, and book clubs, and readers that have decided to support my novels. You will never know how much your words of encouragement and continued support means to me. For this, I'm grateful.

Finally, I cannot forget to acknowledge my family (they'd break my writing fingers if I did). A special thanks to my daughter, Erin; new grand baby, Amarrea; my mother, and my niece, Diamond, for traveling the world with me while I promote my books. I would also like to thank my sister, Debra, and my cousins Kim and Schilala, for believing in me and helping me to accomplish my dreams. At times, this has been a hard journey, but family makes the difference.

Dedication

To my two month old granddaughter,
Amarrea Lillie Harris.
You have truly been the Lilly in my valley,
and I am blessed among women just to know you.

Prologue

The assassin trained the scope of his rifle toward the preacher's head and hesitated. His client had paid him to not just kill the preacher, but to make it a headshot. But, as he sat in the empty room on the third floor of the office building across the street from The House of God Christian Church, he couldn't muster up enough evil to carry out his client's order. He lowered his rifle, and walked the length of the small room deep in thought. He had no problem with killing the preacher. He'd do that in a heartbeat. But, what kind of cold monster could shoot a man in the head while he knelt down in prayer with his head bowed to God? The preacher had been in prayer for the past thirty minutes, and the assassin doubted that he would be done anytime soon. The preacher seemed so engrossed, happy, and so at peace with his time in prayer.

An idea struck the assassin and he smiled. He could shoot the preacher in the heart or the throat and tell his client his rifle slipped. He smiled as he walked toward his rifle, confident that he could finish the job. After all, this preacher man had done nothing to him. He never even met the man.

So, why should he shoot him in the face? His wife and children wouldn't recognize him. It didn't seem right. It would be an extremely cruel act that would cause the man's congregation to wonder for years to come if the preacher was truly dead or not. Closed casket funerals didn't bring closure to family and friends. Those kinds of funerals enabled miracle seekers to imagine that their dead might be just like Tupac—in a witness protection program or some other nonsense.

The assassin wasn't cruel enough to do that to the preacher's grieving family and friends. As a matter of fact, in the ten years he'd been an assassin, he'd never done a headshot. He wouldn't have taken this job either except for the fact that he'd already taken and spent his client's money by the time he received the call asking for a headshot.

He hoisted the rifle back onto his shoulder and peered through the scope to find his mark. Just as he suspected, his mark was still on his knees with his head bowed in prayer. But his mark now had company. A huge man stood behind the preacher. He was dressed in this long white gown. A belt hung at his waist with this long golden sword attached to it. The assassin wondered what was wrong with this freak. Why didn't the preacher stop praying and greet the weird looking man?

Before the assassin could ponder this weird turn of events, the man clothed in white pulled the sword from his side, lifted his massive body from the ground and flew. The assassin thought his scope allowed for some type of 3-D effect, because it appeared as if the man with the sword was flying toward him. Then, a strong wind blew into his room and knocked him down. He dropped his rifle and watched it violently slide against a wall while he was being thrown against a wall on the opposite side of the room. As the assassin slid down the wall and landed on his buttocks, he tried to focus his eyes so he could find his opponent. No one else was in the room with him. The assassin wasn't fooled though. He didn't knock himself down or throw himself against the wall. And, he'd seen that flying freak through the scope of his rifle.

The assassin wondered where the weirdo was as he started to crawl toward his rifle so he could look through the scope. But, in the next instant, the assassin watched as his rifle crumbled into a thousand little pieces as if the very hand of God had reached down from heaven and crushed it.

Angels, the assassin thought as his mouth hung open in awestruck wonder. He figured the guy must be an angel sent to protect the preacher. At that moment, the assassin realized two simple truths: there was a God in heaven, and he would pay a great price for all the wrong he'd done. He braced himself for the blow that would shatter him into a thousand little pieces like his rifle. When the blow didn't come, the assassin stood, calmly brushed off his clothes, and for the first time in his life, walked away and left a job undone.

The majestic glory of God shown bright as He sat on His throne looking down at His enemy. That old serpent, who'd tricked Eve in the garden, poisoned the minds of a third of the angels in heaven and aided millions of earthly souls in their descent to hell stood before God accusing Isaac Walker of not being a true servant of God.

"Lord, I understand that You are pleased with this preacher man's progress, but do You truly believe that Isaac Walker is crusading for You? What about the glory and accolades he himself receives?" Satan asked.

The Lord had heard it all before. Satan was a creature of habit. Each time one of God's warriors became too much of a threat to Satan's kingdom, he would ask God for permission to send that warrior through the storm to prove whether he or she would still praise God in the midst of tragedy. Time and time again, God's warriors had stood against Satan's assaults and brought joy to God's very being. But, He'd also lost a lot of good men and women during this shaking process. So once His enemy left the throne room, thunder and lightening sparkled from the throne of Grace, then Michael's glorious nine-foot form stood. His colorful wings glistened as they flapped in the air. "Yes, my Lord," he said, as he received command from the Lord.

Michael left the throne room and walked from the inner court toward the outer court of heaven to convene with Aaron, the captain of the host. He past unnumbered mansions in the inner court; where there was room enough for everyone. But, Michael knew that the beauty and splendor of heaven would only be enjoyed by the few that served God. As he passed by the room of tears, he glanced in and shook his head in wonderment. It still amazed him that humans had tears so precious that God would bottle and preserve them in a room as glorious as this. He stepped in and looked at the tear bottle with Isaac Walker's name on it. It was not full yet, but before it was all over, Isaac and his family would cry a river of tears. Michael shook his head as he walked out of the room and continued on his journey toward the inner court.

A great multitude of warrior angels stood in the outer court waiting on their assignments. Their appearance was that of beauty and majesty. They wore white radiant garments with gold edged trim that embellished the front of the garment. At their waist hung a huge golden sword, and large white wings flapped from behind. Michael's sword was longer and heavier than the other angels'. Jewels were embedded throughout the handle of this massive sword, a symbol of his many victories. The belt that held his sword sparkled with the gold of heaven. Michael had defeated the Prince of Persia more times than he cared to remember. But, the enemy was getting stronger as his time drew near.

Michael eagerly awaited their next meeting. It would be their last.

"We're going to have a fight on our hands this time, Captain Aaron. I need you to pull together a host of heaven's best for this assignment," Michael said as he handed Aaron the scroll that was in his hand.

Aaron took the scroll, looked at it and then reported, "Brogan just stopped an assassination attempt on this preacher's life. Are you saying we are facing even more trouble than that from the enemy?"

Michael patted Aaron on the shoulder. "You may lose some soldiers on this one, my friend."

Aaron unsheathed his mighty sword and declared, "We will still fight, sir. For all that is holy and all that is right."

Chapter 1

Pastor Isaac Walker smiled as he instructed the sorrowful man standing before him to raise his arms and surrender to the Lord. "Repeat after me, Joey," Isaac said as the man lifted his tatted arms. "I believe that Jesus Christ is the Son of God and that He died and rose again so that I might be saved."

Joey McDaniels lived a life of hustling, drug dealing, and womanizing. The scars on his face told stories of knife and cat fights. Joey's sunken cheeks proclaimed that he started getting high on his own supply of drugs. This meant he was about to lose his hold on the ghetto kingdom he worked years to establish. Isaac knew Joey only had six good months of street life left in him, that's why Isaac and his evangelistic team ministered to Joey every time they caught him on the street. The evangelistic team's persistence paid off. Joey, the drug dealer, stepped into The House of God Christian Church today, and Isaac preached a message that caused Joey to believe he could change his ways. Joey walked down the aisle when the call for salvation went out to the congregation.

And now as tears streamed down his scar tarnished face, Isaac hugged him and said, "You did it, Joey. You did it."

Joey wiped the tears from his face as he stepped out the Godly embrace and asked, "I'm saved? You mean it?"

"God has saved you, Joey. He's not likely to change His mind about that," Isaac assured Joey just before sending him to the prayer room to have an altar worker pray with him again and give him a Bible and information concerning the Bible classes Isaac developed with his wife, Nina, for new converts.

"My life is going to be different now, I can feel it," Joey declared as he walked toward the prayer room with an altar worker.

The moment a new convert began to understand that God was truly with him or her always thrilled Isaac. At sixty-one, he had been a soldier in the army of the Lord longer than he had been a destroyer in the devil's camp. Life was good. Isaac hadn't experienced a sleepless night in over a decade. He was winning souls into the kingdom, after sixteen years of marriage, his wife was still in love with him, and his son was the youth pastor at his church. Isaac only had one problem. His daughter Iona Walker was threatening to bring back his insomnia. Isaac walked away from the joy of his pulpit, and walked toward his office to meet his wayward daughter.

As he opened the door to his office, an involuntary smile crossed his lips at the sight of his son, Donavan. His son was six feet, the same height as his old man. Donavan had the same chocolate complexion as Isaac. As a matter of fact, both his children had his chocolate kiss complexion and deep dimples. However, Donavan had his mother's hazel eyes and small button nose. Donavan was standing near his desk talking with the church secretary, Diana Milner. Diana had the schedule of events in her hand and Donavan was asking about certain dates. His daughter was seated on his black leather couch looking through her palm pilot.

The couch had been placed directly underneath a huge picture window. Isaac loved sitting there and watching his congregation. He liked seeing the expression of joy on their faces as they entered God's house. At times, the people looked as if they had allowed God to carry the weight of their world, if only for the two hours during Sunday morning worship service. Yes, Isaac knew that most of the people would continue to carry their own burdens once the service was over, but if they could forget for just a few hours; they would be free for a little while at least.

The parishioners that Isaac did not enjoy viewing through his window were the ones who walked into the house of God filled with scorn and puffed up with attitude. But, he didn't have to look out his window to see that. The queen of attitude turned off her palm pilot, and glared at him as he took a seat behind his mammoth size mahogany desk. She had dark cold eyes just like his. Of the two children, Iona, looked more like him.

"Hey, Dad," Donavan said as he moved from Ms. Milner and sat down next to his sister.

Ms. Milner put the schedule of events on Isaac's desk and said, "All the dates that have been requested for special events such as singles meetings, marriage retreats, and so on have been highlighted on your calendar. I just need an okay from you, so that I can let the auxiliaries know if their dates are approved or not."

"Thank you, Ms. Milner. I'll look over this and get it back to you some time next week," Isaac said.

Diana Milner made no attempt to leave until Iona glared at her and said, "That will be all." Iona pointed to Donavan, herself, and then extended that pointer finger to Isaac and continued, "We need to talk right now." No one in the room missed the meaning in Iona's words. Diana was not a part of their inner circle.

Diana's high yellow cheeks turned red with embarrassment as she lowered her head and walked out of the office. Iona didn't care. She wasn't fooled one bit by long skirt-wearing-praise-dancing Diana Milner. She was after Donavan, but if Iona had anything to say about it, that snake would not be slithering into a princess cut diamond ring purchased by Donavan Walker any time soon.

"Was your rudeness necessary, Iona?" Donavan asked when Diana closed the door.

"Forget her," Iona said as she picked up one of Isaac's crystal eagles off of his credenza and stood. "I want to know what's on Daddy's mind, and why he feels the need to constantly summons me to this office like I'm ten years old and on the principal's naughty list."

Isaac leaned back in his seat and studied his twenty-six year old daughter. Nothing about her was like the ten-year old child who'd given her life to Christ. She was now about 5'7 with a lean athletic body and a go-to-Hades expression on her deep chocolate face.

"Calm down, Baby Girl." Isaac said. "I just need to talk with you for a minute."

Iona's chestnut eyes flashed with fire as she put the crystal eagle back on the credenza and strutted over to her father's desk. She clenched both sides of his desk and leaned in closer to Isaac and said, "You want me to calm down, Daddy? Then please stop calling me Baby Girl, and stop summoning me to your office."

Still seated on the leather couch, Donavan leaned forward and said, "Stop trippin', Little Sis—you know Dad isn't trying to treat you like a child."

Iona whirled around to face off with Donavan. Her thick shoulder length hair fell back into its perfect layers, when she came to an abrupt stop. With one hand on her left hip and her pointer finger shaking in Donavan's face, she declared, "See what I mean. You and Dad are always coming to my office with this Baby Girl and Little Sis stuff. I'm a professional, and beyond that, I'm a grown woman. And, I'm tired of the two of you making me seem like less in front of my peers."

Donavan laughed as he said, "Drama queen."

"Golden boy," Iona spat back at him.

Isaac looked at his children. Well no, not children—these were adults that happened to come from his seed. Donavan, his oldest, was mild tempered and humble like his mother. Iona was all spit and fire, totally confrontational, and didn't care who knew it. Maybe that's why she went to law school, and Donavan went to seminary. Isaac raised his hand and said, "All right, all right, you've made your point. I won't call you Baby Girl when I come to your office. But when you're in my office . . ."

He let that thought trail off and Iona caved with a smile. "Okay, Daddy, you win. When I step foot in your world I'm Baby Girl."

"Okay, so can we get down to the reason I asked you to meet me in *my* office?" Isaac calmly asked his Baby Girl.

Iona had gotten her point across, so there was no more reason to fight. She sat back down on the couch next to her brother and said, "What's up, Daddy? Nothing's wrong with Nina-Mama is it?"

Nina was Isaac's wife and Donavan's mother—Iona's mother was Cynda Williams. Although she was beautiful, she had been a cantankerous woman who'd caused a whole lot of problems for Isaac and Nina until they all learned how to get along for the sake of the children. Iona had lived with Isaac and Nina since she was ten years old, so Iona had taken to calling her stepmother Nina-Mama. Because it just felt right to her.

"Everything is fine. Nina just has a touch of the flu, so I told her to stay home this morning. But the first thing I want to know from you is how Joey's case is going?"

Iona rolled her eyes. "Daddy, will you please stop asking me about Joey McDaniels? I have an investigator looking into everything right now—but he doesn't even go to court until August. This is February, so I don't have any updates. Okay?"

Isaac's eyes lit up as he asked Iona and Donavan, "Did you see him walk down to the altar today? That boy is saved!"

"You didn't give up on him, Dad. You should be proud," Donavan said.

"No, son, I'm not proud; I'm humbled that God would even allow me to help people like Joey." Isaac turned back to Iona and said, "Speaking of which." He opened the top, left side drawer on his desk and pulled out a picture and newspaper clipping. He stood up and walked it over to Iona. "I have another client for you." He handed Iona the material and reclaimed his seat.

Iona shook her head. "Oh no, not this again. I told you from the jump that I became a lawyer to get rich. I'm not interested in handling these pro bono cases you keep bringing me."

"Look at the information, Baby Girl. The man is innocent," Isaac told her.

"So was Vinny the three time loser and Robbie the preschool drug dealer," Iona said without looking at the information in her hand.

Isaac nodded. "Okay, I was wrong about those two, but you have to admit, the other clients that I sent to you have been innocent, right?"

"Innocent and broke," Iona whined.

Donavan took the stuff out of her hand, turned the picture and newspaper clipping right side up and then placed it back into her hand. "This guy needs your help, Sis. We're asking you to do this for the family," Donavan told her.

"There you go trying to put somebody on a guilt trip," Iona said as her eyes fell on the photo. It was a Most Wanted picture printed off the internet. Iona's eyes widened. "That's Clarence Mason."

"Donavan went to high school with him," Isaac said.

"I know that. I also know that Clarence just pulled off a three million dollar jewelry heist." She held up the newspaper clipping knowing exactly what it was about. "He can afford the best attorney that money can buy. Why would he want me? I mean, I know I'm good, but I've only been practicing law for two years."

"First of all, Clarence doesn't have any money, so he can't just hire any attorney he wants. And, I told him that you would be his best bet," Isaac said, and then added. "Look, Iona, I've been witnessing to this guy for months, so when Johnny arrested him, he used his one phone call to get in touch with me."

Iona held up her hand. "Wait. You're telling me that Johnny Dunford arrested this guy and now you're trying to get him a lawyer?"

Johnny Dunford was a deacon at the church and one of Isaac's most dedicated members. He also happened to be a cop.

"Johnny will understand. I'm just trying to help someone in need of a break," Isaac stated.

Iona rolled her eyes. "You're not just trying to give a guy a break. You're doing the minister thing; down at that prison preaching Jesus as always. When are you going to finally wake up and realize that some of these guys aren't worth saving?"

"Iona! What's wrong with you? This is our life. We preach to these people because we believe God can make a difference," Donavan angrily said.

Holding up the five finger disconnect to Donavan, Iona said, "You are such a suck up. When will you ever have a thought that doesn't originate in Daddy's head first?" She then turned to Isaac and said, "I'm not mad at you, Daddy. Preach Jesus to all the criminals in the downtown jail. Hey," Iona said with a smile, "it's admirable."

"Then take the case, hon," Isaac said.

"Dad, you know how busy my schedule is right now?"

"This case will be a huge deal, Iona. Think of how it will look on your resume if you get Clarence off," Isaac said.

Iona sat quietly for a moment looking at the mug shot, and the newspaper account of the robbery. Then she smiled to herself. She looked back up at Isaac and said, "You know what, Daddy?"

"What, Baby Girl?"

"I think I will take this case." She stood up and headed toward the door. "Now if you gentlemen will excuse me, I have to go buy some new outfits. I bet there will be tons of reporters at the courthouse for this case, and I must look my best for the cameras. This might even end up on Court TV," Iona said, giddy with excitement as she closed the door behind her.

Donavan leaned back on the couch and shook his head.

"That's my Baby Girl," Isaac said sarcastically. "Always doing the right thing for the right reason."

Chapter 2

Iona strutted into the Dayton Municipal Courthouse at 8:50 am, ten minutes before the judge would be seated. She was wearing a Michael Kors eyelet trench with a matching MK satchel. Underneath her coat, she wore a pale blue pants suit that gave her butt that J-Lo look. Her hair was neatly and professionally pulled back, giving her face an exotic look that caused the handcuffed, red jumpsuit wearers and the gun totting boys in blue to stop and stare. Hey, if she was going to be on TV, she might as well look good. She might even end up with her own TV show like Star Jones. From attorney to television personality—Woo Hoo!

"Good morning, Ms. Walker. You're looking very nice today," a dreadlock wearing security guard told Iona.

"Thanks, Malcolm. How's that new baby?" Iona asked the security guard as she handed him her satchel and briefcase and prepared to go through the metal detectors.

"He's about thirteen pounds now," Malcolm told her as she walked through the metal detector.

"Thirteen pounds? I thought he was only two months?" Iona asked as she took her satchel out of Malcolm's hand.

Malcolm smiled and rubbed his big stomach. "What can I say? He got his appetite from his old man."

Iona laughed as she got on the elevator heading to the third floor. She was never nervous when going through the medal detectors, because she kept her gun in the glove compartment of her Lexus. She had a license to carry the gun, and with all the criminals she worked with, Iona thought it quite prudent to have it handy when she was out and about.

She walked into courtroom B, where Clarence the jewel thief was shackled and in a red jumpsuit waiting for her to arrive for their first date. That's what she called the court appearances she made with her felony clients—dates. She smiled at the bailiff and sauntered over to him. He'd actually asked her out a few times. So, she was a little uncomfortable that she couldn't remember his name. Poor bailiff with the afro. Hey, maybe that's what she should call him–Afro Man. She rubbed her chin as she wondered if he would respond well to his new name. Anyway, she turned Afro Man down every time he'd asked and she didn't have the heart to tell him that, for the last two years, she only dated her clients.

Afro Man smiled as she inched closer. Iona's smile brightened when she noticed that Afro Man did indeed have his name tag on today. "Hey, Stan, how's it going?"

"Not too bad. But, I would be a lot better if you'd go to dinner with me," he replied.

Iona leaned in as close as she could without touching him and whispered, "Stan, you know I would love to go out with you." She lifted her briefcase. "But, I'm just so busy trying to clear all these cases that I don't have time for myself, let alone a dinner and a movie."

Stan leaned down and whispered into her ear. "Well, you let me know when your load gets lighter, okay?"

That's what she wanted to hear. She smiled coyly at him. "Actually, my load could get a little lighter right now if you want to help me."

Stan opened his arms wide. "Hey, you name it. If I can do it, it's done."

Too bad he wore an afro, Iona thought as she said, "I need to speak with my client in the holding cell."

He took a step back. "You're too late, Iona, Judge Eden is about to come to the bench."

Iona had a problem with time. Her law professor and her hair stylist told her that she didn't respect other people's time. She was working on it. Iona put her hands together in a steeple as if praying to the bailiff god. "Please, please, please help me. I'll never ask again."

He hesitated, but only for a moment, then said, "Okay, two minutes and that's it. What's your client's name?"

"Clarence." Iona almost called him Clarence the jewel thief, but managed to reign herself in long enough to say, "His last name is Mason."

The guard led her back to the holding area. Iona sat down next to her shackled client, and took out her notepad. Clarence was a high yellow freckle faced man. He stood about five-seven and weighed no more than a hundred and sixty pounds. He was definitely too short and thin to do a dime in prison.

She didn't bother to introduce herself. If he didn't re-member her from high school, too bad. Iona took a pen out of her purse and asked Clarence, "Do you have family? A wife? Children?"

"Hey, Iona, thanks for helping me. It's nice to see you," Clarence said with a smile and a friendly tone.

"Family? Wife? Children?" Iona repeated.

The smile left Clarence's face as he responded, "I've been married for nine years. We have two boys and a new born baby girl."

Iona jotted down the information. "Do you have a job?" Iona asked, trying to ignore the loving way Clarence said 'baby girl'.

"Yeah. That's why I don't understand why the police think I would jeopardize a job I've worked on for seven years to pull some robbery."

She didn't look up. Her face and ink pen were still trained on her note pad as she told him, "Save the outraged indignation for the witness stand." Then she asked, "Place of employment?"

"I'm a computer analyst for Rite Stop."

Iona put the pen down and finally looked at her client. "Okay, I've got what I need. Today, we're entering a plea of not guilty and will try to get you out on bail. We'll discuss our strategy once you're out of here."

Exasperated, Clarence clenched his fists. "I didn't do it. Just get me out of here. I don't belong in jail."

"Whatever," Iona said, and then added, "Look, if the judge grants bail, will you be able to come up with it?"

"My wife and I already discussed this; we'll put up our house."

Iona stood. "One last thing." She pointed her finger indicating the direction of the courtroom. "This right here, it's our first date. And, it's on the house. You can thank my father for that." She put her hand on Clarence's shoulder and added, "But, if you want to go steady with me, it will cost you a minimum of twenty-five thousand. So, either get my money, or find yourself another lawyer." With that, she went back into the courtroom to handle her date's bail hearing.

It took two hours for her case to be called. *There is definitely too much crime in this city*, Iona thought as she shook her head. Once before Judge Eden, it only took fifteen minutes to plead and have a hundred thousand dollar bail set. It might have been a lot of money for some, but Iona was sure a jewel thief like Clarence could come up with the ten percent bond without batting an eye.

Clarence shook Iona's hand with one of his shackled

hands. "Thank you. Your dad said you were the best. You don't know how much this means to me."

Iona smiled as she leaned closer to Clarence's ear while still holding his hand. "You like what I did for you today? You want to take me to the prom? Then get my money when you get the bail bondsman his." She let Clarence's hand go, put her file back in her briefcase and then attempted to walk out of the courtroom to get her five minutes of fame with the reporters that awaited her outside.

Assistant District Attorney Jerome L. Tyler tapped her on the shoulder. When she turned he asked, "I thought you were trying to build your career. Why would you take on this loser of a case?"

Iona stared at the three piece suit in front of her. His wire rimmed glasses only further displayed how uptight he was. His mustache and sideburns were trimmed and well groomed. Although he claimed he was Black and Native American, his hair was processed.

"Refrain from meddling in my business, Jerome," Iona told him.

His face tightened. "I asked you not to call me Jerome."

That's right. Jerome preferred to be called JL, because Jerome was too urban. But, who was she to judge? If her mother named her Chiquita or something equally fruity, she would have had her name legally changed rather than using initials. "Look, JL, I've really got to go."

He lightly wrapped his hand around her arm, halting her exit. "All I'm saying is, this is the wrong case to try to build a name for yourself. Clarence Mason robbed that jewelry store, and you're going to look like a fool in court."

She pulled her arm from his grasp. "Get off my back. I'm doing a favor for my father. So, whether it's a dud or not, I have to take the case. Okay?"

When Iona stepped outside, the paparazzi was waiting. The bulbs of cameras flashed in her face as she recited, "No comment" to every question asked about her client or the case. By the time she reached her car, Iona's adrenaline was pumping. Forget Star Jones, she was going to be the next Johnny Cochran, and Clarence the jewel thief was her very own OJ. She just hoped that the prosecution would find the gloves used for the jewelry heist. "Lord, God if you're listening, please don't let the gloves fit," Iona mumbled as she drove off.

Chapter 3

When Iona arrived at the offices of Smith, Winters & Barnes, her secretary, Vivian Stellar, handed over a stack of pink telephone messages. Iona put her briefcase on her desk, sat down and went through the messages. There were two from her mother. But, Iona couldn't deal with Cynda Williams right now. She sat those messages on her desk, and continued to sort through them. Three calls came from Larry the assassin. Iona laughed as she crumbled up the messages and threw them in her waste paper basket. Iona might represent thieves, dope heads, drug dealers, and the like, but she absolutely refused to represent anyone who killed people for sport.

The Porsche dealership had left her a message. Iona currently had a two-year old creamy white Lexus. She loved her car, but felt there was no harm in keeping her options open. Never know when the right case would land in her lap and offer up enough money to make it possible for Iona to upgrade. She would call him once Clarence the jewel thief paid up. The law firm would get their cut, but she'd still have a hefty amount to put in her bank account. All the other messages were from her second, third, fourth, and fifth offender clients.

She picked up the telephone and started returning calls, only to discover that her clients needed her assistance yet again. Whoever said crime doesn't pay hadn't checked a defense attorney's financial records. The last call she returned was to Stan, the TV star. He had been caught on tape and millions of people viewed him on *America's Dumbest Criminals*. Now, he wanted her to get him out of the jam a water pistol and saggy pants got him into.

Stan had walked into the all-night convenience store on Main Street, demanded all their money, while holding one side of his pants up with his free hand. The clerk gave up the money, but as Stan was walking out the door, he accidentally squirted his water gun, slipped, fell in the puddle of water and then couldn't get up because his pants kept falling down. The store owner grabbed his bat and commenced to beating Stan like he'd stole something, which he had, until the police showed up. Now Stan wanted to sue the store owner for attacking him. She was in the middle of explaining to stupid Stan that they needed to get through his criminal case before worrying about suing the man he was caught on tape robbing when she heard a commotion at her secretary's desk. Iona and Vivian took karate classes together, so Iona knew that Vivian could take care of herself, but she still wasn't going for anyone messing with Vivian.

Iona got up and angrily swung the door to her office open. Vivian was saying, "I have already told you that I gave your messages to Ms. Walker. I cannot make her return your calls."

Larry Harris or better yet, Larry the contract killer, leaned his big bulky linebacker body over Vivian's desk and got in her face. "And I already told you, I demand to see her right now!"

Vivian stood and got back in his face. That's what Iona liked about Vivian. She didn't back down to anybody.

"Like I said—"

Iona interrupted. "I got it, Vivian." Iona then turned to Larry and said, "Come into my office, Mr. Harris." She opened the door wider so Larry could get his meaty head and bulky shoulders through the door.

Larry had to be at least an inch shorter than Iona, no more than five-six, with a shiny bald head and muscles that made Mr. Clean look like a wimp. He sat down in front of Iona's desk and said, "Thank you for seeing me. Now, can we get down to business?"

The last time Larry had been in her office, Iona had wanted to give him a lecture. Something like: *Killing is bad, stop it!* Iona sat down behind her desk. She stared at Larry for a moment. He was totally self-absorbed and in love with his whole persona. Iona, however, was not impressed. She had never liked men with big bulky biceps; always thought they had to be compensating for some physical or mental flaw. With this guy, she got the impression that he was definitely compensating for mental flaws. "What business do we need to get down to, Mr. Harris?"

He snapped at her. "Would you cut the Mr. Harris crap? When we spoke last week I told you to call me Larry."

Iona nodded but said in a calm even voice, "I prefer to keep this meeting as professional as possible if you don't mind, Mr. Harris."

"Whatever." Larry scratched his nose. "You takin' my case or what?"

"The last time we spoke you had not been arrested for any crimes. Has that changed, Mr. Harris?"

"Naw, the police are still clueless. But, who knows what tomorrow brings. Any minute one of the dudes that hired me to murder a rival could get popped. Hustlers don't always go gently into that goodnight, if you know what I mean."

"No, Mr. Harris, I don't know what you mean," Iona confessed.

He looked at her with an 'are you kidding me' expression on his face, but explained himself nonetheless. "One of my former employers might rat me out, and then I'll be hot and have no time to find a good lawyer. So, I'm one of those— what do you call it?" He snapped his fingers and then said, "Proactive kind of guys."

Iona rubbed her temples, warding off the headache that was threatening to attack. She informed Larry, "Are you aware that, by law, I have to report anyone who tells me about a crime they plan to commit?"

Larry's face was blank for a second, then he asked, "What about attorney–client privilege stuff?"

Iona laughed at him, not caring how unprofessional it was to laugh in the face of a potential client. "I hate to break it to you, Mr. Harris, but even your priest would have to re-port you to the police, if you went into his confessional and said, 'When I leave from here, I'm going home to hack my wife up into a million little pieces. So, who am I if even your priest can't protect you from premeditated murder?"

"Well, what about the stuff I've already done? Will you represent me if anything should come from that?" Larry reached into his pocket, and pulled out three bundles of cash and sat them on Iona's desk. "There's thirty thousand dollars. All you have to do is come get me out of jail when I call."

In truth, Iona wanted that money. She could call the Porsche dealer right now and order her midnight blue Cay-man S. But, she honestly couldn't see herself on a date with Larry. It wasn't just that she found big bulky biceps distaste-ful, but this whole business of killing people that never did a thing to you just didn't sit well with her. "Please take your money and leave my office, Mr. Harris."

He leaned back in his seat with this evil smirk on his face and said, "You think you're untouchable?" Iona didn't reply. "Think because your daddy is the infamous Isaac Walker that you've got a free pass."

Yes, her father had been one of the top gangsters in his day. Iona was proud of the fact that she was a gangster's daughter. She would never tell her attorney friends how much her father's past thrilled her. But, secretly she thought their story was kind of like one of her favorite old books, *Chances* by Jackie Collins. In the book, this guy, Gino, becomes this big mobster and nobody messed with him. Gino had a daughter named Lucky, and that was Iona. The only trouble Iona had with being Lucky was that *her Gino* had grown a conscience and had given his life over to Jesus. Now, instead of terrorizing the streets, Isaac was evangelizing them and setting the captives free. Hallelujah and amen.

Iona stood, picked up the money, and threw it into Larry's lap. "Get out of my office and take your blood money with you."

Larry stood and put his money back in his balloon pants. He pointed his finger in Iona's face. "You're making a big mistake, lady. You don't know all the misery I could cause you and your family."

"Oh yeah, well bring it on. My family hasn't seen enough misery yet," she said with her chest puffed out.

They were about nose to nose. His tone was low and menacing as he told her, "Watch your back, Iona, you're as good as dead."

Iona grinned, and tried not to giggle. Her father always told her that you never threaten a man—just do it. Obviously, this guy missed the killing session in his hustler 101 class. Maybe he was out having his head waxed during that class.

"Keep laughing and I'll put my fist down your throat."

The grin left Iona's face as she asked, "You sure you want to do that, and ruin your day?"

Larry swung.

Iona blocked his fist with her arm and sent a karate chop to his neck with her free hand. She kicked him where it hurt, then let out a battle cry that she'd learned in karate class as she kicked up her legs and landed a blow that bent Larry over and caused him to yell out in pain.

Vivian opened Iona's door, and came running in just as Iona was taking Larry's arm and twisting it behind his back. Vivian grabbed his other beefy arm and twisted it backward also. "I knew you shouldn't have let him in your office," Vivian said as she almost yanked Larry's arm out of socket.

With her free hand, Iona opened her top desk drawer and took out a pair of handcuffs. She clamped them down on Larry's wrist before he could think about getting out of their grasp.

"Now what are you going to do? How are you going to put your fist down my throat now?" Iona said.

"Uncuff me," Larry yelled as he struggled with the cuffs. Still bent over, he toppled and fell head first on the ground. Larry cursed and threatened them from his seat on the floor.

"Where did you get those cuffs?" Vivian asked.

"You know I used to date a cop."

Iona and Vivian laughed.

"What in the world is going on in here?" a voice from just outside her office door asked.

Iona looked up and the laughter in her voice died immediately. At her door was her brother, Donavan the golden boy. But, Donavan hadn't been the one to stop Iona from smiling; it was the smooth talking, chocolate coated, brown eyed man standing next to her brother; Johnny Dunford, the heartbreaker. Iona thought it might be unfair of her to label Johnny *the* heartbreaker. After all, he hadn't gone around town breaking hundreds of women's hearts. Johnny hadn't even broken ten, five, or three hearts. But, he had broken hers. Iona glued a false smile on her face and said, "Officer Dunford," she put an emphasis on the word officer while looking pointedly at Larry. "Thank you for coming to pick up our little felon. I'm sure Mr. Larry Harris has some warrants out on him."

"What happened?" Johnny asked as he walked over to Larry and lifted him off the floor. Larry was bulkier than Johnny. Although Johnny definitely had a six pack, his muscles were obviously not enhanced by the use of steroids.

Larry turned to Johnny and said, "I want to press charges." He pointed at Iona. "She assaulted me."

"Oh that's rich," Iona blurted out. "Our trial will make headlines all over the world; the assassin who got beat up by a girl. You sure you want to do that, Larry? It might be bad for business."

Johnny looked from Iona to Larry and then back to Iona. "Did you just call this man an assassin?"

Just then, Iona's boss, Mr. Gregory Winters, stepped into her office. "What is all the commotion about, Iona?"

"We've got it under control, Mr. Winters. This man threatened to kill me because I refused to represent him," Iona recited the entire story for her boss's benefit as well as Johnny's. Mr. Winters backed out of the room admonishing her to take care of the matter.

Johnny was hauling Larry out of her office, but he stopped at the door and looked pointedly at Iona and said, "So you finally found something you won't do for money?"

"What's that supposed to mean?" Iona asked in her most indignant voice, but then she raised her hand and waved him out. "Nevermind, don't answer that. Just do your job and arrest that sociopath." Iona knew exactly what Johnny meant. It was the reason he stopped seeing her. Johnny thought she didn't have a moral compass, and that she would represent anyone as long as they had enough money. Guess she proved him wrong today.

But, he hit her between the eyes as he pulled Larry out of her office and said to him, "Come on, Larry, no date for you."

Iona's mouth hung open. How did he know that she called her court appearances with her client's dates? He claimed he didn't want to be with her, but he was spying on her. Men. She was about to tell Johnny to keep his nose out of her business, when Donavan spoke, causing her to close her mouth and turn her attention to her brother.

Donavan said, "I think you need to go into corporate law. I'd sleep a lot better if you made the switch."

Iona laughed as she sat back down. "There are just as many crazies in Corporate America as there are on the street. But, Vivian and I can handle them." Iona turned to Vivian and said, "Ain't that right?"

Iona and Vivian high-fived. "I got your back, girlfriend," Vivian said, then left the office so Iona could be alone with Donavan.

"What's up, golden boy?"

"Hey." Donavan pointed at her. "If you don't want me to call you little sis at your office, then don't call me golden boy."

"How can I resist? You're just so good. Dad is always pleased with everything you do." She rolled her eyes and then added, "Well, at least one of us has made him proud."

Donavan sat down and pulled his chair up to Iona's desk. "Dad is very proud of you. And besides, I'm not perfect, sis. I've made my mistakes and I'm still trying to get over some of them."

She waved that comment off. "Whatever. Daddy thinks the sun doesn't come out until you get out of bed, so don't tell me about making mistakes."

The light in Donavan's eyes dimmed a bit as he looked away from his sister. He picked at some imaginary lint on his dark blue jeans as he said, "Anyway, I'm not here to talk about me or you. I came about Clarence."

"Clarence the jewel thief?" Iona asked.

Donavan laughed. "You are amazing. How can you continue to come up with names for all the people you meet?"

"They make it easy. I label them by what they do or who they are, not who they say they are," she told him.

"Okay then, what name did you give Mr. Larry? Was he Larry the assassin?"

"No. But you were close." Then she told him, "Larry the contract killer."

They both laughed. Then Donavan said, "Okay, I know I'm the golden boy, so what name did you give Daddy?"

"Daddy's the crusader."

"What about Johnny? What's his name?"

Laughter left Iona and her eyes clouded over as she answered, "Heartbreaker."

For a moment there was complete silence in the room. Donavan loudly scratched his throat and said, "Clarence came to the church this morning, sis. He said you told him if he wanted to go steady with you, he'd have to come up with twenty five thousand dollars."

Iona's eyes widened. "Did he tell Daddy that?"

"No, Daddy wasn't there. He had left the church about five minutes before Clarence showed up. He had to go with Mom to a doctor's appointment."

Iona visibly exhaled. "That ingrate! I get him bonded out and the first thing he does is run to my daddy to tell on me." But then Iona's mind trained on the other thing Donavan had said—something about Mom and doctor. "Is something wrong with Nina-Mama?"

"I don't think so. I know she hasn't kicked the flu yet, so maybe they're trying to see if the doctor can prescribe something. That's the least of your worries, sis. You better be glad Dad wasn't there. Some of the things you say to these people—it's outrageous."

"I'm letting these little criminals know where I stand. Nothing in this world is free, Donavan. And, I definitely want them to understand that I didn't get in this business to do pro bono."

"Just like having a prom date will cost you the corsage, the limo and dinner, an attorney will also cost you," Donavan said.

Iona smiled, knowing Clarence had spilled the beans on that little prom date comment too. "Exactly," she said, then asked, "Hey, did you tell Johnny what I said to Clarence?"

"My car is in the shop, so he gave me a ride over here." Donavan hunched his shoulders. "We had nothing else to talk about on the way over. Oh yeah, I'm going to need a ride back to the church."

Iona gave him the evil eye. "I should let you catch the bus. You know I don't want that man in my business."

Donavan became serious as he turned back to the subject at hand. "Clarence doesn't have any money, sis."

"Stop being so gullible, Donavan. Clarence and his buddies stole three million in jewelry. He can get the money."

"He's innocent. You are his only hope of proving that. Come on, Iona. Do the right thing."

Chapter 4

After work, Iona and Vivian went to a kickboxing class at the YMCA. Vivian kicked higher and harder than anyone else in the class. Iona was a close second and strived to be number one. Just before the class began, Iona's cell rang. It was Keith, her mother's husband.

When Iona was a kid, she was confused by all of her parents. Mama Cynda, step-daddy Keith; daddy Isaac, step-mama Nina. Or, was it the other way around she had wondered? Adults didn't understand the turmoil they put their children through. How could she not be a mess? She didn't even know that her father was alive until the day he came to take her to his home not long after her tenth birthday . . . and, oh yeah, right after her mother got arrested. Iona decided not to answer the call. She just saw Keith and her mother at Christmas time and she had her fill for a few months.

When they finished their episode of beating and kicking the air as if they were beating on one of Iona's clients, they sat down at one of the tables near the kid's playroom and chatted as they always did when they finished karate or kick-boxing.

"So what's up with you and Michael?" Iona asked Vivian.

"Not much," Vivian responded.

"Look," Iona told her. "You've got to give me more information than that, I'm living vicariously through you. You know I don't have a man, so don't hold out."

"You may not have a man, but you have an awful lot of dates," Vivian joked.

"Yeah, well, a girl's got to have her fun. I still can't believe that little criminal went and squealed on me."

"Look at it this way, at least you don't have to go to the prom with him," Vivian laughed.

"Shut up, it's not funny. And I do still have to represent the little squealer. My daddy would blow a gasket if I left Clarence hanging like that."

"I don't understand you, Iona. As long as we've known each other, I've never known you to be afraid of anyone or anything, but Pastor Isaac Walker."

Iona took a sip of her bottled water. "I'm not afraid of my father. I do, however, have a great deal of respect for him."

And that was true. Since Iona was a fifth grader and Pastor Isaac Walker marched into her principal's office after she'd been suspended for spitting in her teacher's face; she tried to get smart with her father, but he assured her that he would beat her until she went into a coma and gladly take the prison time before he'd allow a child of his to disrespect him. Iona had gotten the message and had learned just how far she could go with her father.

"However you want to put it." Vivian then added, "If you ask me, your father is the reason you don't have a man. You can't find anyone to measure up to his greatness."

That wasn't exactly true. Iona had indeed found someone to measure up to Isaac Walker, but he'd seen through her just as her daddy always had. "Enough about me, I want to know what you and Michael have planned for the upcoming weekend."

Vivian whispered, "I think we're going to the Bahamas on Saturday morning."

"What do you mean, you *think* you're going?"

A conspiratory smile crossed Vivian's lips. "I saw the tickets after he laid his jacket on my sofa and then went into the restroom. He hasn't said anything yet, but I think he is going to surprise me tomorrow night."

"Girl, this is Thursday, and he hasn't said anything? How do you know those tickets aren't for some chickie babe he has on the side?"

"That's what I like about you, Iona; you always see the glass as half empty."

Iona shrugged. "Hey, I'm just saying."

Vivian opened her bottle of water and told Iona, "Those tickets better not be for anyone else. I would kill him if he tried something like that."

"And I would defend you with everything I've got," Iona told her friend. "They raised their bottles of water in the air and toasted one another.

"I don't want to talk about Michael anymore. What's going on with that handsome brother of yours?"

Iona shrugged. "Nothing much. The church secretary is throwing herself at him. She thinks she's slick, but I see right through her."

Vivian laughed. "Does Donavan seem interested?"

"I don't know. But I'm going to talk with him about that woman. I really think he needs to steer clear of her; Something is not right about that one."

"You're just over protective of Donavan."

Iona shrugged again, then her phone rang. It was on the table so both she and Vivian looked down at the caller display at the same time. Vivian laughed and said, "I want to see you ignore his call."

It was her father. Iona stuck her tongue out at Vivian as she pushed the talk button on her cell phone. "What's up, Daddy?"

"Why haven't you returned any of your mother's telephone calls, Iona?" he asked without saying hello or asking how she was doing.

"Which mother would that be, Daddy?"

"Always with the smart mouth, huh? Well now it has backfired on you. Your mother is in the hospital."

Iona sat up straight in her seat. "Donavan told me you took Nina to the doctor this morning. What's wrong, Daddy."

"No, baby," his voice became gentle. "It's not Nina. Cynda is in the hospital. You need to get to Chicago immediately."

Iona wondered why her father said, *immediately?* It sounded as if he were trying to tell her that if she didn't get to her mother soon, she might miss her opportunity to say . . . "What's wrong with her, Daddy?"

"Your mom wants to discuss this with you herself. I can't leave Nina right now, we have something we need to work through. But Donavan can ride with you."

"No, don't worry about it, Daddy. I'll book a flight as soon as I get home." She hung up the phone wishing that she had made time to call her mother today.

Chapter 5

Iona ran into St. Francis Hospital and practically begged the baby faced woman at the information desk to tell her what room Cynda Williams was in.

"She's in room 6021," the clerk said.

Iona turned away from the woman and ran past the information desk. She jumped in the elevator, moved to the left to let a young all business, corporate-type couple in. She punched six. The man punched number four, then looked at his watch, the woman checked her blackberry. Iona had been moving on auto pilot since her father told her that her mother was in the hospital. Go online, order airline ticket, pack a bag, go to the airport, rent a car, and get to the hospital. She couldn't tell one thing about anyone she'd come in contact with during the last twelve hours, and that wasn't normal for her. She noticed everything about everybody. But she didn't want to think about strangers today. Her mind was stuck on Cynda Williams; the woman who'd birthed her, smoked dope and prostituted her body until Iona was ten years old.

The elevator opened on the fourth floor and the corporate couple stepped out. Iona moved to the middle of the elevator and prepared to get off herself. As the elevator opened and Iona stepped out and began looking for room 6021, she almost gagged at the smell of sickness that accosted her senses.

She passed room 6001 and watched as a group of nurses worked to resuscitate a patient. At that moment, Iona wished she hadn't wasted so much time holding a grudge against her mother. To be quite honest, Iona had forgiven her mother for her drug usage and prostitution. It was what she had done once she'd given up drugs, married Keith and given her life to the Lord, that Iona hadn't been able to forgive her for.

As she turned the corner, moving away from room 6001 as fast as she could, she came face to face with the reasons she hadn't been able to forgive her mother. Keith stepped out of room 6021 with her three younger brothers; Keith Jr., who was now fifteen, Joseph, thirteen and Caleb was ten.

Sometimes Iona admonished herself for being angry with her mother for getting married and having three more children. But doggone it, she had been the one to suffer through her mother's ten year span of drug addiction and everything else that came with it. When her mother finally got clean, Iona had still been left on the outside looking in. Yeah sure, the courts had taken Iona away from her mother and given custody to her father; essentially turning her into a summer and holiday visitor at her mother's house, but it still burned Iona that these children never had to cope with a drug addicted mother. She might not be sharing her with drugs and pimps anymore, but she was sharing her with a bunch of men called brothers and a step father; and oh yeah, the other man in her mother's life was God, and He took His share of her time as well. It just wasn't fair.

Keith walked over to Iona and put his arms around her. "It's good to see you, honey. I know Cynda will be real happy that you are here."

He said it as though he hadn't been sure that she would come, so she replied, "I wanted to be here."

The boys ran up to her and started jumping on her. Where she was little sis to Donavan, she was big sis to this group. They clung to her. She closed her eyes wishing that she felt for them what they obviously felt for her.

"Okay guys, let your sister go. She needs to go see your mother." Keith turned back to Iona and said, "I'm taking them to school. I'll be back in a little while."

"All right." Iona pointed to Cynda's door. "I need to get in there." She walked past them and then hesitated at the door for a moment. She wanted to turn back to Keith and ask him what had happened to her mother. How could her beautiful, vibrant, laugh out loud mother be in a hospital where patients were being resuscitated? She took a deep breath, then knocked on the door. Her mother's soft, tired voice bided her to come in. She opened the door wide and stepped in.

Just as Iona opened a door that would forever change her world, so did Isaac. He received an email from Donavan. In the email, Donavan had asked to meet with him at his house. Donavan's email stated that he wanted to discuss something that was critical to his future in the ministry. Isaac jumped in his midnight black Hummer and headed south to meet Donavan.

Isaac smiled every time he opened the door to this vehicle. Although the Hummer wasn't his only car—he also had a silver Mercedes and Nina had a dark blue two-seater convertible Mercedes—the Hummer was by far his favorite. God had been good to Isaac over the years. He and Nina had followed God without wavering and the Lord had prospered them. Although Isaac did receive a modest income from the church, that paycheck did not pay for the upgraded lifestyle he and his wife now enjoyed. With the help of his wife, Isaac had written a series of *New York Times* bestsellers that dealt with overcoming addictions and strongholds in life.

Isaac marveled over the way in which God had chosen to use his life to inspire others to be overcomers. It was laughable when he thought about it. After all, Isaac had spent more than two decades of his life making sure that people became addicted to drugs. That was how he made his money. And now God chose to prosper his family with something Isaac would have gladly done for free.

He parked his Hummer in front of Donavan's condo. Isaac thought it was strange that Donavan's Oldsmobile was parked in his carport, but his email had indicated that Isaac should let himself in. Isaac and Nina had a key to both Donavan's and Iona's condos. They were constantly running errands for the kids and dropping things off to them. But Isaac didn't like to just let himself in when they were at home. He wanted them to feel as if they were king and queen of their own domain; even if he was big Papa.

Isaac knocked on the door and waited about a minute. When Donavan didn't answer, Isaac concluded that his son's car was still acting up, so Donavan probably borrowed one of his friend's cars to run his errands. He put the key in the lock and opened the front door. Before Isaac could step into Donavan's living room, he heard the laughter and giggling—the voices of a happy man and woman, then his son came running into the living room with just a towel covering the lower half of his body. He had obviously just gotten out of the shower because his upper muscular half still had droplets of water on it. Running in behind him was Ms. Milner, the church secretary. The only thing she had on was the black and gray robe that Nina had given Donavan two

Christmases ago. Her hair was wet as if just getting out of the shower also.

Isaac was too stunned to speak. The pair obviously hadn't noticed him, because Ms. Milner tackled Donavan from behind and they both fell to the ground. Then Ms. Milner, sitting on top of Donavan said, "I've gotcha. Now what are you going to do about it?"

Donavan reached up and pulled her into an embrace. Isaac could take no more. This was his son rolling around on the floor, being very intimate with a woman that he was not married to. He had ordained his son into the ministry two years ago. Had given him an office at the church and hired him to preside over the children's ministry. Donavan was serious about ministry. He loved the Lord. What had Iona called him, *the golden child*?

Isaac felt ill as he uttered, "Son!"

Cancer.

How could a beautiful woman like Cynda Williams not have a blemish on the outside but be tarnished inside? That's what Iona wanted to know.

"I'm not going to beat around the bush, honey. The doctors don't think I have much time left," Cynda told her daughter.

Iona sat in the chair next to her mother's hospital bed wondering if it was possible to feel pain that was deeper, more gut wrenching, than the one she was feeling right now. Tears rolled down her face as she opened her mouth to ask how, why, what would make something like this happen, but nothing would come out. Her chest began to heave as a furry of tears drizzled down like a storm upon her face.

Cynda reached up and wiped the tears from Iona's face. "No, baby, don't cry like this. I'm okay, I really am. I don't plan to die today, tomorrow or next year for that matter."

Iona had last seen her mother two months ago. And

though she'd thought her mother had dropped a few pounds, she was skeletal now. This sickness had drained the beauty from her face and taken the laughter out of her eyes. How could her mother think she wasn't dying anytime soon when it was plain to see that she was wasting away?

Through blubbering lips, Iona said, "B-but Mama, you j-just told me that the doctors don't think you have m-much time left."

"Stop all that crying, Iona. I'm telling you I'm going to live." Cynda lifted her head off the pillow to cough. Her body visibly shook from the effort of lifting up. When she laid back down and spoke again, her voice was hoarse and forced. "Now, whether my living is going to be done on earth or in heaven—God hasn't given me all the details yet. But I have a strong feeling that my work on this earth isn't done yet." She gave Iona a weak smile. "Your mama will be around. And I would love for you to make more time for me."

Iona had allowed herself to become so jealous over the time her mother spent with her brothers that she'd wished that Nina had been her only mother. But Cynda refused to be replaced no matter how much Iona pushed her away. After all the things her mother had done to her, once she made changes in her life, Iona was sure that Cynda would spend the rest of her life making everything up to her. But what did her mother go and do? Cynda had not one, not two, but three more children, a husband and a bunch of God obligations. And everything and everybody came before Iona. So Iona covered up her hurt with resentment, and as she got older and could make her own decisions, she spent less and less time with her mother.

Iona's elbows were on her knees as she put her face in her hands and cried some more. How she wished she could turn back time. If she could, she would spend every waking moment finding out everything there was to know about her mother. "Oh God, give me back the last sixteen years of my life," Iona wanted to scream. But would God listen to her?

"Mama," Iona said when an idea struck her. She clutched the bed railing and said, "You talk to God all the time. Tell Him that you don't want to die. Tell Him that I don't want you to die."

Cynda put her hand atop her daughter's and patted it. "I have, baby. It's in the Master's hands now. He won't fail us whatever the outcome."

Chapter 6

Iona spent the night in her mother's hospital room. She pulled two chairs together and the nurse gave her a pillow and a blanket. The nurses normally didn't allow visitors to spend the night, but Iona knew why the nurse let her do it; they thought her mother was dying.

It seemed that Cynda knew why they allowed the overnight visit also, and she wasn't having it. When Keith came back to the hospital early Saturday morning, Cynda told him that she wanted to go home.

Keith stood at the side of his wife's bed and brushed his hand along the side of her face as he said, "I don't know, baby. Dr. Noelman wants you to stay here for observation."

"Dr. Noelman has me on a death watch." Cynda's voice was weak but there was no missing the sound of determination as she told Keith, "I want to live. Take me home, husband."

Iona watched as this six-foot-two, Arnold-Schwarzenegger-muscle-built man's chin began to quiver.

Cynda put her hand on his arm. "No tears, husband. I need you to believe with me."

Keith nodded and headed toward the door.

Once his back was to Cynda, Iona saw him wipe his face. His shoulders slumped as he opened the door, but Iona knew that no matter how weary this whole situation had made Keith, he would not rest until Cynda was released from this hospital. It seemed to Iona that since the day Keith married her mother, he lived to do her bidding. Iona's father was like that with Nina also. And she knew that Donavan would be the same way when he finally found his wife. She was surrounded by knights in shinning armor—she just didn't have one of her own.

"Iona," Cynda called out to her daughter.

Iona stood up and walked over to her mother's bed. She looked so frail, Iona ached just looking at her. She reached her arm over the bed rail and touched her mother's hands. She felt the bones protruding upward. In recent years, her mother had weighed a healthy hundred and fifty pounds. Since she was five-seven, the extra weight didn't make her look fat, just like a woman who'd borne four children and worked at keeping herself in shape. She was now about a hundred and fifteen pounds. Cynda looked like one of those anorexic runway models—like she was about to pass out at any moment from starvation.

"Yes, Mama?"

Cynda's voice was low and ragged as she said, "The Lord has shown me what to do, baby. Don't you worry, I'm going to live."

Iona had stopped trusting God to handle the things that concerned her during her first year of law school. She had allowed a very persuasive law professor to put doubt in her mind about the omnipotence of God. How could God be in all places at all times? So she asked, "What can we do for you, Mama?"

Cynda smiled, her eyes weren't focused on Iona though. They were looking heavenward as her body seemed to sink deeper into her hospital bed. "I'll tell you tomorrow, I need to rest right now."

Cynda napped for about two hours. Iona went down to the cafeteria to get her and Keith some lunch as he continued to work on getting Cynda released. By the time Iona had eaten her grilled chicken salad and purchased a cheese burger and fries for Keith, her mom's papers had been processed and she was released and ready to go.

Cynda slept peacefully in her own home Saturday evening. When everyone woke Sunday morning, Cynda told Keith to take the kids off to church so she could spend some time with Iona.

Keith let out the sofa bed in the family room and then carried Cynda in there. He scrambled some eggs and toasted a few slices of bread; took the plate in the family room with a glass of orange juice and asked his wife, "Do you need anything else, honey?"

She lovingly touched her husband's hand as she said, "Can you bring me my Bible and the concordance?"

As Keith walked back to their bedroom to get Cynda's Bible, Junior, Joseph and Caleb came over to Cynda carrying a large paper that the kids used in art class. Cynda smiled and said, "Hey, handsome," to all three of them.

Junior told her, "Caleb and Joseph made something for you."

Cynda tried to lift up, but wasn't strong enough to do it. Iona was walking into the family room with a cup of coffee in her hand. Keith was also coming back into the room with Cynda's Bible and concordance in his hand. Iona put her coffee down on the table next to the sofa bed and Keith put his stuff down as they both helped to pull her into a semi-sitting position.

Joseph showed Cynda the picture. It was of a woman dancing with her arms joyfully lifted up. "This is you, Mom."

Cynda's eyes misted. "I certainly have a lot of energy on that picture."

"You used to always have a lot of energy, Mom," Joseph told her.

"And I will again, Joseph. I promise," Cynda told her son.

"So you're not going to die?" ten year old Caleb blurted out.

"You know what?" Iona said as she took the picture out of the boy's hands, "I'm going to help Mom hang this picture up. That might help her regain her strength, don't you think?"

A big smile spread across Caleb's face. "Yeah! Let's hang it up."

Cynda turned to Junior and asked, "Do you have anymore of that art paper left?"

"Yes, ma'am, we have a bunch," Junior answered.

"Can you bring it to me?" Cynda asked. Then as Junior started to walk away to get the paper she added, "Bring me some tape also."

Joseph brought back the paper and tape. Keith kissed Cynda and then took his sons to church.

When they were alone, Iona asked Cynda what she wanted the art paper for.

Cynda said, "I'm going to live, Iona."

In a reassuring tone, Iona said, "I know. You told me that yesterday."

"I need your help. Can you look up the word 'live' in my concordance?"

Iona opened the concordance and searched out the word live. "I've got it, now what?"

Cynda closed her eyes and shuddered for a moment. When she opened her eyes, she began panting as she spoke. "I need you to find scriptures about living, rather than dying. I also want to look up scriptures on healing. When we find ones that we like, can you write them on the art paper and hang them all over this room? Don't forget to hang that picture of me dancing."

Iona did as her mother asked. She searched the concordance for phrases surrounding 'live' and 'healed' that might relate to Cynda's situation. She found one in Psalm 118: 17 that read: I shall not die, but live, and declare the works of the Lord."

She read it to her mother and Cynda smiled. "Put that one on the art paper."

Iona found a black marker in Joseph's room and used it to write her first scripture. She put tape on all four sides of the paper and hung it above the TV straight in front of Cynda.

As Iona walked back to the Bible, concordance and art paper that she had sprawled on the floor Cynda asked, "Do you think Caleb will believe that I'm going to live when he reads that poster?"

"I certainly hope so. I thought you were going to break down when he asked you that."

"Thanks for stepping in. I was a little dumbstruck."

"Not a problem," Iona said as she continued looking for scriptures. When she came across Ezekiel 37: 3-5 she said, "Listen to this Mom: And he said unto me, Son of man, can these bones live? . . . . Oh ye dry bones, hear the word of the Lord: Thus saith the Lord God unto these bones; Behold, I will cause breath to enter into you, and ye shall live." Iona looked up from the Bible and asked, "Isn't that how you feel right now? Like you've got dry bones?"

Cynda nodded.

"Then this is it. You've got to speak to your body and tell it to live. I'm going to put this one on a poster also," Iona said and began to write. But a funny thing happened as she put the word of God on paper this time; Iona began to believe that this just might work.

Chapter 7

On Sunday afternoon, Nina and Isaac sat in his office waiting on Donavan to join them. When Isaac found him on the floor of his condo with the church secretary, Isaac had told both of them that he wanted to meet with them in his office after Sunday service. He and Nina met with Diana at two in the afternoon. They explained to her that her actions were in violation of the conduct code of the church. Nina allowed Diana to review the employment agreement she had signed two years earlier. Then Isaac said, "We are suspending you without pay for two months. If after that time period you believe that you can conduct yourself in the manner in which God requires of His people, you will be welcomed back to your position at this church with open arms."

Diana squirmed in her seat. She kept her head down as she asked, "What am I supposed to do for the next two months?"

Isaac told her, "We hope that you will seek the Lord during this time and ask Him to cleanse your heart. You are more than welcome to continue coming to this church during your suspension period. But if you would like to attend another church during this time, we will understand that as well."

With her head still slightly lowered, Diana asked, "How am I supposed to pay my bills?"

Isaac answered matter-of-factly, "You'll probably have to get another job during this time period."

When it was Donavan's turn, he sat across from his father. Nina got up from the couch and handed her son the employment agreement he had signed when he started working for the church. "Please read over this information before your father speaks with you." She patted him on the back and then turned and reclaimed her seat.

Isaac saw the tears floating around his wife's eyes as she turned from Donavan. He hesitated for a moment, giving Nina time to adjust to what he was about to do. Donavan's head was still bent as he read through the employment agreement. Isaac's eyes were on Nina. Her head was bowed as she prayed, then she looked at Isaac and gave him a reassuring smile and nodded.

All right, she had his back, and that was all he needed to know. He and Nina had gone back and forth on this issue over the weekend. They'd prayed, talked and fussed about what they would do with Donavan. They had finally made the only decision that could have been made in this situation. They had to do to him what they would do to any other staff member caught in the same predicament.

"Your mother and I set this meeting with you this afternoon because we need to inform you that your conduct has fallen below the Godly standard you agreed to uphold at the time of your employment," Isaac began.

Donavan laughed nervously, "At the time of my employment? Dad, why are you talking to me like I'm just some employee here? I'm your son."

Nina stood and walked over to Donavan and put her hand on his shoulder. "Let your father finish, hon."

Donavan both feared and respected his father. Isaac went to prison when Donavan was eleven months old for drug trafficking. Donavan was four years old when Isaac had been released from prison. Prison changed Isaac to the point where he now wanted to live right and love the Lord. As Donavan grew older, he heard stories about how infamous his father had been during his drug running days. Knowing what his father had been capable of always made Donavan hesitate and check his words before speaking. Even now, as Donavan looked across the desk at his father, he decided it would be best to just shut his mouth and listen.

Isaac's voice was calm but forceful as he said, "We are suspending you without pay from your responsibilities at the church for four months."

Donavan shook his head as if he'd just heard something really wrong and he had to get it out of his mind before it somehow became right or true. "B-but you only suspended Diana for two months? I don't understand how you can do this to me."

"You are in a position of authority at this church, and that makes your offense much worse in my book. Therefore, you will pay a higher price for your sins," Isaac told him.

Donavan turned to Nina. "Mom, come on. I'm sorry about everything. I'll do anything to make this right, but don't send me away like this."

Nina wasn't even trying to hide her tears now. The saltiness of tears tasted bitter as she opened her mouth to say, "We're not sending you away, Donavan. This is still your church and we are still your parents. We just believe that you need time to rebuild your relationship with God before trying to minister in the children's church."

Donavan turned back to his father. "Is this really what you want, Dad? You know me. You know I love God and you know that I'm good with the kids in Children's

Church." When Isaac said nothing, Donavan continued to plead his case. "Don't do this, Dad. I'm your son. I know I messed up. I'm sorry; I really am."

Isaac asked Donavan, "Are you truly sorry, son; or just sorry that you got caught?"

Donavan stepped back as if he'd just been punched by his father. "Okay, then. Throw me out of here. But, tell me this—how am I supposed to pay my bills without a paycheck for four months?"

Isaac hunched his shoulders. "There are consequences for our actions. You should have had a plan in place since you knew you were living contrary to the will of God."

"Isaac, you don't have to be so harsh," Nina admonished.

Isaac was fed up. "You know what, Nina? I've had it up to here," he lifted his hand above his head then continued, "with this boy's attitude. He messed up, but then he comes in here and expects us to just act as if it never happened." He pointed a finger at Donavan as he said, "But, you forgot one thing, didn't you? You forgot that I don't work for myself. I answer to God about everything that goes on in this church, so even if I did want to forget about it, I can't. Because God saw what you did long before I walked in and caught you playing house with the church secretary."

Donavan was fired up. He forgot about how much he feared his dad as they stood nose to nose, and Donavan huffed, "What about forgiveness, huh, Dad? Yeah, you're so up on what God says and what God wants, so tell me what the Bible says about forgiveness?"

Isaac calmed himself and sat back down. "We are more than willing to bring you back to your current position after your suspension period, if you are willing to conduct yourself as a man of God."

"Are Godly men homeless, Dad? Because that's what I'm going to be without an income for the next four months."

Nina wiped away her tears as she told her son, "Why

don't you move back home for the next few months and rent your condo out?"

That idea earned an angry, bitter laugh from Donavan. "I wouldn't step foot in your husband's house," he told his mother. He put his hand on Isaac's desk and leaned down so that he was in his father's face again. "You win, Pastor Walker, I'll get out of your church, but I want you out of my life. Do you hear me, old man? Don't you come near me."

Donavan stepped away from his father. Nina tried to hug him. He brushed her off by saying, "Not now, Mom. I just need my space right now, okay?"

Nina's blubbering response indicated that she understood.

Donavan angrily strutted by his mother and father. When he reached the office door, he swung it open and then turned back to them and said, "Matthew 6:15 says 'if you do not forgive men their sins, your father will not forgive your sins'. Can you afford to not have your sins forgiven, Dad?" With that, Donavan slammed the door behind him.

Chapter 8

Donavan was throwing his personal belongings in the open boxes on his desk and floor of his office when Johnny walked in. "Man, what's going on around here? Diana and the other ladies on the administration team are in the front office crying; you're in here throwing all your stuff in boxes. What gives?"

Donavan turned to his friend. He and Johnny had been best friends since Johnny came to the church two years ago. Donavan threw the 'Best Coach of the Year' plaque he'd received for coaching the peewee football team in his box as he told Johnny in a very loud voice, "My father, the pastor of this great church, fired me!"

A look of astonishment crossed Johnny's face. He closed the door and said, "Donavan, please tell me you're kidding?"

Donavan sat down and put his head in his hands. He rubbed his face and then looked up at his friend. "My mom didn't even have my back, man. Do you know how that makes me feel?"

Hurt and pain was etched on Donavan's face. Johnny

wanted to back away and let Donavan deal with his pain, but he had to know, so he asked, "What did you do?"

Shame replaced hurt on Donavan's face. He lowered his head and turned away from his friend.

"Man, what happened?" Johnny pressed.

Donavan turned back to Johnny and said, "Dad caught me with Diana."

Johnny pointed in the direction of the front of the church. "Diana Milner?" Donavan nodded. "Well what exactly did he catch you doing?"

Donavan gave his friend a look that said, "What do you think we were doing?"

Johnny backed away from Donavan. "I don't believe this. I know you've been struggling with this, but you told me that you had it under control. And, you promised me that you would not approach anyone at this church. Do you remember promising me that?"

A year ago, Donavan confided in Johnny about the woman he slept with. Donavan told Johnny that he was going to stop seeing her, but most of all, he'd promised that he would never approach a woman at his father's church until he had gotten himself together.

"I didn't approach her. Diana came after me. I kept telling her I wasn't interested, but she wouldn't let it go. You see how she looks. How could I just let it go?"

Johnny folded his arms. "Oh, so it's her fault? Boy, you are an elder at this church and old enough to know better than that."

"Now you sound like my father." Donavan mimicked Isaac as he buttoned his suit jacket and sat stiffly behind his desk. "Your penalty is greater because you are in a position of authority."

"So what was the penalty?" Johnny asked.

"He suspended Diana for two months and me for four."

"You said he fired you. That doesn't sound like you've been fired."

"It's without pay, Johnny. He knows I'll have to get another job in order to pay my bills. Who would leave a new job to come back to a place they were basically in exile from?" Donavan pointed at his door as if someone was standing behind it. "He knows I won't come back here, but he can still keep a happy home by telling my mom, '*I didn't fire him, honey. I gave that son of yours a chance to repent—he just won't do it*'."

"Donavan, excuse me for saying this, but you're acting as if you didn't do anything wrong."

Donavan lifted his hands to the heavens. "I know I was wrong," he yelled. "But where is the forgiveness that my father always preaches about?" Donavan shook his head. He picked up some of the papers on his desk, crumbled them, and threw them in the trash. "I'm just angry right now."

Johnny ran his hand over the top of his head. He stood in the middle of the floor, not sure what to do, then he made a decision. "I'm going to talk to him."

"Talk to who? "Donavan asked.

"Your father; I'm going to tell him how you've been struggling with this situation."

Standing, Donavan asked, "Are you crazy? You can't go in there and tell him that."

"Well then, tell me what to do, because I don't know how to help you with this one," Johnny said.

"If you really want to help, I do need you to do something for me."

"You name it, buddy; I'm there."

By the time Diana Milner left the House of God, she didn't feel angry like Donavan. Diana was repentant and humbled by the way the staff at the House of God treated her. When she walked out of Pastor Walker's office and told her office mates that she'd been suspended, they didn't look at her as if she was a leper. They huddled around and prayed for her. One by one, each of them wished her well. By the time they were finished, they were all in tears.

Pastor Walker called her back to his office and apologized for what his son had done to her. If only he knew.

What she remembered most clearly was Pastor Walker telling her that although men make mistakes, God would never fail her. And then he admonished her to put her trust in God.

Diana had not come to the House of God for some big spiritual experience. She had a job to do and that had been her single focus. However, each Sunday as she listened to Pastor Walker deliver the Word of God, she felt something stirring in her heart. She hadn't allowed the stirring to grow into a meaningful relationship with God. She was too busy chasing after Donavan to worry about developing a relationship with the Lord.

But now, as she sat at her kitchen table with the Bible in front of her, Diana decided to find her way back to God. The telephone rang and she almost let the answering machine pick it up, but then decided to just get it over with.

"So how did it go? Did he fire you?" the voice on the other end of the phone asked.

"No he suspended me and Donavan," she said.

After a slight pause, the caller said, "It doesn't matter, we can still sue. I'll get you one of the best lawyers. That church will be closed and penniless by the time we get through with them."

"He had just cause to suspend me. I violated the rules of conduct in the employment agreement I signed," Diana told the caller.

"It doesn't matter. We might not win the case, but we will bankrupt them with litigations." The caller laughed and then told her, "And if you get a jury of people who like to fornicate and don't want some Bible-thumping preacher telling them it's wrong, you just might win."

"I'm not suing Pastor Walker. I'm done with this whole mess. Do you hear me?"

"Look, we had a deal. You can't just quit now."

"I don't want anything else to do with your little plot. Don't call me ever again or I'll call the police." She hung up the telephone, took a deep breath and then opened her Bible.

Betrayal happened all the time. This was a fact of life that he was only too aware of, but he still hadn't expected Diana to back out of their deal. Forget honor among thieves, he knew all of her dirty little secrets and could expose her anytime he wanted to. That was the reason he thought she would do as he said, when he said. And she had followed his instructions line upon line, precept upon precept—until now.

Diana had joined the House of God Christian Fellowship Church, applied for the administrative assistant position and gotten it, then she started cozying up to Donavan just like he'd told her to do. But he doubted if that part of the assignment had been a big hardship for her. Donavan looked like Morris Chestnut with a Bible and youth group followers instead of star struck fans following behind him. Now it had all blown up and he thought this would be his moment of glory, but the turn coat refused to bring charges against the House of God Christian Fellowship.

He shook his head as if shaking off a bad dream and picked up the phone. He might be down, but he was certainly not out. There were always two jokers in a game of spades. Diana had been his little joker, the most expedient means to an end, but he was about to play the big daddy joker; the card that always made the other players gasp as it was smacked down on top of their punk bust-a-move-thought-you-won-this-hand-but-you-didn't cards. He dialed the numbers that he'd promised not to call until the time was right.

When his big joker answered he said, "It's me. We need to talk."

"I'm not so sure about that," the big joker told him.

"What do you mean?"

"I don't think I will be able to help you."

"Haven't you been doing the things I asked you to do?"

"Yes, and he's totally clean. The man doesn't have a corrupt bone in his body."

This had to be some kind of record. Twice in one day he had been refused. That just didn't happen to him. People got in line and did what he told them to do or he exposed them. "I don't think you want to disappoint me. You know what this could mean for you, right?"

His big joker might as well have been a deuce as he told him, "I refuse to harm an innocent man just to save myself. So you do what you have to do." He hung up.

The man put the phone back in its cradle after being hung up on by yet another betrayer. Someone would have to pay for all that had gone wrong. Yes, he would take care of Diana and his big joker, or big joke as he turned out to be, but first he had to make Isaac pay.

Everyone seemed to think that Isaac Walker was some sort of prince, but he knew the preacher to be a monster, and he was going to expose that fact to the world.

Chapter 9

Iona grabbed her suitcase from the baggage claim and stepped outside of the Dayton Airport terminal to look for Donavan. She hadn't talked with him since she left for Chicago but he had agreed to pick her up before she left town; and Donavan never forgot an obligation. As Iona stood outside waiting on Donavan's black Oldsmobile to pull up, her thoughts were still in Chicago. She just couldn't get her mind off of all those posters she hung in the family room of Cynda and Keith's house.

Iona smiled as she remembered one of the scriptures on healing that she hung on the wall. It seemed as if one half of the scripture was for her mother, but that God was speaking to her with the other half of it. Jeremiah 17:14 read, Heal me, O Lord, and I shall be healed; save me, and I shall be saved: for thou art my praise.

It was as if God was reminding her that she had given her life to the Lord when she was a child; and if God saved her, she was saved. How could that be? She certainly hadn't felt saved for a good seven years. But maybe what God was trying to show her with that scripture was that He hadn't taken

His salvation away from her. And that the ball was still in her court. Like God was saying, come back and you will be saved. But saved from what? And did she really want or need what God could offer her at this point in her life?

A Blue Bonneville pulled up next to Iona. The blowing of the horn caused her to stop thinking about her mom, God and salvation. She looked into the familiar car and saw Johnny. What was he doing here she wondered.

He rolled his window down and yelled, "Get in."

Iona shook her head. "I'm waiting on Donavan."

"He sent me to get you," Johnny told her.

Iona rolled her eyes as Johnny got out of his car, unlocked his trunk and took her suitcase out of her hand. He then opened the passenger side door for her and swept his arms into the air gallantly. "Madam, your carriage awaits," he said as Iona hesitantly strolled forward. When she reached the car, she braced her hands on the window sill and said, "I hope you don't think this nice act of yours is going to make me want to date you again."

Johnny let go of the car door and laughed to the point of being obnoxious as he walked all the way around the car. He didn't stop laughing until he had buckled his seat belt.

"What's so funny?" Iona asked, boring into him with menacing dark eyes.

He snickered, but waved his hand in the air and said, "Nothing."

"Obviously something is hilarious. Let me in on the joke."

"You wouldn't want to know. Just let it go," Johnny said as he put the car in drive and pulled off.

Iona harrumphed, folded her arms and then asked, "Where's Donavan? Why didn't he come to get me?"

Johnny didn't respond for a moment, but when he did open his mouth to speak, his voice was gentle and kind. "I'm sorry that I have to tell you this, but I know Donavan would rather not have to tell you himself."

Iona's eyes rolled. "What's big brother done now? Did he win the Nobel Peace Prize while I was gone? Is my father at the church turning cartwheels for his good little son?"

"Your father fired Donavan yesterday."

Shock and disbelief crossed Iona's face. "What? You're lying, I don't believe that."

Johnny steered the car with his left hand, and with the other, he lightly touched Iona's shoulder. "Look, Iona, I know that you joke around a lot, calling Donavan the Golden Boy. And I also know that you have a lot of respect for him, and at times, you have attributed hero status to Donavan. But he's just a man, Iona. And he messed up."

"Messed up how?" Iona asked.

"I don't know if it's my place to tell you Donavan's business."

"Why are you lying like this? Donavan couldn't have done anything bad enough to make my father fire him." She pulled out her cell phone and dialed Donavan's number. The phone rang six times then went to voicemail. "Donavan, where are you? Call me as soon as you get this message."

"You need to give him a couple of days, Iona. He doesn't want to talk with anyone right now."

Iona turned fiery eyes on Johnny but she didn't say anything to him. She opened her cell phone and dialed her father's number. He answered on the first ring. Iona noticed that her father's voice lacked its normal upbeat God-is-on-your-side cheerfulness he always displayed when answering the phone.

"Daddy, what's going on? Johnny said that you fired Donavan," Iona said into the phone.

"How was your trip, baby? How is your mother doing?" Isaac asked, side stepping the question.

Iona wasn't going out like that. "We can talk about Mama later. Tell me what's going on. Please, Daddy." There was desperation in her voice and she hated that Johnny heard it, but what else could she do? Her family was falling apart.

"Baby, I can't discuss that with you right now. Donavan is going to have to tell you what happened," Isaac told her.

Feeling dejected, Iona hung up with her father and turned to Johnny with tears in her eyes. "My mother has cancer. Did you know that?"

"Yeah, I know. I was sorry to hear it."

"The doctor's think she might die. And it took that for me to realize that I really do want that woman in my life." Her hand went to her head and she massaged her temples. "I can't deal with something bad happening to Donavan too. Please tell me what happened. Please Johnny."

Johnny sighed, and as he turned the car onto Iona's street he said, "I really don't want to get in the middle of this, Iona. But I know you won't let this rest until you know what happened, so I'm going to tell you." He took a deep breath and said, "Your father caught Donavan having sex with Diana Milner."

Iona's mouth hung open for a moment. When she recovered she said, "No way that happened. There has to be some mistake."

"Your father is the one who found them."

Iona closed her eyes and then reopened them. But it was hard for her to see with the bubble of tears in her way. "Donavan must feel awful. All he ever wanted to do was please my father. Something like this could destroy him." She wiped away the tears and then said, "I knew that woman was up to no good. I just knew it."

Johnny parked the car as he said, "Donavan is a grown man, Iona. He made the choice to sleep with Diana."

"I thought you were supposed to be Donavan's friend. But look at you, all high and mighty as if you never slept around."

He angrily turned toward her. "I am Donavan's friend. What happened between me and you happened before I got saved. When God saved me, He saved me, Iona. I understand how a Christian is supposed to act."

She turned away from Johnny's piercing gaze and pushed the car door open. His words had convicted her, and caused her to think on that scripture she'd read this weekend; the one where the writer declared: *save me, and I shall be saved.* God had saved both Iona and Johnny, but she hadn't stayed saved. She had backslid. And now she had to get away from Johnny and his perfection. She grabbed her purse and took off running toward her condo.

Johnny got out of the car and took her suitcase out of the trunk. He followed behind her calling, "Wait up, Iona. You forgot your suitcase."

Iona opened her door and then swung around to face off with Johnny. "You've got some nerve judging me, Johnny Dunford. You didn't even know anything about God until I brought you to my father's church. You had never even read the Bible for goodness sake."

Johnny looked around just to make sure that none of Iona's neighbors were coming out of their condos to find out who Iona was screaming at. "Calm down, Iona. Just go in the house."

"No, no. You're not better than me! You are not better than me—do you hear me?"

He pushed her door wide open and nudged her inside. When he closed the door, he turned back to her. "Iona, will you please stop. You're making a fool out of yourself."

"No, I'm not. I made a fool of myself when I thought we were in love *together*."

Johnny lifted his hands, halting Iona's tirade. "This isn't the right time to go there, Iona. So let's just leave it alone for now. Okay?"

She started walking toward him, determined to show him that he was no better than she or Donavan. He had once been hers and he would be again if she willed it. "I don't want to leave it alone." She put her hands around his neck and seductively told him, "I don't want you to leave me alone." She pulled him toward her, and as her lips met his, she felt his need for her.

Johnny's eyes were closed as he willingly returned Iona's kiss. He pulled her closer and sunk deeper into her embrace.

Iona said, "See, you don't want to leave me alone either."

Snapping out of the trance Iona's kiss had put him in, Johnny reopened his eyes and stepped out of her embrace. "I can't do this."

"Why not?" she protested. "What's so wrong with being with me?"

"I'm not going to sleep with you."

Iona took a deep breath and exhaled, then ran her hands through her long hair. "Why are you being so difficult? You want this as much as I do."

Putting his hands in his pocket Johnny said, "To tell you the truth. I don't think I can afford you."

She put her hands on his chest and said, "What are you talking about? I'm sure you don't earn much more than you earned when I dated you two years ago, and we didn't have a problem then."

He removed her hands from his chest and stepped away from the fire. "Well, let me put it this way, counselor. I don't pay for dates, okay? And no, I don't want to take you to the prom either."

So there it was; big mouth Clarence Mason strikes again. "Look, we both know that I'm not dating my clients, and what I say to them is my business—not yours."

"Who are you kidding? You put on this big act when we first met; telling me how much your mother ruined the first ten years of your life by prostituting. But look at you. You're not a lawyer, you're just as much the prostitute that your mother was."

Iona backhanded Johnny so hard, blood sputtered from his lip. "I should kick your black behind for saying something like that to me."

Johnny wiped his lip, saw the blood and then said, "Be careful, baby. Don't let them karate and kickboxing lessons get you knocked out."

She posed. Left foot firmly planted, right foot taking the lead, slightly bent. Her hands were lifted, ready to strike. "Make a move. Ain't nothing between us but air and opportunity."

Johnny backed up and opened Iona's front door. "You're not thinking clearly right now, so I'm just going to get out of here."

She broke her stance and told him, "Just know that if you call me out my name again, I'm not going to give you a chance to back up, flip it and reverse. You're going to get beat down as soon as you open your mouth."

"You're what?" Isaac asked his wife.

Nina stood in front of the window of their bedroom wondering how life could be so cruel to her time and time again as she said, "You heard me the first time, Isaac. I'm pregnant."

"B-but you're fifty-four."

Nina wanted to say, 'No duh,' but this wasn't the time to be sarcastic; because she had been asking God the same thing. How could she be pregnant now? She would have welcomed this pregnancy sixteen years ago when Iona came to stay with them. Nina had done everything to try to conceive. She'd begged and implored God to give her and Isaac another child. But those prayers had gone unanswered. Nina would have even welcomed this pregnancy ten years ago. A lot of career women have children in their forties. But Nina didn't know one single woman who'd had a baby in her fifties. This was a Sarah and Abraham joke that the Lord was playing on them.

"Say something, Nina."

"What do you want me to say?" Nina put her arms

around her stomach and thought about the numerous doctors that had proclaimed her womb dead. Years ago, Donavan had gotten involved with the wrong crowd and he'd done some things that had angered an evil man. That man shot her son and as Nina tried to protect Donavan, she'd been shot also. When she woke up in the hospital, the doctor told her that she would never be able to have another child. Then after years of praying for God to open her womb, Nina's doctor informed her that she was headed for early menopause. Nina had cried herself to sleep night after night, until she had finally decided to accept God's will for her life and be happy. Now a decade after she'd given up hope, could it be true that she would now give birth to another child?

Isaac lifted his six foot form off of their king-size bed, walked over to the window, stood behind his wife and wrapped his arms around her. "Thank you, babe."

Nina turned around in Isaac's arms. He squeezed her tighter as she put her head on his chest. "What are you thanking me for?"

He lifted her head and kissed her. "Thanks for being my babies mama."

She laughed, then swatted his shoulder. "It's not funny, Isaac. "This child is going to think something is wrong with us. I mean come on, I'm fifty-four and you're sixty-one. We're like a modern day Sarah and Abraham. We'll be dead before this child goes off to high school."

"Speak for yourself, woman. I plan to live to be at least ninety-five."

Nina stepped out of his embrace and sat down on the edge of their bed. Her shoulders slumped as tears formed in her eyes.

Isaac followed his wife and got on his knees in front of her. He wiped the tears from her face. "It's going to be all right, baby. I guarantee you that we will live to see this child grow up."

Chapter 10

On Tuesday morning, Iona got out of bed, dressed in a dark brown skirt and jacket, and went to work. Truth be told, she wasn't feeling work today, but the bills had to be paid. She had her first meeting scheduled with Clarence the jewel thief and snitch. He earned the added label of snitch for what he told Donavan. Even though Clarence was snitching on her, she wasn't going to give up his case. It had the potential of being front page news.

As part of her five year plan, Iona really needed a front page news type of case. She was banking her money and she was right on schedule, with about thirty thousand in the bank. But Iona knew she would need at least five times that in order to get her law firm off to a good start and let this community know that she was about business.

Vivian was behind her desk in the reception area. She handed Iona her messages and told her good morning.

Vivian looked sad, like somebody pimp slapped her mother and made her watch. Iona wanted to ask her friend what was wrong, but she couldn't take another sad song right now. So she closed herself in her office, took a deep breath and reviewed her messages. The message on top was from Keith, her mother's husband. She had ignored his call last week. She would never make that mistake again.

She picked up the phone and dialed Keith's cell number, not wanting to wake her mother if she was tired or sleeping. Keith picked up on the first ring.

"Hey, what's up," Iona asked.

"Nothing much. I just wanted to check on you and see how you're holding up," Keith told Iona.

That was Keith. Always making sure everyone else was taken care of. *But who's going to take care of you, Keith, if Mama doesn't survive this battle, who will take care of you?* Iona wanted to say, but instead she told him, "I'm holding up. I arrived home to find out about a bunch of drama going on with Dad and Donavan that I still haven't received the whole story on, but I plan to get to the bottom of it today." She picked up her coffee cup. It was dirty. She put it back down and asked. "How's Mom doing today? I was going to give her another hour or so to sleep before I called."

"She got out of bed this morning and started walking around the house reciting each of those scriptures you hung on the wall for her this weekend."

Iona could hear the hopeful excitement in Keith's voice. It made her smile. "Well, just make sure she doesn't over do it, okay? Faith is one thing; foolishness is another."

"Don't worry, I'm watching out for her." Keith hesitated for a moment and then asked, "Will you be back out to see her this weekend?"

"I'll be there Friday evening."

"Good, your mom wants to take you somewhere on Saturday."

Iona laughed. But it wasn't a ha-ha very funny laugh; it was more of an I-wish-this-was-somebody-else's-life kind of laugh. "She's not in any shape to take me anywhere. I know you don't like to do this where Mom is concerned, but you are going to have to put your foot down and tell that woman she can't go out of the house."

Keith calmly told Iona, "If she doesn't appear to be able to make the trip, I'll make sure she stays home. You make sure you get here on Friday. I think seeing you has given Cynda that extra boost she needed to fight this thing."

"I'm glad, Keith. I'll see you on Friday," Iona told him before hanging up the phone.

Iona grabbed her coffee cup and left her office to go to the restroom and wash her cup out. As she was turning off the water, she heard someone sniffling in the stall behind her. There were three stalls in the bathroom. Two of them were empty, but Iona recognized the navy blue Prada shoes underneath stall number three. She had helped the wearer shop for those shoes during a weekend shopping trip to New York last summer.

"Vivian, are you crying?" Iona hated asking obvious questions, but sometimes she opened her mouth, and stupid stuff came out anyway.

Vivian opened the stall door and slowly walked out. She was carrying a string of wet tissue like Linus on Charlie Brown carried his dirty blanket. Her eyes were blood shot and puffy. Yeah, Iona answered her own question, Vivian had been crying.

Iona hugged her friend and asked, "What happened?"

"Michael b-broke up w-with me," Vivian said through tears and stumbling attempts to control her breathing. Vivian pulled her inhaler out of her pocket and took a puff. She leaned against the bathroom wall and took deep easy breaths.

"You okay now?" Iona asked.

Vivian lifted her inhaler. "I don't leave home without it."

"Did Michael take someone else to the Bahamas?"

"You guessed it."

"That's low down. You've been with him for two years. I really thought he was going to ask you to marry him."

"Yeah, me too." A small bitter laugh came out of Vivian's mouth as she said, "I think I'm going to kill him."

Iona leaned against the wall next to Vivian as she remembered how she thought Johnny was the man of her dreams when she met him a few years ago. She knew the pain Vivian was feeling, because she had endured it herself. She turned to her friend and suggested, "Why don't you go home? Take the day off and just come back tomorrow morning."

Vivian blew her nose. "If I leave, who is going to answer the phone and get your case files together?"

"Look Vivian, I'm not handicapped. I can handle this office for a day." Iona opened the bathroom door and ushered her friend out. "Come on, let's get your coat and your purse. Go enjoy this cold wintry February day."

"Girl, it's minus two degrees out there. Instead of going home to nurse my broken heart, I'll probably die of frost bite."

Iona laughed. "Well, if you're still alive in the morning, I'll pick you up for breakfast—my treat. Okay?"

"All right, I'll see you then. But if it's your treat, I want to go to the Marriott for breakfast. I love their waffles and omelets," Vivian told her as she gathered her belongings and left.

Iona looked at her watch. It was 9:45 in the morning. She had about fifteen minutes before her meeting with Clarence and she hadn't even gone over his file yet.

Back in her office, Iona opened the file that JL's office had sent over last Friday while she was in Chicago. She went up against JL in one other trial. He had played dirty and withheld evidence until it was too late for her to do anything about it. In short, her drug dealing client was now doing federal time. Therefore, she planned to go over all the documents JL sent to her and then she was going to petition the court for any other documents that might have somehow been misplaced. How does that saying go? Fool me once, shame on you; fool me twice, and I might have to cut you.

According to the documents JL sent over, Clarence was not spotted on the surveillance tapes inside the jewelry store at the time of the heist. What messed Clarence up was the fact the jewelry store had cameras installed on the outside of the building. Those cameras clearly showed two masked men jumping into a red Monte Carlo, Ohio license plate number DDU-1470. When the police ran the plates, they discovered the car was registered to Clarence Mason. They picked him up on his job. Clarence claimed he was at work all day and someone else had his car. But, when the detectives pressed him about the identity of the person who had his car, Clarence stopped talking.

"That's why his stupid self is heading to prison. If he didn't do it, why didn't he just tell the cops who had his car?" Iona said to herself then jotted that question down on a note pad to ask Clarence when he arrived.

She looked at her watch again. He was five minutes late. Her telephone rang. Iona almost didn't pick it up then she remembered that Vivian had left for the day. "This is Iona Walker. Can I help you?"

"Thank God you picked up. You're my one phone call; I just got popped," a voice on the other end told her.

Iona recognized the voice. The caller was Vinny, the petty thief. If someone looked up the phrase "repeat offender," his picture would be next to the definition.

"What did you do this time, Vinny?" Iona asked.

"They got me down here on a bogus breaking and entering charge. But, they don't have any witnesses." He sighed as if he was just so tired of being falsely accused. "I need a date, Counselor. Are you available or what?"

The words Vinny spoke made Iona feel dirty. She shivered in her seat as she replayed Johnny telling her that she wasn't a lawyer, but a prostitute, and she snapped. "Why don't you just call it what it is, Vinny? A court appearance. Why do you need a lawyer to make a court appearance for you? Could it be because you can't stop stealing? Well, guess what, Vinny? This time I have better things to do than to try and keep your sorry self out of prison."

"Now wait a minute," Vinny said, raising his voice. "You're my attorney. You're supposed to help me. I need your advice."

"You know what, Vinny? I'm going to give you some free advice. Stop stealing and get a job," she told him and then hung up the telephone.

She sat behind her mahogany desk looking at her bookshelf full of serious, no-nonsense leather bond case law books, she determined that she would never again refer to a meeting with a client as a date. She was a professional. She earned her right to be an attorney and she would start acting like it.

Her telephone rang again. Iona snatched it up, hoping that it would be Clarence with some explanation about his tardiness.

It was Vivian. "I know I'm supposed to be crying my eyes out and not calling the office for the rest of the day, but I had to tell you what I saw."

"What's up?" Iona asked.

"When I left the office, Clarence was walking toward our building, but then this black sedan with smoked out windows pulled up and Clarence got in the car."

"Who did he get in the car with?" Iona asked.

"I don't know. But I did get the license plate number. Do you want it?"

The second line on Iona's phone rang. "Hold on a minute, Vivian." She clicked over. "This is Iona Walker can I help you?"

"Hey, hon, it's your dad."

"Hey, Dad, what's up? You ready to tell me what's going on with Donavan?"

Isaac's voice sounded hurried and a bit disturbed as he said, "We'll have to talk about that later. But I need to know if Clarence is there with you. He told me he was meeting with you this morning."

"No. He blew our meeting off. Probably out hiding the jewels with his accomplices."

"I don't think Clarence is with any accomplice," Isaac told her.

"How can you be so sure? Vivian just told me she saw him getting into a car right in front of my building this morning."

"Honey, I just received a call from someone claiming to be holding Clarence. He said he was going to kill him."

"Daddy, what are you talking about? Why would anyone want to kill Clarence?"

"I don't know. This guy said that he was going to kill Clarence for me—like I asked him to do it or something."

Iona stood up and frantically looked around the office, as if something within would help her solve this dilemma. "Daddy, listen to me. You need to hang up with me and call the police. I'll go to Clarence's house and talk to his wife."

"No. I don't want you going anywhere by yourself. If this maniac has really killed Clarence, who knows, he could be after you next. I'll pick you up in front of your office. We'll go together."

"Okay, Daddy, I'll wait for you downstairs," she said, then hung up the phone. As Iona cleared off her desk and then reached for her purse, she noticed that line one on her phone was blinking. She hit her forehead with the palm of her hand as she realized she had left Vivian on hold. She picked up the telephone and hit the line one button. "Vivian! Vivian!"

No answer.

"Vivian, can you hear me?!" Iona yelled. When Vivian first told her that she'd seen Clarence get into a car right outside her law office, Iona assumed he was bailing on her. After talking with her father, she was concerned Clarence may have been abducted or even worse. She needed that license plate number from Vivian like she needed to breathe. "Vivian, please say something."

Iona hung up and tried her friend's cell. No answer. She dialed her home number and didn't get an answer there either. Alarm swept through her. What if the abductor saw Vivian when she saw him?

Chapter 11

"We need to go to Vivian's house first, Dad," Iona told Isaac as she jumped in his car. "Vivian told me she wrote down the license plate number of the car Clarence got into. I'm worried that if Clarence really was abducted, maybe the person who did it saw Vivian writing down his license plate number."

Iona gave her father the address and they sped off in that direction. Isaac picked up his cell and dialed. It rang twice and then was picked up.

"Dunford here," Johnny said.

"Johnny, I think we may need some police back up." It was funny to Isaac that he would voluntarily contact the police to help with anything. For more than thirty some years, he avoided the police. Now in his sixties and a law abiding citizen, he reached out—worked with the police to prevent crime. "We're headed over to the Salem Woods apartments over by Cub Foods." Isaac gave him the full address and then asked, "Can you meet us over there? It's one of Iona's friends and we think someone might have attacked her."

"I'm on my way," Johnny told Isaac.

"Thanks, son. We'll see you when you get there."

Iona rolled her eyes when Isaac hung up the phone. She asked her father, "Why'd you have to call *him*? We could have dialed 911 if we needed the police."

"I trust Johnny. He knows what he's doing, and if anyone can help your friend, it'll be him."

Iona wasn't going to waste her breath discussing her ex-boyfriend with her father. She knew good and well that Pastor Walker thought the sun rose and set in Johnny Dunford; that a finer man had not been born, except of course Donavan. "Daddy, have you talked to Donavan?" Isaac gripped the wheel tighter. Iona knew that her father's tight grip on the steering wheel was his way of trying to grab hold of a situation that had spiraled out of control; like trying to bottle a whirlwind. She patted her father's shoulder to comfort him.

"He won't return my calls," Isaac finally told her. "He messed up, but it's as if he blames me for catching him. Like I sent that email to myself."

"What email?"

Isaac took his eyes off the road for a second and looked at his daughter, then turned his eyes back to the road. "You haven't talked to your brother?"

Iona sighed. "He won't return my calls either. But, he can't avoid me for ever. I'll talk to him sooner or later. But right now I need you to tell me about this email."

Isaac shrugged. "Nothing to it. Donavan emailed me. Asked me to meet him at his house. His email indicated that I might get there before he did, so I needed to let myself in. Which I did, and I don't even want to discuss what I saw when I opened that door."

"Daddy, are you telling me that my brother told you to let yourself into his house when he knew you would find him in a compromising position?"

"Sounds crazy, I know. But I think he wanted me to catch him."

"Not in a million years, Daddy. It didn't happen like that."

"You explain it to me. I saw everything with my own eyes."

"I can't explain it right now. But I'll get to the bottom of this. You better believe I will." She snapped her fingers and said, "Oh yeah, Vinny got arrested again."

"I don't want to hear that," Isaac told Iona.

"I know. That boy is his own worst enemy. I'm done. I'm not taking his case this time."

"Iona, you need to understand something about Vinny. I don't think he wants to be the way he is. He just needs someone to believe in him. His entire family is a bunch of criminals; that's all he knows."

"I don't care. I'm done."

"All right, all right. I'll find someone else to take his case."

Iona turned and looked at her father as if he just stunned her by saying he was going to divorce Nina or something else crazy like that. "I don't understand you, Daddy. When do you finally throw in the towel on some of these guys?"

"I used to be just like them, Iona. I wish someone had gone out of their way for me. Maybe I would have come out of that life sooner than I did, and caused less destruction."

They pulled up in front of Vivian's apartment. Iona got out of the car, ran over to her friend's door, and started banging on it. When Iona didn't receive an answer, she turned to Isaac and said, "The manager's apartment is right next door, maybe he can open the door for us."

Johnny pulled up next to Isaac's car. Isaac waved him over. As Johnny approached, Isaac pointed in the direction of the manager's door and asked Johnny to go see if the manager could open the door for them.

The manager was still in his robe when he came down the stairs. The man appeared to be about fifty, but Vivian had told her that her manager was well into his seventies. He slowly walked over to Vivian's door, and unlocked it after the officers told him that they needed to get in.

They entered Vivian's apartment and Iona ran in. She put her hand to her mouth and screamed as she spotted Vivian stretched out on the floor.

Johnny called for an ambulance.

Iona noticed the bruise on the side of Vivian's head and screamed louder.

"Get out of here, Iona," Johnny said.

Isaac grabbed Iona by the arm and tried to pull her out of the house.

"She needs her inhaler!" Iona screamed. "Get her inhaler." Isaac was pushing her out the door when she said, "It's in her pocket!"

Isaac put his arms around Iona and told her, "Let him do his job, Baby Girl. Just wait here with me."

Iona hugged Isaac. "What have I done, Daddy? What have I done?"

"You didn't do anything, Baby Girl."

"Yes, I did," Iona said through tears. "I sent her home. I'm the reason she saw something she shouldn't have. Do you want to know something, Daddy? I sent her home because I didn't want to hear about her problems."

Isaac hugged his daughter tight and said, "Don't do this to yourself. You couldn't have known what would happen."

"I'm an awful person, Daddy. I'm an awful friend."

Johnny ran back outside with a frantic look on his face. He asked Iona, "Does she have a breathing machine?"

She pulled herself out of Isaac's arms and said, "I-I don't know. Can't you just use her inhaler?"

"She doesn't have an inhaler."

"She keeps it in her pocket," Iona said.

Johnny told Iona, "It's not there, I looked."

Iona rushed back into the apartment and checked Vivian's

pockets herself. Nothing was there. She turned back to Johnny and shouted, "You've got to do something. She's turning blue."

Isaac said, "Move out of the way, Iona. Let me pray for her."

Isaac got on his knees and put one hand on Vivian's forehead and the other at the top of her chest and began to pray as Iona stood up and moved out of his way. "Father God, we need you in this situation. This young woman's air passages are blocked, but I believe that you can breathe life into her. So, right now in Jesus' mighty name, I speak life into Vivian's body. Do you hear me Vivian? Live, in Jesus name."

Iona expected her father to hoop and holler over Vivian's body and spit all over the girl while trying to get God to revive her. But his prayer was more like a conversation; like he was in direct communication with God and he knew that God heard him even without all the hoopla. Like when Lazarus had died and Jesus simply said, 'Lazarus, come forth' and Lazarus got up out of the grave just like that; because God always heard Jesus.

The bluish/purple tint to Vivian's skin color began to subside and Iona could see Vivian's own honey skin tone again. Vivian's eye lids fluttered.

Johnny pumped his fist in the air as he said, "Thank God. Oh, thank God."

The paramedics came through the door, put Vivian on the stretcher and carted her out of the room. Iona ran to her father and hugged him. "Thank you, Daddy. Thank you so much."

Isaac pulled Iona's hands from around his waist and held them in his hands as he corrected her. "No, baby, thank the Lord. He is the healer."

Tears streamed down Iona's face as the realization of what her father said sunk in. God was more than able to bring a person like Vivian back from near death and He was able to heal her mother from this cancer that was eating away at her body.

"Okay, Daddy. Okay. I will thank the Lord for all He did for Vivian and for what He will do for my mother also."

"Never stop believing in the power of prayer, Iona."

The problem for Iona was that she had stopped believing. As she sat in the hospital waiting room with Vivian's parents waiting to find out if her friend would live or die, she desperately wanted to believe again. Iona found herself questioning the decisions she made her whole adult life. When had she become the master of her own fate? When had she decided that she didn't need God anymore?

Iona couldn't point to a certain date or even a particular situation. She could only remember that when she went away to college, prayer time had taken a back seat to all the other activities and school work that concerned a young college student. Then, she discovered sororities and frat parties, and within a year of being away from home and at her college, Iona never noticed she lost her Bible. Or, maybe it had been stolen. She didn't know for sure what had happened to the leather bound Bible that Nina had engraved with Iona's name on it.

Her family believed in God. Nothing had ever swayed them from what they believed, so how did she get so messed up?

Iona put her feet in the chair she was sitting in, and hugged her knees to her chest as she pondered the twists and turns of her life. She was a young, black professional woman with money in the bank. Iona knew that no matter how much money she had, she couldn't help Vivian now, nor could she help her mother with her fight against death. All of that was in God's hands. "Please be merciful," Iona mumbled.

Johnny sat down in the seat next to Iona's. He had two cups of coffee in his hands and offered one to her.

"Thanks." She grabbed the cup and then asked, "Where did Daddy go?"

"He had to go take care of something with your mom. He said to tell you that he would be back in about an hour."

"Which mom?" Iona said with a half-smile.

"Nina," Johnny answered.

Iona took a sip of her coffee and then told Johnny, "I was just kidding. That's just my own private joke. I think of Nina as another mother. I love them both. I just don't know how to show it when it counts."

He sipped his coffee then asked, "Why is Vivian's father so angry with her?"

Iona turned to Johnny. "Her dad isn't angry with her—he's probably upset about what happened to Vivian and you're just reading it wrong."

Johnny glanced over at Mr. Stellar. He had his feet propped up on the coffee table and a pillow cushioning the back of his head as he leaned back and took a nap. "Vivian is back there fighting for her life and he doesn't seem to care. When I tried to get some information out of him, he acted as if I were bothering him. Maybe I should list him as a suspect."

"Johnny, that's just crazy," Iona said.

"No it's not. And you know something else? I don't think Mr. Stellar is Vivian's real dad. They don't look anything alike."

Iona's eyebrows furrowed as she glanced at Mr. Stellar, then turned back to Johnny. "Not everyone looks like their dad, you know?"

"He probably knows that Vivian isn't his child."

"I'm not going to sit here and listen to you insinuate that Vivian's mom cheated on her husband."

"It happens every day," Johnny said then raised his hand. "But hey, it's not my business—just trying to make sense of the things Mr. Stellar said to me and his need for a nap at a time like this." He pulled out a note pad and then changed the subject. "Look, I need to ask you a few questions before I get back to the station. If you're not up to talking about this right now, I can talk with you later this evening."

Iona shook her head. "I don't want to put anything off. I want to help. I'm tired of just helping myself and never doing anything for anyone else."

"I think you're being too hard on yourself, Iona."

She unfolded her legs and let her feet drop to the floor as she said, "Okay, well then answer this for me, Johnny. Why do you jump every time my father asks you to do something?"

He shrugged. "I believe in everything he's trying to do with these young thugs. I look at some of them and think how lucky I am that I didn't turn to a life of crime. God knows I didn't have much to influence me in the right direction."

Iona nudged him. "Boy, who are you kidding? Your father was a cop. He would have beat your behind if you got into any trouble."

"Yeah," Johnny agreed. "But he died before I reached my teens, so I had a lot of opportunity to get into trouble. I guess I jump for your dad because I wish I had one just like him."

"See what I mean?" Iona shook her head. "He *is* my father and I don't jump like you do when he needs something. I always give him a hard time. I am completely self absorbed. And you know something else? You were right about me."

Johnny brought his hands to Iona's face and wiped away the tears that were rolling down her cheeks. "Iona, you're at the hospital crying about what happened to Vivian, so you can't be completely self-absorbed."

Iona brought her hands to her face and rubbed her eyes. She then turned and looked at Johnny. "Do you know why I became a lawyer? I mean, why I even went to law school in the first place?"

He sat the notepad in the empty seat next to him. "No, why?"

"Well, my whole family is in the ministry in some way shape or form. Ministry was all I knew from the time I was ten years old. Whether I was in Dayton at my father's house or in Chicago at my mother's house, they taught me how to win the lost to Christ. I knew my parents had trouble with the law before they came to Christ.

"So I wanted to be an advocate for people like my mother and father. People that had been on the wrong side of the law, but just needed a chance; somebody to help them pick another path."

"Well, isn't that what you do now?"

Iona shook her head. "I didn't fulfill my mission. I was supposed to get these criminals off and help them turn their life around. The only time I even come close to doing something like that is when I take a case that my father forces on me. And he's the one that tries to get them to turn their life around. I just take as much of their money as I can."

They sat in silence for a few minutes. Uncomfortable with the silence, Iona scratched her throat and then said, "You had some questions for me?"

"Um, yes," Johnny said as he picked his note pad and pen back up. "What exactly did Vivian tell you when she called?"

Iona leaned back in her seat and told Johnny everything that happened that day. But just as she was finishing her story, the doctor came out and spoke to Vivian's parents. Iona jumped up and hurried over to them.

"She's weak," the doctor told them. "But she'll make it."

"Oh thank God," Vivian's mother said as she fell into her husband's arms and wept.

Then the doctor asked, "Is there someone by the name of Iona out here?"

Iona raised her hand. "I'm Iona."

The doctor looked at Iona and said, "Come with me, ma'am. My patient is refusing to go to sleep until she speaks to you."

Johnny turned to Vivian's parents and asked, "Do you mind if I go with Iona. We think Vivian might have been attacked. Hopefully she can reveal something that might help us find the person who did this to her."

"Please go," Vivian's mother said. "I want that animal caught."

Vivian's father rolled his eyes as if his wife was being a drama queen. He shook his head and told Johnny, "Go ahead, young man. Hopefully you can get the truth out of her."

With that, Iona and Johnny headed through the emergency room double doors. The doctor directed them to room number ten and they walked in.

Vivian was stretched out on the hospital bed. The right side of her face was swollen. She reached out her hand and Iona bent down and hugged her friend. "He took my inhaler," Vivian told her.

Iona stepped out of their embrace and said, "I figured that when I couldn't find it."

"I just don't know why he took my inhaler. He'd already knocked me out when he hit me. When I woke up; I was having trouble breathing, so I reached for my inhaler. But it wasn't in my pocket. I searched for it on the floor, but then I passed out again."

Johnny stepped closer to the bed and asked, "Did you get a look at the person who hit you." He wanted to ask, *was it your dad?*

Tears sprang into Vivian's eyes as she shook her head. "No. He hit me from behind."

Iona spoke up. "Vivian, you always keep your inhaler in your pocket. Since the motive wasn't robbery, this guy wouldn't have a reason to go in your pockets unless he knew that you used an inhaler. So I'm guessing that the person who kidnapped Clarence and then came after you has to be someone familiar with you, me or the firm. What do you think?"

Vivian turned to Iona with a thoughtful look on her face. "I'm not so sure it's someone we know," she said after a moment. "The guy did steal something from me. He probably went into my pocket looking for the license plate number and found the inhaler in my pocket."

Chapter 12

Donavan stood in his front yard and looked around. He loved the well manicured lawn that he'd spent numerous Saturday mornings creating. He'd replaced the outdated bushes in the front lawn with Japanese Maples and put a deck on the back that he used in the summertime when he had cookouts for his youth group. His mom and Iona had planted an assortment of flowers around his condo to beautify the place. This was his home and he loved everything about it.

He stuck the 'For Rent' sign in the front yard near the curb. He hung his head and closed his eyes for a painful moment. He then turned to walk back into his condo. But just as he was opening the front door, he felt as if someone was watching him. He turned around and saw a black sedan with tinted windows stop in front of his house. He closed the front door and walked toward the car. Donavan was hoping that the driver was writing down the telephone number on his 'For Rent' sign. Maybe he had a taker already. But before he could get to the car, it sped off.

Turning back around, he wondered what that was all

about. Had he scared a potential renter off? He knew he was messed up, but was he really that ugly? *Oh well*, Donavan thought, *someone would call*. He put his mother's cell number on the renter's sign because his suitcases were packed and he was about to get on I-75 South and keep it moving. He needed to get away, and the reunion his fraternity was having in Atlanta was reason enough to shake the Ohio dust off his feet. He knew his frat brothers were going to be in the partying mood—lots of drinking and night clubbing. Donavan had never gotten into that stuff when he was in college. His frat brothers used to snidely ask him to pray for them before they headed out on a night of mischief. Donavan knew they didn't really want prayer, but he'd prayed for them anyway. He wondered what his frat brothers would think of him this trip when he went out drinking and clubbing with them. Because that's what he intended to do.

Nina pulled up as he was loading his car. She opened the driver side door of her Mercedes and strolled over to her son. Her hands were in her pocket as she leaned against his car and said, "Do you really have to go, son?"

Donavan put the last bag in the trunk of his car and closed it. He walked over to the side of the car, and stood next to his mom, whom he deeply loved and respected. That's why he couldn't look her in the eye as he said, "It's too hard for me to stay here Mama. I can't deal with you and dad, knowing I failed you."

Nina took her hands out of her pocket, grabbed hold of Donavan's face and turned it so he looked her in the eye. "Who did you fail, Donavan?"

He tried to look away, but she wouldn't let him. He closed his eyes, took a deep breath and then admitted, "I failed myself—and God."

"That's right, son. God is the only person that can judge you on this. You will have to figure out a way to forgive yourself for failing Him." She gently brushed his face with her hand, and as tears fell from her eyes she told him, "You have never failed me, son. I love everything about you, and I accept the good and the bad. Do you understand that?"

Donavan nodded, then he lifted his arm and wiped his eyes with the sleeve of his shirt. "I just need to get away, Mama. I need to figure some things out. Okay?"

Nina stepped away from her son and said, "You're a grown man, son. Not a day will go by that I won't pray for you. Promise me that you won't forget your foundation."

He'd told his mother that he didn't know how long he would be away, that he might look for a house while in Atlanta. That's why she looked so unsure and sad right now. So he tried to reassure her. "I won't, Mama. I haven't stopped believing in God, trust me on that."

"I'll be praying that the Lord guides you back home." She opened her purse and pulled an envelope out and handed it to Donavan. "Take this. Your father and I want you to have it."

Donavan looked around and asked, "Where is my father, huh? He knew I was leaving just like you did, right mother?"

She nodded.

Donavan stretched out his arms and turned to the left and then to the right. "Why didn't he come with you to wish me well, if he really cared?" Nina started to respond, but Donavan waved her off. "Forget it, I don't want anything from him. I just want to be left alone." He opened the car door and got in.

Nina grabbed the door before he could close it. "Donavan, your father is on his way here. He had an emergency with Iona. That's the only reason he's not here right now." She put the envelope in his lap. "Take this check, it was signed by your father—and you know the man as well as I do. If he didn't want you to have the money, he wouldn't have signed that check."

He opened the envelope and turned back to his mother, astonished. "This is five thousand dollars."

Nina straightened. "I know what it is. God has prospered me and your father in the last five years. So at the end of each of those years we put five thousand in an account for you and five thousand in an account for Iona. It was meant to help you start your own business or whatever you want to do. We planned to give it all to you when you turned thirty anyway."

"Why didn't you give it all to me now? Are you and Dad trying to keep me on a short leash by showing me what could be mine if I shape up?"

"No, son. The money is yours and we will give you the rest when you turn thirty. I just wanted to make sure you didn't starve while you were out there figuring things out. After all, I am still your mother," Nina said with a half-hearted smile.

His voice caught in his throat as he said, "T-thanks, Mom. I appreciate it." He closed the door and turned his eyes away from her as he backed out of the drive.

Davison and Brogan stood on top of Donavan's roof, surveying the land. They were God's angels charged to watch over Nina and Isaac. Davison was Nina's angel and the first to arrive at Donavan's condo. He was there because of Nina's concern for her son. Whether it was a premonition or a prodding from the Lord, Nina had been in fervent prayer for Donavan. That caused Davison to race to Donavan's to find out what was going on.

When he arrived, Satan's instrument of destruction was parked in front of Donavan's condo. The man Satan chose sat in his car with a gun trained on Donavan as he walked out toward the car. Donavan couldn't see the gun, because of the dark windows on the car. Davison quickly used the forces of God to instill fear in the assassin's heart. The assassin put the gun down and sped away.

When Brogan arrived, he let Davison in on the reason why the assassin set his sights on Donavan. The evil one was back in play. His attack against Isaac had failed and now he had set his sights on the preacher man's family. Someone working for the evil one had ordered Donavan's murder.

"We're going to need more help," Davison told Brogan. "If Nina hadn't been praying for Donavan like she had, I wouldn't have been here in time enough to scare that guy away. We don't know the way these evil minds work, so there's no way we're going to be able to fend off every attack."

"The evil one picked the perfect assassin. It is the sin that Isaac forgot about that has come back to haunt him."

"Do you think we have a chance of winning this battle?" Davison asked.

Isaac had been Brogan's charge for more than thirty years now. Brogan had been through many battles in his quest to protect Isaac. The evil one had become angrier each time Isaac brought a lost soul over to the kingdom of God, and had therefore sent attack after attack. Brogan guarded his charge with his very life. He saw no reason why he would lose Isaac at this late stage in the game.

Brogan unsheathed his long golden sword and lifted it in the air. He allowed it to glisten in the air to ward off any demon that would dare come near his charge. He turned to Davison and said, "I came to win, how about you?"

Davison smiled and unsheathed his golden sword and lifted it to the sky also. "Let's do this."

They both said in unison, "For all that is holy and all that is right."

Isaac wished some force—wind, or something—would have helped him get to his son's house on time. He stood in Donavan's yard with Nina looking lost and heartsick. He ran his hands through his hair as he turned to Nina. "How could he leave without saying goodbye to me? Let me see your cell phone. I'm going to let him know what I think of his behavior."

Nina glided her hand up her husband's back. "He's hurting right now, honey. We just have to give him some time."

"We didn't do this to him, Nina."

"I know that and you know it, but Donavan has to figure that out for himself."

He scratched his forehead and then looked to heaven for guidance. When he turned back to Nina he told her, "Okay, I'll give him time to cool off. I don't have time to worry about it right now anyway, I've got to get back to the hospital and pick up Iona."

"I'll follow you. I wanted to check on her friend anyway."

They got in their respective cars and drove to Good Samaritan Hospital, neither comprehending or knowing the fatal danger their son had just avoided with the help of the Lord and His angels. They also had no clue that tomorrow would be a world rocking day for Isaac either.

Chapter 13

Isaac stood behind his pulpit delivering a message designed to change the very hearts and minds of the listeners. Isaac knew that many street hustlers, con artists, prostitutes, and thieves attended his Wednesday night Bible study and Sunday morning worship service just so they could say they were trying to live right. They felt comfortable coming to the House of God, because the preacher was a former hustler himself, and could relate to their struggles.

Isaac understood the struggles a hustler faced when it came to going straight. The struggles were green with dead presidents on them. When a hustler is at the top of his game, he has street power and respect that he will never have washing cars or working a nine to five. He had been his own boss. He sets his own clock. He told other street hustlers what time to get up, where to go, and how long they should stay. Hard to convince a man like that to work for seven dollars and twenty five cents an hour.

Isaac was looking directly at Ron Holmes, a street hustler who'd managed to stay one step ahead of the police and rival hustlers that wanted to take his place. Isaac had been ministering to him for more than three years. He had never had any indication that he had gotten through to Ron and didn't expect to see him at church tonight, but here he was. Isaac knew this might be his last chance to convince Ron of God's goodness.

But when Isaac opened his Bible to preach, he didn't concentrate on the obstacles that stood in the way. Instead, he concentrated on God's ability to soften the hardest heart. He held onto both sides of the pulpit and looked out at the people gathered for Wednesday night Bible study and surmised that quite a few hustlers were in attendance tonight.

"Open your Bibles to Luke seven. We're going to begin reading at verse number thirty six," Isaac instructed.

Pages began turning. When they stopped, Isaac then read from the scriptures:

"Behold, a woman in the city, which was a sinner, when she knew that Jesus sat at meat in the Pharisee's house, brought an alabaster box of ointment,

And stood at his feet behind him weeping, and began to wash his feet with tears, and did wipe them with the hairs of her head, and kissed his feet, and anointed them with the ointment.

Now when the Pharisee which had bidden him saw it, he spake within himself saying, This man, if he were a prophet would have known who and what manner of woman this is that toucheth him: for she is a sinner."

Isaac lifted his eyes from the Bible and told his congregation, "This is a typical response that most church folks have when people who are not Bible totting scholars come into the house of God. They decide which sin is worthy of forgiveness and which is not, without asking God what He thinks. But if we go down to verse forty, I'll show you what the Lord thinks." He bent his head and began to read again.

"And Jesus answering said unto him, Simon, I have somewhat to say unto thee. And he saith, Master, say on. There was a certain creditor which had two debtors: the one owed five hundred pence, and the other fifty. And when they had nothing to pay, he frankly forgave them both. Tell me therefore, which of them will love him most?

Simon answered and said, I suppose the one to whom he forgave most."

Isaac looked at the congregation and said, "The one who was forgiven the most, loved God the most. How about it? Is there anybody out there that has messed up so bad that you could never earn enough money to pay your debt? What if Jesus decided to pay the debt for you? Would you accept His free gift or would you walk away as if the Lord had done nothing at all for you?"

Isaac's sermon continued for about ten minutes. He implored his listeners to give God a try; to trust the Lord with all their baggage. By the time he finished and made a call for all who wished to come to Jesus and leave his or her sins behind, twenty people stood at the altar. Not only were women at the altar crying, but grown men were crying and declaring their love for the Lord also. Ron Holmes had been one of the men standing at the altar with tears streaming down his face.

Isaac felt like walking on water when he entered his office after service. He took off his preaching robe and hung it in the closet, then he walked over to his leather couch to lay down and bask in the glory of what God had done this evening.

Just as he was sinking into the softness of his cushion and about to say, "Aaah," his door swung open and Deacon Harris ran in. Deacon Martin Harris was a portly man who'd never met a burger he didn't enjoy. But he'd also never entertained the thought of getting on a treadmill to shed some of the pounds all that good eating blessed him with. Consequently, running to Isaac's office left him out of breath. He bent down with his hands touching his knees and his oversized backside in the air and panted for air.

Isaac jumped off the couch and asked, "What's going on, Deacon Harris? What's the problem?"

Still panting, Deacon Harris managed to raise himself to an upright position as he said, "We need you out front, Pastor." Unable to move himself one step further, the deacon pointed to the front of the sanctuary. "Just outside the front door . . . Johnny is waiting on you out there."

Isaac left Deacon Harris in his office and walked toward the front of the sanctuary. When he reached his destination, he noticed a group of people standing outside staring down at something that was on the ground. Isaac opened the front door and stepped outside. As he turned his eyes in the direction that seemed to be holding everyone's attention, he to became mesmerized.

The body of Clarence Mason was on the ground, propped up against the wall next to the front door. He had a bullet hole in his forehead and a piece of paper taped to the front of his tan polo shirt. The note read, 'We don't like thieves, do we, Pastor Walker'?"

Isaac turned to Johnny and asked, "Who would do something like this?"

"I have no clue. In all my years on the police force I have never seen anything as bold as this," Johnny told Isaac. He then turned to the people standing around the dead body and told them, "Okay everyone, we're going to have to ask you to leave. This is a crime scene now and the homicide detectives are on their way here."

The crowd began to leave. Isaac went back into his office. Nina came in behind him with her arms folded and a horror stricken look on her face. "What's going on, Isaac?"

He was too stunned to answer. Even if he wasn't in a state of shock, he wouldn't be able to explain this unthinkable act. What type of person would be sick enough to kill a man and leave him on the church steps with a note pinned to his chest?

What about that note? 'We don't like thieves, do we, Pastor Walker?' Why did this madman leave a note for him on a dead body?

Nina pressed him. "Isaac, do you remember our conversation last night?"

"You're pregnant. Of course I know what we discussed last night. What does that have to do with what just happened here?"

Nina began wagging her finger in his face. "I told you I couldn't do this alone. I begged you not to get involved in anything that would bring harm to this family."

"Nina, how is this my fault?" Isaac asked exasperated.

"This type of stuff just seems to follow you around." Nina began to cry as she continued wailing at Isaac, "How could you let this happen? Why is this happening to us— now?"

Isaac hugged his wife. He gently stroked her back and said, "I don't know why this happened, baby. I didn't do anything." He stepped back from her and looked in her eyes. "Please believe me, Nina. I wouldn't do anything to jeopardize spending the rest of my life with you and our new baby. Do you really think God would finally allow you to conceive, just to take me away from you?"

Nina calmed herself, then as she wiped the tears from her face she said, "Okay, Pastor Walker. Just don't get involved in this. Let the police take care of it."

"That's exactly what I intend to do. The only thing I have to do is call Iona." When Nina gave him a questioning look as she sat down on the couch he told her, "Clarence was her client. She needs to know what happened to him."

This was Wednesday night, and the church had Bible study. So, as a member of the House of God Christian Fellowship, Iona should have been in attendance. She hadn't attended a Wednesday night Bible study in years. Iona was a Sunday go-to-meeting type of worshiper, and it hurt Isaac every time he had to admit that fact to himself.

Iona's phone rang twice before she picked up. "Hey, Daddy, what's up?"

"Clarence just turned up, Baby Girl."

Her voice had an excited lilt to it as she asked, "Are you kidding me? No, of course you're not kidding." She answered her own question and then asked, "Did he come to church? How was he acting? Like nothing happened and he hadn't caused any problems I bet."

"Iona, Clarence is dead."

She gasped.

Isaac continued, "Someone dumped his body at the church during Bible study. I thought you should know since he was your client."

"Y-yeah, s-sure, Dad. Thanks for telling me," she managed to stammer out.

"Do you need to come down here?" Isaac asked.

"How did he die?" Iona wanted to know.

"He was shot in the head." He heard Iona gasp. He didn't want to further shock her, but he told her the whole story. "There was a note pinned to his shirt. It said, 'We don't like thieves, do we Pastor Walker?'"

"What? Why would somebody leave a note like that on a dead man?"

"I wish I knew," he told her.

There was a knock at his office door. Nina walked over to the door to open it, and in walked Johnny with two men behind him.

Isaac ended his call as Nina was asking, "What can we do for you?"

"These men are homicide detectives out of my precinct." Johnny pointed to a tall, thin white man with curly, blonde hair and said, "This is Alex Matthews." He turned in the direction of the shorter, bald, black man and said, "This is Malcolm Gordon. They want to ask you a few questions."

Isaac offered them a seat and then told the detectives everything he knew about the situation, which wasn't much. When he was done, Detective Gordon asked Isaac, "And you don't have any idea why this maniac is doing this?"

Isaac shook his head. "I have no idea at all."

"Well, what's this problem you have with thieves?" the other detective asked Isaac.

"I don't have a problem with anyone, officer. I try to treat everyone the same, and I help the people that go astray."

"What type of firearms do you own?" Detective Matthews asked.

"I don't," Isaac said.

Gordon asked, "When's the last time you had a gun in your possession, whether you borrowed it or whatever?"

"Hold up a minute," Johnny said. "Pastor Walker had nothing to do with this. Your questions are way off base."

"Let us do our job, Johnny," Detective Gordon admonished. He then turned back to Isaac. "We are not accusing you of anything, Pastor Walker. We're just trying to get all the facts straight."

Isaac nodded and then told him, "I haven't had a gun in my possession in almost twenty years. I rely on the Lord to protect me now. I left all that other stuff alone a long time ago."

The detectives rose. "Thanks for the information, Pastor Walker. We'll be in touch if we need anything further."

"Thank you. If I think of anything else, I'll let you know," Isaac told them.

"You do that," Detective Gordon said as they exited the room.

Chapter 14

Iona sat behind her desk and called the assistant district attorney's office. When Jerome, or JL as he preferred to be called, picked up the phone, Iona told him the awful news concerning Clarence. JL had been the prosecutor on the case and Iona thought she should let him know that he wouldn't be getting a staring role on the nightly news based on the Clarence Mason case.

JL seemed to take the news pretty well. He managed to gloss over the dead body between them and turned it into a win-win situation for himself. "You know, Iona, since we are no longer opposing each other, why don't we work together?"

"How can we work together JL? You're a prosecutor and I'm a defense attorney."

"I'm not talking about the courtroom."

"What exactly are you talking about then?"

"Come on, Iona. You know I want to take you out. I've been giving you signals every time I run into you. Why won't you give a brother a try?"

Was JL a brother? Iona thought he was just a deeply

tanned white man. That assessment was unkind. JL was an assistant District Attorney on the fast track to becoming *the* District Attorney and then a Judge, so maybe he had to be stiff and guarded when in the public eye.

"I don't know JL; I've never thought about you in that way."

"Fair enough. Why don't you let me take you out to dinner and see if I can change your mind?"

Iona picked up a pencil and tapped it on her desk as she thought about this. The more she tried to imagine JL as her man, images of Johnny kept coming to mind. Iona was drained. This past week had worn her out. "I'll tell you what. Let me think about it, and I'll let you know. Okay?"

"I can live with that. I'll get back with you next week."

"All right, I'll talk to you later." She hung up the phone and picked her mug off her desk and walked out of her office to get coffee. She stopped just outside her door and almost dropped her mug at the sight of Vivian sitting behind her desk. "What are you doing here? You were just attacked on Tuesday and released from the hospital yesterday. I specifically told you to take the rest of the week off."

"I watched the news last night, Iona. So, I know that Clarence is dead. All night long I kept imagining that psycho sneaking into my apartment and finishing the job he started on me. I had to get out of there." Vivian told her.

"You're a martial arts expert, Vivian. If someone breaks into your house, break his arm."

Pure terror swept across Vivian's face at the mention of someone breaking in on her. "That's just it, Iona. I know how to defend myself, but this guy was still able to sneak in my house and knock me out. Things like that just make you realize that you're not invincible after all."

"Look, if you're really worried about someone coming back to your place, why don't you come stay with me for a little while?"

"Thanks for the offer, but my mom and dad are moving my stuff out of my apartment as we speak. I'm going to stay with them until I feel comfortable enough to move out on my own again."

Iona walked around the desk and gave Vivian a hug. Vivian leaned into her friend as Iona said, "Don't worry, you'll get your footing back."

"I sure hope so. Because I don't know how long I can last under the same roof with my father."

Iona ended their embrace and then asked, "What's going on with you and your father. He seemed a bit upset with you the other day."

"He's been upset since the doctor told him I was a girl." Vivian waved her hand in the air and shook her head. "Anyway, now you don't have to worry about things not getting handled in the office tomorrow when you leave for Chicago."

Iona needed a hug. She had tried not to think about her trip back to Chicago and her mother's illness. She went to the coffee pot and poured coffee into her mug. Neil Morgan, the law firm's private investigator, came over to her with a file in his hand.

"What's up, Neil?" she asked while stirring some cream and sugar into her coffee.

He laughed, and Iona got the distinct impression that he was laughing at her as he held up a file and she read the name on it.

"Where do you get your clients from? I mean really, Iona. Do you take an ad out in Criminals R Us or what?"

She grabbed the file out of his hand and rolled her eyes. She hated working with Neil, but unless she was going to pay for investigations out of her own pocket, she had to use the company jerk boy. That was his name as far as Iona was concerned; Neil the jerk boy.

"Let's discuss this in my office," she said while walking

back to her office. Neil would love to tell her all the misdeeds of her clients in the coffee area for any and everyone to walk by and hear, but Iona wasn't having it.

She sat down behind her desk and invited Neil to take one of the chairs in front of her desk. The name on the file was Joey McDaniels. Iona was very familiar with this case. Joey had been a big time drug dealer who had flunked Drug Dealing 101; don't get high on your own supply. Short on cash and in line for a bullet in the head if he didn't come up with the money he owned some Detroit hustlers, Joey stuck up a crack house. During the commission of the crime, Joey shot the drug dealing house sitter. The dealer later died after a week in intensive care.

"His finger prints are not only on the murder weapon," Neil told Iona, "they're all over the front entrance of that crack house and two of the crack heads in the house put down their pipes long enough to positively ID Joey as the shooter. Your boy is going down."

Iona rolled her eyes. She took this case as a favor to her father. Isaac Walker was on the salvation war path. She saw Joey walk down the aisle and give his life to the Lord at her father's church a couple of weeks ago. As Joey walked toward salvation, Iona remembered how Isaac begged her to help Joey with his criminal case. Joey reminded Isaac of someone he should have helped when he was younger. Her father admitted that he turned his back on a friend.

"Why do you keep taking on these losers when you know you can't possibly win?" Neil asked.

I'm going to wipe away my father's guilt with this case. When we help Joey, my father can stop thinking about the friend he neglected to help in his younger days, Iona thought as she took the file out of Neil's hand. "I'm sure that people thought the same thing about Johnny Cochran and F. Lee Bailey."

Neil smirked. "Do you consider yourself a Cochran or a Bailey?"

"You're a non-believer? Well, watch me work, Doubting Thomas. When I'm done with this case, that smirk on your face will be turned into respect. And you know what else, Neil? I won't even make you grovel for work when I open my own law firm off of these loser cases of mine."

Neil stood and held up his hands. "Look, you don't have to get uptight. I'm just saying that you've got a long way to go before you can claim you're just as good as the defense attorneys you named."

Iona just stared at him.

Neil walked backward toward the door. "Well, I gave you the information you needed. If you have any other cases you need me to look into, just let me know."

Iona couldn't stand the little weasel, but in truth, she did need him to look into something else for her. "Wait, Neil, I do need you."

The smirk returned to his face as he strutted back into her office. "What can I do for you?"

Iona handed him the file she had been reviewing on Clarence Mason. "I need you to check out his story."

Neil briefly looked over the file and then he turned to Iona with a questioning glance. "Didn't this man get killed last night?"

"Yes, but something doesn't sit right with me on this one. When he was arrested, he claimed that he didn't have his car that day. He said that someone had borrowed it, but he wouldn't tell the police who that person was. I want you to find out."

"Come on, Iona, what do you think he would say?"

"You might be correct. Clarence could have lied, but I want to know for sure. Can you check on it, or do I need to find someone else to handle this?"

Neil clung onto the file. "I can take care of it. I'll get back with you next week," he told her and then walked out of her office.

Now that Clarence was dead, Iona felt guilty about not believing him. What if someone else did borrow his car? What if he tried to protect that person and was murdered because he was going to tell her the truth during their meeting yesterday.

Iona turned her thoughts back to her mother. She looked at the telephone for several minutes trying to decide whether or not to call her. Iona didn't know what she would do if her mother had gotten worse. She decided she wouldn't wait until tomorrow to talk to Cynda.

She picked up the telephone and dialed, laughing to herself as she remembered telling friends in high school about her *summer home*. Back then she tried to make the fact that she split her time between her mother and father's homes seem like something out of the *Lifestyles of the Rich and Famous*. If her high school friends had seen the small one-story house Keith had back then, she would have been the laughing stock rather than the homecoming queen of her high school class. But Keith's construction business had prospered and they now lived in a seven thousand square foot mansion. Her mom called their home, The House That God Built. Iona wondered if God would re-build her mother.

Cynda picked up the phone and said, "Hey, honey, I was just praying for you. What's going on down there?"

"You don't even want to know, Mom. And I didn't call to discuss the craziness going on in this town. I want to know how you're doing."

Cynda sighed. "I have good days and bad. Today has been a bad day for me, hon. I haven't been able to get out of bed, so I've just been praying where I lay."

Iona closed her eyes and brought her hand up to her head. She ran her hand through her hair as she said, "I hate to hear that, Mom. Do you think I should come out there today instead of tomorrow?" In other words, do you think you're going to die tonight?

"No, baby. I wouldn't be good company today. You go on and take care of your business there. I can wait until tomorrow to see you."

"Are you sure, Mom?" *Please don't die on me.*

"I'm sure. Let me rest today. And we can throw a party tomorrow. Okay?"

Iona laughed. "Okay. I'll bring the party favors."

A hulking figure unseen by Iona sat huddled against the wall in her office. His assignment was just to watch. Iona had not yet yielded herself to the Lord, and because of that, she was vulnerable to all the attacks of Satan. The angel was bold and fearless, well able to defeat the demonic forces sent by the enemy, but he could do nothing until Iona began to believe.

Miguel had been assigned to Iona when she was just a young child. He hadn't been able to enter into many battles on her behalf. Her mother and father covered her with their prayers when she was younger, but Iona had long since reached an age where she needed to cover herself. Until she learned how to do that, his angelic protection meant nothing to her. That was a shame, because the angel knew that Iona was in grave danger. He wished she knew it. If she knew the danger that lurked just around the next corner, maybe she would begin to pray, and then he could unsheathe his sword and do battle for her. These heavenly and hellish battles were not meant for humans to fight. The Lord wanted His angels to fight battles for humans, but people like Iona just wouldn't pray; wouldn't seek God.

A burst of light entered the office. The angel saw Iona blink twice and then rub her eyes trying to adjust them to the brightness that was suddenly apart of her world. But the angel knew that Iona would never be able to adjust to the light the commander angel, Arnoth, exuded. He even had trouble with it at times.

The angel stood and Arnoth's light began to dim. He lowered his head, ashamed of the position of inactivity he'd been in for more years than he wanted to admit.

"Commander, what brings you here?" the angel asked.

Arnoth glanced over at Iona as she adjusted the blinds in her office then came back to her seat to look over the files on her desk. Cynda Williams was his charge, and he had been knighted because of the battles he endured during her journey back to God. He turned back to the angel before him and said, "Miguel, your wait is over. Cynda has been praying fervently for this one," he pointed to Iona. "The Lord revealed to me that a great battle is about to take place and she will be right in the midst of it. So get ready to unsheathe your sword. The All Mighty has commanded that you protect her."

When Miguel put his hand on his sword and lifted it above his head, there was joy on his face. He was unleashed to help Iona fend off the attacks of the enemy.

Chapter 15

Vinny Thompson walked out of the county lock up early Thursday morning after his baby's mama came up with the bail money. His public defender thought he had a good chance of beating the charges against him. Like he'd told Iona; no witnesses.

Thursday night he sat in his girlfriend's Toyota checking out a two-story house in a suburban section of town. This job was going to go better than the last one. Basically, as long as it ended without him getting arrested, it would go down in his book as a better job. No one was home at this fancy-dancy five bedroom house that could easily house his two sisters and four brothers. Maybe they'd have to double up, but they could make it work. If his family had received breaks like this wonderfully blessed family, maybe he wouldn't have turned to a life of crime. Maybe he would have gone to college to become a doctor or something else slick like that.

So, really these people owed him for the good life they had. Every now and then they needed to give to the poor. And Vinny was about to help them do just that. He put on his gloves, opened his car door and grabbed his tools. His mark didn't have a fence around the house, so he walked right up the driveway. It was dark outside and he wore all black and had a black cap pulled over his head, so he wasn't worried about anyone being able to ID him as he walked to the back of the house.

He bent down in front of the back door and opened his kit. This would be a piece of cake. Rich people, living in so called safe neighborhoods always thought they were safe. So they didn't bother using half the high-tech equipment provided by their security system. Just as he started working the racket wrenches on the door jam, he heard footsteps behind him.

At that moment, Vinny wondered if he should find another line of work. Breaking and entering wasn't going too well for him. Did a neighbor call the police that quick? Vinny dropped his tools and lifted his hands. "I lost my key. I'm just trying to get into my house, officer."

Vinny felt the the butt of a gun as it connected with his head. He knew it was a gun, because it happened to him before. He fainted, and when he woke up, he realized it wasn't a cop who hit him. It was Chico, the supervisor from the car wash he'd worked at. For some reason, Chico had thought he'd broken into his house and he wanted all his stuff back.

As Vinny blacked out, this second time he wondered who had followed him to this house. Who wanted their stuff back now?

Cynda was laying in the bed in the family room singing praises to the Lord when Iona walked in. Keith had picked her up from the airport and seemed to be in good spirits. Iona didn't understand this since his wife was at home struggling to stay alive. So she had asked Keith, "What's got you in such a good mood?"

Keith smiled as he grabbed her bag. He then turned to

Iona and said, "Nothing in particular. I just love the Lord, and I was thinking about that all day today."

And now as Iona stood in her mother's family room and watched her struggle to raise her hands as she sung, "You are great; You do miracles so great," Iona wanted to remind her mother that she was giving praise to the same God that had allowed her to be stricken with cancer.

Iona rolled her eyes and stormed upstairs to her bedroom and slammed the door. She wanted to block out her mother's and Keith's delusions of this great God coming to their rescue. Her mother couldn't even get out of bed for God sakes.

Iona sat down on her bed, picked up her pillow and covered her face with it as she bent her head toward her knees and screamed into the pillow. She screamed and screamed and screamed until Keith swung her door open and knelt down in front of her.

He pulled the pillow out of Iona's grasp and pulled her into an embrace. But Iona broke free and stood up. Tears were flowing down her face. She defiantly wiped them away.

"It's okay, Iona. Calm down, honey," he told her.

She wiped more tears away but they kept falling. "I don't want to calm down. I'm angry." She pointed at him and said, "And you should be too. But no, you are here thinking on the goodness of the Lord and my mother is down there praising His holy name."

Keith reached out to her. "Iona, come to me. Okay?"

"No," she shouted. "I don't want you to comfort me. I want my mother to live. Can you do that for me, Keith? Can you get that prayer through to God?"

Even in the midst of Iona claiming that she did not want to be comforted, Keith walked toward her with his arms wide open. He pulled her back into his arms and held her as she cried.

"Please, Keith," Iona clung to him and said, "Can you get that prayer through?"

"God knows, baby. I've done nothing but pray about this."

Iona was running out of steam. She felt overwhelmingly tired and in need of rest. She stepped out of Keith's embrace and told him, "I'm a little tired, Keith. Let me take a quick nap and then I'll come sit with Mama so you can pick the kids up from school. Okay?"

"All right," Keith said and then walked out of the room and closed the door.

Iona laid down and tried to imagine what the world would be like if she still believed in knights in shining armor, good things coming to those who wait and happy endings to disastrous beginnings. She didn't know where, how or even when, but her innocence had been stolen—and Iona wanted it back. She closed her eyes hoping that when she reopened them she would believe again.

It was two in the afternoon when Iona woke up. She had slept about an hour and a half. She yawned and stretched. She then got out of bed and went downstairs to check on her mother.

Cynda was reciting scriptures from the verses Iona had put on the wall during her last visit, she turned from the poster to smile at Iona as she entered the room. "Did you sleep well, honey?"

Iona nodded and then sat down next to Cynda's bed. She noticed that her mom looked even thinner than she had last weekend. The silk gown she was in seemed to swallow her. Iona willed herself not to cry as she asked Cynda, "Have you been back to the doctor, Mama? What is he saying now?"

Cynda smiled and said, "Sure have, hon. Doctor Jesus visits me everyday. He says that everything is going to be all right."

In frustration, Iona put her head in her hands as she realized that she had not awoke in belief of happy endings as
she had hoped. She removed her hands and lifted her head
to the reality of her mother's condition and said, "I don't
think you understood my question, Mom. I want to know
what your real doctor has to say. Are you going to force me
to call him myself?"

Cynda put her bone frail hand over Iona's and patted it.
"You've got to trust me, Iona. Mother knows best in this situation. Okay?"

Iona didn't respond

Cynda then told her, "I'm sorry that I won't be able to
take you to the church tomorrow."

"That's okay, Mama. I probably wouldn't have been very
good company at the event anyway."

"Yes you would have," Cynda said, then an idea struck
her. "They're having the Prayer Journey next Saturday also.
Promise me that even if I can't take you, you'll go anyway."

Iona wanted to tell her mother that she was summoned to
church enough in Ohio; she didn't need to come to Chicago
and be treated the same way. she wanted to spend all her
time in Chicago with her mother, not at church. She looked
into her mother's imploring eyes and couldn't refuse her.
"I'll do it on one condition," Iona said.

"Name it."

"You have to be well enough to go with me."

Cynda turned her head from Iona and looked heaven-
ward. She said in a loud voice, "Did you hear that, Lord?
You've been given a challenge. Don't let me down, Lord.
We've got to get this girl to that Prayer Journey."

Iona sat in silence, as she wondered if her mother would
still be alive next weekend, let alone well enough to go to
some Prayer Journey with her. Iona decided that she wanted
to spend the time her mother had left right here with her.

"I have three weeks of vacation. So when I go back home

on Monday, I'm going to clear out my schedule and then I'm going to spend those three weeks with you. Would that be okay?" Iona said.

"Of course I'd love for you to stay with us. Since I've had to compete with your father for your attention, I've always felt like I was fighting a losing battle and that you'd rather be with him than spend time with me."

"You didn't have to compete with Daddy, Mama. I think it was just that I had been your only child for ten years, and then suddenly you had three more kids and I didn't know where I fit in all of that."

"But your dad has another son," Cynda said.

"That was different. Donavan had been there before I came. So I guess I knew I had to share with him." She hunched her shoulders and continued, "And I guess it didn't hurt as much to share dad and Nina with Donavan. But it sure bothered me to have to share you."

"I'm sorry, Iona. I never meant to do anything to cause you more hurt than I had already caused."

"I know that, Mama. Anyway, that was my issue. I'm just sad that it took me this long to get over it." Iona's voice cracked and tears crept into her eyes as she said, "I miss the time I didn't spend with you."

"Me too, baby. Me too," Cynda said just before she fell asleep.

The rest of the weekend went by in a blur. Iona didn't just spend time with her mother, Keith and her three brothers hung out with them in the family room as well. Consequently, they were stuck watching cartoons and sports. It was torture that Iona grew to love.

On Sunday evening the telephone rang. Keith got up to answer it and Iona knew right away it was Isaac.

Keith said, "Hey knuckle head, what's going on with you?" Keith and Isaac had been boys since they were in their early teens. Nothing ever came between them accept when Keith informed Isaac that God had instructed him to marry Cynda. Since she had been Isaac's ex-girlfriend, the two had bumped heads over the matter. God's will prevailed and Keith and Isaac's friendship survived and grew stronger.

Iona couldn't hear her father's side of the conversation, but she saw Keith's face turn from happy, to puzzled, to terror stricken as he continued his conversation with her father. Finally Keith looked at her and said, "Hon, your dad needs to talk with you. You might want to take this upstairs."

"Okay," Iona said as she stood up and took the telephone out of Keith's hand. She put the receiver to her ear as she walked up the stairs. "What's going on, Daddy? Did something happen to Donavan?"

"No. Donavan is fine as far as I know. How's everything going with your mom?"

Iona caught the false chipper sound of Isaac's voice and refused to let him drag out whatever news he had to deliver to her. "She's kind of weak right now, but I want to know what's going on with you. So spill it."

The fake chipper tone left Isaac's voice as he said, "I do have something to tell you. But I want you to know right up front that the only reason I'm telling you now is because I didn't want you to come home to any surprises."

"Fair enough. What is it, Daddy?"

"It's Vinny, Iona. Someone killed him."

"What?" she exploded.

"That's not all, Baby Girl." Isaac took a deep breath and trodded on. "The killer sent me an email Friday night."

Iona sat down on her bed. "You're kidding me, right, Daddy?"

"I wish I was. The email said, 'Thieves deserve to die'. Then it gave directions to the place where Vinny's body was."

"I don't get it, Daddy. Why is this whack job killing people just because they like to steal? I mean, there are all sorts of other crimes out there, why is he so fixated on thieves? And why is he so fixated on you?"

"Maybe he believes that stealing is the worst crime of all. I don't know," Isaac said, then added, "Maybe he also thinks I will agree with him since I'm a pastor and he is trying to justify his actions. Iona, the detectives that were at the church last week have requested that I come to the precinct."

Now Iona was confused. "Why do they want to talk with you?"

"I called them as soon as I opened the email—that's how they found the body. He was right where the killer told me he would be."

"How sick," Iona said.

"Tell me about it. Anyway, I was hoping you would go with me after I pick you up from the airport tomorrow. Johnny doesn't think I should go without my attorney."

Those stupid detectives must suspect her father if Johnny is advising her dad to bring an attorney. What did they think? He was sending notes to himself? "Of course I'll be there. What time do they want to meet with you?"

"Ten in the morning."

"Let me check Orbitz and see if I can change my flight to get there sooner. I'll call you back and let you know what time you need to pick me up from the airport."

"Thanks, Baby Girl. I'll see you in the morning."

Chapter 16

Iona and Isaac sat in the interrogation room waiting on the detectives to come in so they could find out why they wanted to speak with Isaac. Detective Gordon came into the room and slammed a file on the desk. He looked at Isaac as if he were a pedophile who was caught on a playground holding hands with a ponytail wearing little girl.

"So what is it, Pastor Walker? You can't stand for hypocrites to come to your church? They sin and you judge and jury them with a bullet?"

"Excuse me," Isaac said.

Gordon put his hands on the edge of the table, and leaned into Isaac. "Oh don't play innocent with me." He pointed at his hair and said, "You see this gray hair? That means I've been around a long time. And I know all about your past. These aren't the first people you've murdered are they, Ike-Man?"

Ike-Man had been one of Isaac's street names and Iona wasn't about to let her father be disrespected by this officer of the law. She stood and got in Gordon's face. "Let me explain a few things to you, Detective Gordon." She pointed at Isaac and said, "His name to you is Pastor Walker or Mr. Walker, in no uncertain terms are you to ever call him Ike-Man. And another thing that you should know," she lifted the business card she'd placed on the table, "I am Pastor Walker's attorney and you can address your questions to me for the duration of this interview." Iona sat back down next to Isaac.

Gordon stared at her for a moment and then took the seat at the head of the table. "Well, I see that *Pastor* Walker sure lawyered up quick."

"Yeah, you're real observant. You should be captain rather than just a detective around here. Now can you please tell us what you want?" Iona said.

"Where were you on Friday night at around 10 p.m.?" Gordon asked Isaac.

"I was at home with my wife," Isaac answered.

Gordon harrumphed. "Convenient, wouldn't you say, Mr. Walker?" Gordon asked.

"No, he would say that is the truth," Iona responded, then added, "Next question please. We don't have all day for this."

Gordon opened the file he brought in and pulled out a picture of the now deceased Vinny Thompson. Isaac looked at the picture. Vinny's body had been found in an open field that was under construction. He was in all black with a small hole in his head. Isaac shook his head, remembering the email he received.

"How'd it feel when you put a bullet in this sinner's head?" Gordon asked.

"What is wrong with you?" Isaac shouted. "How can you think that I would do something like—"

Iona held up her hand. "Don't say another word, Daddy." She stood up. "You have nothing linking my client to this murder or you would have already arrested him. I'm not about to allow you to badger him simply because you don't have a clue how to investigate a murder case." She looked at her father and said, "Let's go. This interview is over."

Isaac stood and followed his daughter out of the interrogation room. He had so many run-ins with the law in his younger days, he kept looking back, half expecting to be stopped, cuffed, and thrown in the little three walled box with iron locks. If it wasn't so tragic, it would actually be funny. Isaac had done so much wrong that he should have spent the rest of his life in prison. In all his life, He only did a three year stint in federal prison. He never paid for any of his other crimes. Would he now pay for the folly of his youth by going to prison for crimes he hadn't committed?

Iona was fuming when they got in the car. Isaac looked over at her as he started the car and pulled off. "Calm down, Baby Girl. I thought you were going to jump on that man in there."

She balled her fist and blew out hot air. "I wanted to smack the arrogance out of his stupid mouth."

Isaac laughed. "I guess no one can say that you're not my daughter. When I was your age, I would have knocked him down and then stepped on his head.

"That's right," Iona said gleefully. "I am my father's daughter and I'm not about to let anybody forget that."

Isaac smiled and then told her, "You did good today. I was very proud of the way you man handled that officer. That's why I always send my people your way."

Iona rolled her eyes. "Yeah, well thanks for that. But do you think you could ever come up with a client that actually has some money?"

"Most of the people I send your way didn't commit the crime they were accused of—so they're not going to have any money to give you. But don't worry, God will reward you for your kindness to people in their time of need."

"You really **believe that don't you?**"

Isaac nodded.

Iona kissed him on the cheek. They drove in silence the rest of the way to her office. Before getting out of the car, Iona told her father, "Don't talk to the police. If they approach you, tell them to call me." She got out of the car and walked into her office building.

Isaac watched his daughter go into Smith, Winters & Barnes and reveled in the beautiful and successful young woman that was his daughter. He helped make her the woman she was today, and as far as he was concerned, he did a pretty good job. He knew she had a mountain load of flaws, but she was yet and still Daddy's little girl. One day, he assured himself as he drove off, she would also belong to the heavenly Father.

When Isaac entered his home, Nina was sitting in the living room waiting on him. She leaped from her seat and ran to him. Before Isaac could get through the door good Nina had asked, "What happened? What did they want to talk to you for? Is everything all right?"

"Whoa! Calm down. Everything is alright," Isaac told her.

Nina pouted, which was something she rarely did. "If everything is okay, why would the police want to see you?"

Isaac took his coat off and headed upstairs toward their bedroom. "I don't understand it myself, Nina. The cops believe that I shot and killed Clarence and Vinny. Gordon accused me of killing them simply because he thinks I don't like sinners."

Isaac hung his coat in their closet and sat down on the bed to take his shoes off. Since he preached on Sunday and often worked on Saturdays with outreach programs, Monday was his day off and he and Nina normally spent it relaxing in their suburban home.

Isaac had moved Nina away from the West Side of town when his first book hit the *New York Times* bestsellers list. He remembered Nina getting mad and saying that she hadn't made the bestseller's list until her eighth book was published. Isaac quickly reminded her that she wrote his book as well. His name was on the book cover, because it was his experiences that had been detailed in the book, but he never would have been able to put together a book without her. Then Nina had smiled and called her friends, telling them how she and Isaac had made the bestseller's list on their first non-fiction book.

"That's preposterous, Isaac. All you ever did was try to help Clarence and Vinny and hundreds of others people just like them," Nina stated.

"Tell that to Detective Gordon," Isaac said.

Nina put her hands on her hips. "I will."

Isaac raised his hands. "Hold on a minute, Mrs. Walker, Iona has already taken care of the detective. So I need you to get over here and take care of your husband."

Nina smiled at him. She took two steps toward him, then stopped and asked, "Are you sure that we have nothing to worry about?"

"I didn't do it, Nina. So I'm not worried about the police finding evidence to the contrary."

She continued walking toward her husband. Isaac stood and pulled his wife close to him. He kissed her and then playfully tossed her onto the bed.

"Careful," she told him while patting her stomach. "This is how we got in the predicament we're in right now."

Beaming from ear to ear, Isaac told her as he joined her on the bed, "Baby, I love the predicament we're in right now."

Later, as they cuddled underneath the covers, Isaac placed his hands on Nina's belly. "When do you think we should tell the kids?"

Nina scrunched her nose. "I don't know, Isaac. I'm a little nervous about how they will react to this news."

"I think they will be happy for us. Everyone knows that we've wanted another child ever since we married."

Nina turned in the bed to face her husband. "Isaac, that was seventeen years ago."

"It's not my fault that you refused to marry me until my son was twelve years old," Isaac told her with a smile on his face.

"You weren't worth marrying until then," Nina reminded him.

Isaac put his hands on Nina's stomach again and asked, "What do you think we're having?"

"One angry child who will think we are his grandparents," Nina said.

Isaac nudged her shoulder. "I'm serious, Nina. I want a girl and I want her to look just like you."

Nina rolled her eyes. "Who are you kidding, Isaac Walker? We both know that your children come out looking just like a body double for you. My genes don't have a chance against the mighty Walker genes."

"Oh ye of little faith," Isaac chided. "I can't believe these things are coming out of your mouth. The woman who believed that God was able to do what doctors said couldn't be done. And now that God has done it, do you still doubt Him?"

"I don't doubt God. I'm just terrified that we won't be around to watch this child grow up. And how fair would that be to this baby?"

"Trust God, baby."

Nina punched Isaac's shoulder. "You keep saying that. But I need you to work with me on this too."

He rubbed her shoulder. "Okay. Whatever you want me to do, I'll do it. Just tell me what you want, and please don't beat me no more."

Nina laughed at her silly husband and then she became serious and told him, "I want you to stay out of trouble."

Iona spent the morning reviewing her files and passing them to other attorneys in the firm so that she could clear her desk and be ready to be with her mother for three weeks. But before she could leave town, Iona would have to work at clearing her father's name. That was the only thing she could think about, and it was driving her crazy.

Iona had no room in her life for unnecessary complications. Her parents were more than enough for her. So when JL called to tell her that he had ballet tickets, Iona told him straight out that it wasn't going to happen.

"I don't think you understand me, Iona. I don't take no for an answer very often," JL said after Iona's negative response to his invitation to the ballet.

"I have too much on my plate right now, JL. I'm trying to clear my calendar so I can go to Chicago for about three weeks to be with my mother" She thought about her father's predicament and her brother being missing in action and then took a deep breath and said, "I'm sorry. I know this sounds like a brush off, but I just can't handle one more thing."

She hung up with JL and called Neil. When he answered, Iona asked him to come to her office.

Neil arrived within moments of hanging up. He was arrogant, but at least he didn't keep people waiting. Iona gave him one point for punctuality. "I need your help with something," she told him when he opened her door.

He bowed gallantly. "I'm at your service."

"If you've been watching the news, I'm sure you are aware that two of my clients were found murdered."

Neil held up his hand to halt Iona. "Wait a minute. I know about Clarence—who else?"

"Vinny Thompson. Maybe you didn't do any work for me on him, but he was murdered this past weekend, and the cops have their sights set on my father as the shooter."

"What cops?"

Iona looked at her notes and told him, "Two detectives came to my father's church last week when Clarence's body was dumped there. The detectives' names are Alex Matthews and Malcolm Gordon."

Neil took a note pad out of his back pocket and a pen from his shirt pocket and wrote the names down. "I'll talk to them and see what we're up against." He looked up from his note pad. "Do you want me to check your father out just the same as I would do any other client?"

Iona glared at Neil and took away five million-zillion cool points from him for having no compassion and no ability to believe that there was actually an honest to goodness innocent man in this world. But then she reminded herself that she had never believed in the innocence of any of her clients—that is, until her father became her client.

"That won't be necessary, Neil. My father didn't do it, so any time you spend on him would simply be wasted."

He looked at her skeptically and then said, "Have it you way."

Just for that, Iona was renaming him. He was no longer Neil the jerk boy. He was now Neil the Doubting Thomas, and just like Jesus, Iona was going to make a believer out of him.

"I'll get back to you as soon as I have something," Neil told her as he turned to walk out.

"Oh, and Neil." He stopped, turned to face Iona and she continued, "I need you to check out Vinny and Clarence. See if there is something that ties the two of them together, besides my father, that the cops haven't come across yet."

Neil tapped the pen to his forehead. "That reminds me; you were right."

Iona looked puzzled. "Right about what?"

"Clarence. He didn't have his car the day of the robbery. I talked with several of the guys on his shift. Three of them saw his wife drop him off at work that day."

"His wife?"

"Yep, his own main squeeze got him killed. How about

that? Clarence refuses to rat her out and ends up getting murdered for being a thief. She's got to feel pretty low right about now."

"Another innocent man," Iona mumbled.

"What?"

"Nothing. Thanks, Neil. Just let me know what you come up with."

When Neil left, Iona leaned back in her seat and wondered how her life had gotten so complicated. She hadn't believed in anything and anyone a few weeks ago. And now she discovered that she had represented an innocent man and didn't even know it. How many other things were right and true in her life? How many were wrong and deceitful?

Chapter 17

Isaac stood behind his pulpit as he did during every Wednesday night Bible study. He declared the goodness of the Lord to his congregation and, once again, implored all who were in need to come to the Lord. A young man in the third row from the back stood up and began walking down the aisle toward the pulpit. His shoulders were slumped as though nothing had gone right for him since he'd been pulled, kicking and screaming from his mother's womb. Tears streamed down his splotch ridden, honey toned face. Recognizing a humbled man in the midst of surrendering to God, the congregation stood and clapped for him.

He stood before Isaac with raised hands and said, "I need Him, Pastor. I need Jesus."

"You better say it," Isaac said as he raised his hands to the Lord also and proclaimed his need for Jesus. The Ike-Man looked pretty un-cool at that moment, but he wasn't living on cool anymore. He was living for Jesus.

An altar worker stepped in front of the man and prayed with him. Isaac observed while the man was being prayed for and noticed how sincere and emotional he seemed. Most men didn't come to the altar with tears and raised hands, so when they were finished praying Isaac asked, "Young man, what is your name?"

The splotchy faced young man looked up at Isaac, wiped his teary eyes and said, "Dwight Johnson, sir."

"Well Dwight, do you know what just happened here?"

Dwight lowered his head as a torrent of tears broke him down. His shoulders shook as an altar worker handed him some Kleenex. Dwight wiped his face and then used the tissue to blow his nose. He kept his head low as if ashamed.

Isaac told him, "You don't need to be ashamed anymore, Dwight. God has forgiven you, and if you had ever done anything to me, I would forgive you. But you can't worry about the people who refuse to forgive the things you did before Christ came into your life."

"But I've done so much to so many people, Pastor."

"Accept God's forgiveness, son, and then go and try to mend the relationships you've ruined," Isaac told him.

Dwight shook his head. "I stole from my own mother, Pastor. How do I mend that? How do I forgive myself for that?"

Isaac stepped down from his pulpit and walked over to Dwight. He hugged Dwight and then told him, "Some of the things we do seem unforgivable by man's standards, but trust God and let Him do a work in you." Isaac turned to Deacon Harris, who happened to be fulfilling his altar worker duties that week and asked him to come forward. Isaac then told Dwight, "Go into the prayer room with Deacon Harris. He's going to pray for you again and then I want to talk with you before you leave church tonight. Okay?"

Dwight nodded and left the sanctuary with Deacon Harris.

Isaac turned to the congregation and dismissed them. As

he walked to his office, he realized something was missing. He should have been feeling joy for a new believer coming to Christ, but what he felt was fear. Dwight had mentioned before the entire congregation that he stole from his mother. And now Isaac worried that something would happen to Dwight. He made a decision. He asked Nina to go on home without him, telling her that he was going to wait so he could drive Dwight home and talk to him some more. He didn't however, tell Nina that he feared that something might happen to Dwight.

Every time Iona watched her father minister she was struck by how charismatic the old man actually was. He could convince a Buddhist to give Jesus a try. He had already managed to convert just about every Jehovah's Witness that knocked on his front door. He turned so many of them on to Christianity that the Walker house was now considered enemy territory for the popular door-to-door witnessing groups.

Iona was about to get up from her seat in the church balcony and go into her father's office to tell him how much she enjoyed his message when she noticed a bald-headed man getting up from one of the back pews. She thought she recognized that fat head. Iona was leaning forward in her seat waiting on the man to turn around when JL Tyler sat down next to her. Surprised, Iona jumped, then she nudged JL's shoulder. "You scared me. What are you doing here?"

"Well, after begging this lovely lady to go out with me and being rejected, I figured I would become a stalker and see if that would cause her to change her mind."

Iona laughed. "Okay, now I'm really scared."

"Come on, Iona. Can't you see how interested I am in you?" He lifted his right hand and did a sweeping motion around the church. "I don't even like organized religion, but I came to church tonight just to be near you."

Iona smiled and then asked, "What did you think of my father?"

"What is that phrase King Agrippa used after Apostle Paul preached to him?" JL hesitated in thought for a moment and then snapped his finger and said, "He almost persuaded me to become a Christian."

"A Bible scholar as well as an attorney. I'm impressed."

"Well, you know." JL popped his collar. "I know a little somethin' somethin'."

Iona remembered the bald man and looked down at the dispersing crowd. He was gone, but she saw her father walk out of the sanctuary toward his office and Nina get up to follow behind him. Then she saw Johnny head toward her father's office also. He stopped and looked toward the balcony. Iona smirked. Johnny always tried to quickly scan the balcony for her and then turn and keep doing whatever he was doing after spotting her.

JL said, "I know you've been busy this week, but are you too busy to go to dinner with me tonight?"

Iona would have turned down JL's invitation except for one thing. Johnny hadn't turned away from the balcony as he normally did. He was still staring in her direction with a look of wonder on his face.

"All right, JL, where would you like to take me?"

JL smiled. "Do you like Italian?"

"Love it," Iona said, still watching Johnny watch them.

JL stood. "I know of a little mom and pop Italian restaurant that will have you acting like you're hitting a crack pipe."

"What do you know about a crack pipe, counselor?"

"Just what your clients tell me."

"Ha, ha, very funny. You're a real funny man," Iona said as she stood and walked down the stairs with JL.

"Do you want to follow me?"

Johnny headed their way as they descended the stairs, so before Iona could answer JL, Johnny stood next to them and nodded at JL. "Nice to see you at church," he told JL, then turned to Iona and asked, "Are you going to check in with your father before you leave tonight?"

Sometimes Iona wondered if Johnny thought *he* was her daddy. "No, Mr. Dunford, I don't have time to visit with my father right now. I have a *date*."

Johnny grabbed her arm and told JL, "I need to speak with Iona for a moment." He then moved her away from JL and said, "I don't think you should go out with this guy."

"What's wrong, Johnny, you don't think JL has enough money to date me either?"

Johnny rubbed his forehead and eyes in frustration. "Forget that I said that, okay?" He was repentant now as he said, "Matter-of-fact, I'm sorry that I said that to you. I was just trying to give myself a reason to leave, because I really did want to stay with you. I was wrong, but please listen to me, Iona. This guy is bad news."

Iona rolled her eyes, walked away from Johnny and ushered JL out the front door of the church. "I'll follow you," Iona told JL when they were outside.

The restaurant was in Kettering, Ohio and Iona had to admit that JL had been right. This was the best pasta she'd ever had. She was licking her lips when JL asked, "So why are you going to be in Chicago for so long?"

Iona put her fork down and looked at JL as she said, "My mother has cancer. I want to be with her in case she doesn't beat this disease."

"I'm sorry," JL said. "I didn't mean to pry."

"Hey, anybody that treats me to the best pasta I've ever had can pry into my life. Don't worry about it."

He sipped his Pepsi and looked at her over the rim of the glass. When he put his drink down he said, "And now you've got to deal with this stuff that's going on with your father."

Defensively Iona asked, "How do you know what's going on with my father?"

"Calm down, Iona. I am the assistant to the DA. I think that makes me privy to things that go on at the police station."

"Okay, all right. I'm just a little suspicious of everybody right now."

"Maybe not suspicious enough," JL said as he brought his glass to his lips and took another sip.

"What's that's suppose to mean?"

JL shook his head. "Nothing. Forget I said anything."

"Oh yeah, that's what I do for a living; I forget what people tell me."

Smiling, JL said, "You seem to forget that your clients are truly guilty easy enough."

She pointed her fork at him. "Hey! Not funny. Anyway, I'm not about to forget this, so just go ahead and tell me what you're talking about."

He hesitated for a second, took a deep breath, blew it out and said, "Okay. Now I know this is going to come as a shock to you, especially since your family seems to trust him so much."

"Wait a minute." Iona raised her hand to halt JL. "Is this about Johnny? Look, I'm out with you so you don't have to dog out the competition. It's been two years since I last dated Johnny, and he dumped me, so you don't have to worry about him trying to win me back."

JL shook his head. "You've got the wrong idea, Iona. I don't see Johnny as competition. I know for a fact that he never cared anything about you."

After a sharp intake of breath Iona asked, "Why would you say something like that? H-how would you even know anything about it?"

He put his hand over Iona's and said, "I didn't tell you that to hurt you."

Iona snatched her hand from JL's and stood up. "I demand to know what you are talking about."

"The reason Johnny started seeing you was to get close to your father. The DA office had been investigating him."

Iona sat back down with a stunned look on her face. "Why would you be investigating my father?"

JL put his hands to his chest and said, "I never wanted to investigate your father. But Johnny wouldn't let it go. He came to my office with all sorts of stories about how your father was stealing from the church. I think his obsession with your father began when the good pastor bought that Hummer."

"But Johnny and my father are so close."

"I guess everyone needs a Judas in their life. I'm told it builds character," JL remarked snidely.

"Why did you ask me out?" Iona demanded.

"I wanted to get to know you."

"You're investigating my father, and you want to get to know me. Are you crazy?"

He raised his hands. "You didn't let me finish. I am no longer investigating your father. Johnny was never able to turn up any incriminating evidence against Pastor Walker."

"Of course he wasn't. My father is the most honorable, upstanding man I know." She looked JL over and added, "Present company included."

"Hey, no need to get upset with me. I'm the one who called off the investigation. I told Johnny that if he hadn't found anything after two years of digging, there probably wasn't anything to find. Johnny doesn't listen. He's not giving up, Iona. So, you and Isaac need to steer clear of him."

Still finding JL's accusations hard to believe, Iona asked, "Why would Johnny do this, huh? What would be his motive?"

JL looked at her with sympathetic eyes. "You really don't know do you?"

"Know what?" Anger was causing Iona's voice to rise. A few people at tables close by glanced at them, but she didn't care.

JL leaned back in his seat and dropped a bombshell on Iona. "Johnny's father is a pastor."

"No he's not. Johnny's father was a cop. Johnny had never even attended church, before I took him to my father's church. He was completely ignorant of everything religious."

"Is that what he told you? Well, I guess that line got you to go out with him." JL leaned forward and Iona could tell that he was enjoying this. "Johnny's father is a married preacher. But he's not married to Johnny's mother. As a matter of fact, Johnny's mother committed suicide after waiting eight long years for that wonderful pastor to divorce his wife and marry her. His mother was a deaconess and little Johnny spent every free moment in church until he was seven years old." JL leaned closer to Iona and whispered. "Do you want to know what happened to Johnny when his mother died?"

Iona didn't answer, but JL told her anyway.

"He was shipped off to an orphanage when daddy never showed up to claim his little boy. That's why Johnny believed your father was up to something. Johnny believes that all preachers are up to something."

Iona stood, composed herself by straightening her dress, pulled her purse strap onto her shoulder and said, "Thank you very much for the good food. Your company, however, I could have done without. I will see you in court, counselor."

"Iona, why do you want to shoot the messenger?" he yelled to her departing form.

Johnny was parked outside of St. Peter Missionary Baptist Church as Iona drove home from her date with JL. He used to sit in front of this church every night when he fin-

ished his shift. But after attending the House of God, he hadn't
needed to come by here every single night. Now he only
made his rounds about once a month. One time he went
two whole months without visiting this church.

Johnny wondered if the church had changed much since
the last time he and his mother attended services. He never
went in. He sat in the driveway like an outsider, and watched
the parishioners file out of the church. Johnny wouldn't
leave until the man of the hour, Bishop Thomas Tewiliger,
opened those huge double doors and stepped out of the
church.

Sometimes the good bishop would look over at Johnny's
car and nod as he headed toward his big Lincoln Town Car.
It was on those nights that Johnny wondered if the man
knew who he was, and if that nod was his simple form of ac-
knowledgment. It was like he was saying, 'Oh there's my son
that I never did anything for. Look, he's stalking me again.
Let me nod so he can go away and I can keep pretending
that I didn't have anything to do with his mother committing suicide'.

Those nods made Johnny angry—made him want to hurt
somebody. Johnny gripped the steering wheel and decided
to leave, because if Bishop Tewiliger came out and nodded
at him, that might force him to do something he would regret.

He turned on his car and drove off. But Johnny knew;
knew with everything in him, that he would one day have to
face down the demon that haunted him.

Chapter 18

Iona was woken at six in the morning by the loud ringing of her telephone. She grunted, rolled over and picked up the phone. "Yeah, what's up?" Iona asked while rubbing her eyes.

"Iona we need—"

Recognizing the voice, Iona said, "Hey, Nina-Mama, what are you doing up so early?" Being a writer and one who could make her own hours, Nina normally didn't get up until eight a.m. She would then spend an hour with the Lord, fix breakfast and then begin working on her current book.

"Your father has been arrested, Iona. I need you to meet me downtown."

Iona sat up, fully awake now. "What did you say?"

"Can you meet me downtown? I have to see about bailing him out of jail."

"What happened?"

"I don't know, honey. This is a nightmare." Nina started crying.

"Don't worry about anything. Just meet me at the police station in thirty minutes."

Iona hung up and bolted out of bed. It took her no more than seven minutes to shower and another seven minutes to throw her clothes on, grab a comb, brush and her keys. She was out of her apartment and rolling down the street in under fifteen minutes of hanging up with Nina. Her mind was so shook-up that she almost didn't stop at the red light as she got off the highway and drove onto Main Street. An elderly man was crossing the street and Iona narrowly missed hitting him. Thoughts of her being arrested for running a red light and killing a pedestrian flashed through her mind as she tried to calm down.

Iona looked to heaven and asked God, "How much more do you think I can take?" Tears streamed down her lovely face as she thought about her mother's illness, her brother's defection, Johnny's betrayal and now her father's arrest. "What? Do you want me to just lay down and die? Do you hate me that much?"

A horn honked behind her and Iona brought her eyes back to the traffic light and saw that it was now green. She wiped the tears from her face and kept it moving. She had to go handle her father's business. If God wasn't going to help her family, Iona decided that she would be all the help they needed. After arriving at the police station, Iona got out of her car and walked into the Dayton Police Station and told the desk clerk that she needed to see her client.

"Client's name?" he asked without looking up from his computer.

"Isaac Walker."

The officer hit a few keys on his computer and then looked up with disapproval in his eyes. "We'll get right on that," he said snidely.

"See that you do," Iona told him as she gave him a don't even try to mess with me today stare down.

She waited for fifteen minutes, all the while wondering what was keeping Nina. Iona went into the visitation room and somberly waited for her father to be brought out. Although Iona knew her father had spent three years in prison for drug trafficking over twenty-five years ago, she had never been able to imagine the dynamic, resilient and charismatic Pastor of the House of God behind bars.

As he walked slowly toward his seat in ankle chains and that awful red jumpsuit, tears sprang forth, and Iona couldn't force them back. This was her father. How could the police think this awesome man was a killer?

Isaac sat down and said, "No tears counselor."

Sniffling she said, "I'm sorry, Daddy. This is just so unbelievable. You would cry too if I had been brought to you handcuffed and shackled."

"Yes, but I'm your father. You're my lawyer, so buck up or I'm going to hire someone else." He smiled as he said the words.

"That's not funny, Daddy." She wiped her face and then got down to business. "But your point is taken. I'll be professional and treat you like a client." She hit her forehead with the palm of her hand. "I forgot to ask what the charges were. Okay. I was thinking like a daughter, but I'll make this work, don't worry. Just tell me what happened. What reason did they give for arresting you?"

The sadness in Isaac's eyes was so apparent, that it caused another tear to cascade down Iona's face as he told her, "Do you remember that kid that gave his life to the Lord at church last night?"

"His name was Dwight, right? He was the one that turned to the congregation and told all his business." Iona slowly finished her comment as she remembered that Dwight had told the congregation that he had stolen from his mother. "No, Daddy."

Isaac nodded. "They found him dead at five this morning. His mother told the police that I was the last person she saw with him."

A look of puzzlement shot across Iona's face. "Why would she say that? Was she at church last night?"

"No. I drove Dwight home and introduced myself to his mother."

"Daddy why would you drive him home? We have a church van. Why didn't you just let one of the van drivers take him?"

"I was worried about the kid. When he said what he did, I started thinking that the person that killed Clarence and Vinny would probably come after Dwight next. So I wanted to make sure the kid was safe. Turns out I didn't help him after all."

Iona rubbed her temples. "Okay, so you gave him a ride home. How did the police then link that to murder?"

"Someone called their house this morning claiming to be me. He asked Dwight to meet him outside. Dwight walked outside and got shot."

Iona hung her head, then as she remembered the bald man that she'd seen in church the night before Dwight was killed, she lifted her eyes toward her father and said, "I think I know who is doing this."

"Who?" Isaac asked.

"This contract killer came to my office wanting me to represent him. I turned him down and we ended up getting into a fight."

"You did what?" Isaac exploded.

"Calm down, Dad. I won the fight." When she saw that Isaac was going to say more about the situation she raised her hands and continued. "Anyway, I think I saw Larry at church last night."

Isaac looked skeptical. "If this guy is a contract killer like you said, then he's working for someone."

"You might be right about that. But if we find Larry, we just might find the master mind, right?"

"Right," Isaac agreed, then added. "But I don't want you looking for this guy, and I especially don't want you in another fight."

Iona stood. "Don't worry about a thing, Daddy. I'm going to get you out of here."

When Iona walked back through the police station, Nina was at the front desk arguing with the clerk about seeing her husband. Iona pulled her to the side and said, "I'm sorry about this, Nina, but you're not going to be able to see Daddy until visiting hours. They won't make an exception."

"What do you mean I can't see my husband? He's an innocent man!" Nina screamed. "He doesn't belong in jail, he belongs at home with me."

"I know. But we have to convince a judge of that, so let's get moving," Iona told her, then asked, "What took you so long to get down here anyway?"

"Girl, I wasn't about to leave the house without praying for my husband. I had to let the Lord know what was going on."

"I thought God was all knowing," Iona said snidely.

Nina shook her finger in Iona face. "Don't you get smart with me today, Iona Walker."

Iona raised her hands and backed away from Nina. "Hey, I'm on your side, remember?"

"Well, then come on. Let's go down to your office and figure out what's what."

"Okay, but first I need to find something out." She turned back to the clerk and asked, "I need to know the charges my client is being held on."

The police officer Iona dealt with earlier was gone and a woman in her mid to late forties had taken his place. She didn't wear a uniform and had a pleasant, helpful look on her tan face as she asked, "Can you give me your client's name please?"

"Isaac Walker."

The clerk stared at Iona dumbfounded then asked, "Pastor Walker?"

"Yes."

"The man is a saint. He helped me turn my knuckle head son around from the drug dealing life he was leading. Why Pastor Walker even helped my Tommy find a job. A saint I tell you; a saint."

"Yes, we know. That's why we're going to get him off. But, I need to know what he's been charged with."

"Oh yeah, sorry," she said while clicking a few keys. "Here it is." The clerk gave Iona another dumbfounded, jaw dropping stare.

Iona prodded. "The charges?"

"First degree murder."

"How many counts?"

"What do you mean how many counts? He murdered more than one person?"

"Focus, okay," Iona told the clerk. "How many counts?"

"One."

"Thank you," Iona said as she turned to walk out of the police station with Nina. But a traitor blocked her way. Johnny was standing at the entrance hugging Nina and earning his Academy Award for the best actor in a church drama.

Iona heard him say, "I just can't believe it. I absolutely can't believe this."

"Why can't you believe it, Johnny?" Iona said while walking toward them.

Johnny released Nina and turned toward Iona. "How are you doing, Iona? I've been worrying about you ever since I heard."

"Why would you worry about me? You've been trying to make this happen for the past two years. I would think you'd be out celebrating."

Shaking his head, Johnny said, "No, Iona, you've got this

wrong. I don't want to hurt your father. I respect him too much."

Iona harrumphed. "Yeah, I know. You respect him so much that you want to see him in prison. Well don't shout the victory yet, because he won't be here for long." Iona grabbed Nina's arm and said, "Don't talk to him, Nina. He'll report everything you say to the district attorney."

Nina turned toward Johnny and asked, "What is she talking about? What's going on with you two?"

Iona pulled on Nina's arm as she headed to the exit.

"Wait!" Johnny commanded. "You can't go out there."

"I can do just what I please and I'll thank you to stay out of my family's business," Iona told him.

"Reporters are out there, Iona. They're lined up just waiting on you to come outside so they can pounce," Johnny said.

With that news Iona's hands began to tremble as fear crept into her eyes. The irony of this situation was not missed for Iona. Her big dreams and her five year plan depended on her getting cases with media appeal. But not *this* case. She could no more exploit her father for her own gain than she could set herself on fire. She didn't want to talk with reporters about Isaac Walker, didn't want to greet them as she and Nina walked away, and didn't even want to see how she looked on camera as she said, 'No comment.' Her voice was weak when she turned back to Johnny and pleaded, "Help us, Johnny. If Daddy ever meant anything to you, help us find another way out of this place."

"Follow me," Johnny told them. Then he guided them through a maze of cubicles, down some stairs that led into the basement and a doorway to freedom. He pointed at the door in front of them. "Go out that way, walk up the steps and the parking garage is to your left. You can't miss it."

"Okay, come on, Nina," Iona said without thanking Johnny.

Nina turned toward Johnny and said, "Thank you. I don't know if I would have been able to deal with a bunch of reporters this morning."

"Why are you thanking him?" Iona asked indignantly. "He's the reason we're running from the reporters in the first place. I guarantee you he had something to do with this frame job."

"Iona, the man's a cop. Do you honestly believe he'd kill all those people just to frame your father?" Nina asked.

"I'm not trying to disrespect you, Nina-Mama. But you're being naïve. Dirty cops are everywhere." Iona grabbed Nina's arm, ushering her toward the door as she'd done upstairs. "Now let's get out of here before he kills us in this basement."

Johnny grabbed Iona's arm. She let go of Nina and swung on him. He stepped back and said, "Girl, you nearly took my head off."

Iona positioned herself for a fight and said, "Yeah, and that was just a love tap. Step to me again and I'll show you what hate feels like."

"I can explain everything, Iona, if you just give me a chance," Johnny said while holding the left side of his head.

"Yeah? How's your father, Johnny?" Iona asked.

Johnny's face turned cold, he clamped his mouth shut and turned away from them.

"Explain that, Johnny. Explain all your lies," Iona yelled at him as he continued walking away. But before he could get out of her presence she gutted him with, "So is that why you were so sure that Vivian's mom tricked her husband—because your mom did the same thing?"

"Iona how can you be so cruel?" Nina demanded.

Turning toward Nina, Iona said, "Johnny is not our friend, Nina. He's been spying on us for the past two years trying to dig up some dirt on Daddy. Now I know how much you and Daddy think of Johnny, but it's true. So don't talk to him. Okay?"

Nina closed her eyes and said a silent prayer for Johnny. Iona knew what she was doing. She used to do the same thing for her and Donavan when they were naughty children. It ticked Iona off that Nina would bother praying for a low-life like Johnny Dunford so she said, "Why don't you just stop praying every ten seconds? Have you looked around at everything that has happened to us? Can't you tell that praying doesn't work?" Iona stormed off toward the door.

Nina wasn't about to let her get away that easy. She caught up with Iona just outside of the station, grabbed her arm and turned her around. "I don't know how you lost your faith after living with us for so many years, but let me tell you something. Your father and I believe that God is up there," Nina pointed to the sky. "Taking note of each and every one of our prayers. And just so you know, I'm pregnant. So, the way I see it, God not only heard that prayer, He answered it. He's a miracle worker, Iona. And I'll never stop praising His name." And with that, Nina strutted off.

Iona stood on the sidewalk with her mouth open, unable to move forward. She knew the tears Nina shed over not being able to conceive another child. She also knew the number of years that had gone by while Nina prayed and believed. Her mind drifted back to the day she walked into Cynda's house and saw her arms lifted in praise to God. Iona heard the song as if she were standing next to her mother. *You are great; You do miracles so great.*

The arraignment was set for two o'clock and Iona was a little worried. The one good thing about this whole episode was that her father wasn't being charged with all three murders. That would have surely labeled him as a thrill or a serial killer, and there would have been no way that she would be able to get bail for him.

The docket was alphabetical, so Iona and Nina sat

through thirteen cases before Isaac Walker was called. JL Tyler stood at the prosecutor's table looking smug and self-assured. Iona was going to wipe that smugness off his lop-sided head when the truth came out. The judge was seated and Iona listened to JL request no bail for her father. She stood and said, "Judge Landon, my client is a well respected pastor with numerous ties to this community. My client is not a flight risk and therefore I cannot understand the DA's need to hold my client in jail awaiting a trial that could be months away, while his congregation and his life's work suffers needlessly."

"Point taken," Judge Landon said as he turned back to JL. "Counselor, would the district attorney's office have a problem with bail if it was set at three hundred thousand?"

Isaac nudged Iona and she shewed him away with the flick of her hand.

"Your Honor, I am currently working with the police to link Mr. Walker to two other murders. And we really don't think—"

"Have you been able to link him?" Judge Landon asked, cutting into JL's pontificating.

"We believe that we will be able to do that within the next few days," JL answered.

"So in other words; no," Judge Landon said.

A bit of the smugness left JL's face as he admitted, "No, judge, we haven't linked him yet."

"Then I see no problem with setting the bail at three hundred thousand," Judge Landon said.

"Thank you, Judge," Iona said. She almost wanted to wink at him. Iona had clerked for Judge Landon and had worked fourteen hour days, six days a week every summer for him. When Iona graduated, it was Judge Landon that recommended her to Smith, Winters & Barnes. As far as Judge Landon was concerned, Iona could do no wrong. But for the two years Iona had practiced law, she had never arraigned a case before him. Maybe there was something to all this praying stuff, because Iona felt sure that Nina had definitely prayed Judge Landon up.

Iona looked toward heaven and silently prayed, *show me what to do, Lord. I need your help on this one.*

Isaac nudged her again and asked, "So what happens now?"

"Nina and I will go to the bail bondsman and pay the ten percent. We should have you out of here soon."

His eyes lit up. "You mean I'm going to get out of here today?"

Iona held up a hand to halt his excitement. "That's only if we can get the bail and get back here in time enough for you to be released today." She looked at her watch. "Honestly, Dad, I don't see you getting out before tomorrow morning."

He patted her on the shoulder. "That's fine, Baby Girl. You go take care of everything and get me out of here as soon as you can."

Iona stood and said, "I will, don't worry." She eyed Nina walking toward them and turned back to Isaac with a huge smile on her face. "Oh, and don't you think you're a little too old to be impregnating defenseless women?"

Isaac smiled confidently and said, "You know how I do it."

Iona laughed. "Just don't expect me to baby sit while the two of you have your hips and knees replaced."

Chapter 19

Just as Iona predicted, Isaac wasn't released until Friday morning. Nina ran to him and hugged her man. Iona watched them, wishing that she would one day find a love like theirs or even the love that her mother had found with Keith.

Isaac and Nina walked toward her, arm in arm. Her father smiled at her and said, "Well, Baby Girl, your daddy's a free man."

"And, I intend to make sure you stay free," Iona told him.

He winked. "I knew I hired myself the best lawyer in this city."

Iona shook her head. "This city is too small. I'm the best lawyer in the world, Daddy. But, that's beside the point. When this is all over, I never want to represent you again. Okay?"

"You got a deal." He put his free arm around Iona's shoulders and said, "Let's go home."

"Wait, Daddy. We need to go out the back way. Reporters are lined up just waiting on you to come out of this place," Iona told him.

"I won't hide from anyone, Baby Girl. I'm an innocent

man. Let them prove otherwise." He turned and walked out the door with his head held high.

Iona had no Johnny Cochran and E. F. Bailey delusions, as she followed her father out the door. She wanted to protect her father, not exploit him. It was at that moment that she faced the fact she had lost her soul to her job. She became a lawyer to protect the innocent. Somehow, she lost sight of that when the money started coming in. She stopped caring who was innocent and only cared if her client could foot the bill. Iona looked at the throng of reporters waiting on her father and she turned her attention to heaven. She promised God that if He would help her get her father out of this mess, she would become the type of lawyer her clients could count on.

A blonde haired, blue eyed reporter Iona recognized from Channel 2 news put her microphone in Isaac's face and asked, "Did you do it, Pastor? Did you kill that young man after he attended your service?"

Another reporter—this one was nappy-headed with brown eyes and a Brooks Brothers suit on—asked, "How do you think your congregation will feel after their pastor has been arrested for such a heinous crime?"

Iona ushered him through the crowd screaming, "No comment! No comment!" as the stalkerazzi continued to pounce on her father.

When one of the reporter asked Isaac, "Why did you murder that young man, Pastor Walker?"

Isaac stopped, turned toward the cameras and said, "I am not this monster you believe me to be. I love this city and the people in it. I have worked for decades to try and make it a better place for all of us. I could never harm Dwight or anyone else."

"But, you did harm someone else, and for that you will pay big, Isaac Walker," JL said as he sat in his office watching the afternoon news. This was the reason he became a prosecutor; to bring one man to justice. When this was all over, JL thought he just might quit his lousy paying job and become a stock broker or a realtor. Maybe he'd flip a few houses and make some real money. Numbers had always been his thing. He never really cared about the weight of justice and all that bull, except when it came to Isaac Walker. That man had to pay, and JL would make sure he did. He picked up the phone and dialed his grandmother. When she answered he asked, "Did you see the news?"

"Yes, I did son," she replied.

"It's finally in motion, Big-Mama. He's going to pay for what he did to us."

"I knew you would get something on him. It just took a little patience."

JL hung up the phone and leaned in his leather cushioned seat. He did it, he did it, he did it. The great Isaac Walker was finally where he wanted him. Well, not quite. If Isaac Walker were to keel over dead of a heart attack or if a family member of one of the murder victims were to plunge a knife in his gut, then he'd be exactly where JL wanted him—but he'd settle for life in prison.

He laughed and the jovial sound echoed off the walls, just as Johnny burst through his office door. Startled, JL sprang up. Once he saw it was Johnny, he sat back down. "Hey, Johnny my boy, I was just about to treat myself to a celebratory lunch. Why don't you join me?"

Johnny ignored the lunch invitation and said, "You've got the wrong man."

"Really? Well then you're talking to the wrong person. I didn't arrest him. Detective Gordon at your very own precinct did that."

"You set him up. It wouldn't surprise me if you had those people killed yourself, just so you could finally get him in court."

JL swiped his two index fingers against each other and made a tis-tis sound. "I wouldn't go around accusing people of things you have no proof of, detective. Besides, this is what you wanted all along. I would think you'd be dancing in the street."

Johnny took a deep breath as he ran his hand over the top of his head. "I wish I'd never listened to you in the first place. Pastor Walker is innocent. He is a respectable man who only wants to bring people to the Lord. You are the one that should be investigated."

"Aren't we high and mighty today? As I remember it, you were more than eager to prove Isaac Walker was stealing from the church. You were just about salivating at the mouth, when I approached you with my plan."

Johnny got in JL's face. "I'm watching you. Do you hear me? If you did anything to bring about what's happening to Pastor Walker, I will see you fry."

Isaac was at his computer in his home office reviewing emails when an email from an unfamiliar address popped up. He was just about to delete it, fearing that it was spam, or worse yet, that a virus was attached to the email. It still amazed Isaac that human beings had so much free time on their hands that they would send out virus laden emails with the sole purpose of destroying other people's property. His mouse clicker was on the X to delete when he read the subject: *Forgive? Forgive?? Forgive????*

The email he received about Vinny had the same subject line. Isaac moved his curser away from the delete button and clicked on the message. There was only one sentence and it read, "No forgiveness for thieves, Isaac. Remember that?" There it was. The killer wanted him to know that he'd done it again. Isaac was dumbfounded. All these years he hadn't had an enemy, but now one was gunning for him and seemed particularly fixated with thieves and the concept of forgiveness.

Isaac's heart was heavy as he slumped into his bedroom

and sat at the foot of his bed feeling discouraged and defeated. He hadn't felt like this in all the years he'd had God in his life. But people were dying; and whether he had pulled the trigger or not, he was responsible. He had to do something to stop the killing, and the only thing Isaac could think to do was something that would destroy his very soul.

His life was about ministry, and he loved every minute of it. This was not a job to him; it was a calling. But how could he continue to seek out lost souls and try to win them to Christ if the very act was putting them in danger of being killed? What was that doctor's creed? *First do no harm.* Aren't pastors responsible to ensure no harm comes to the people they minister to?

Nina walked into their bedroom with a basket of folded clothes and spotted her husband sitting on the bed. "Shouldn't you be working on your sermon for Sunday?"

Isaac shook his head.

"You've already got it done?"

He lowered his head as he confessed, "I'm not going to preach on Sunday. I'm going to ask Elder Unders to do the sermon."

"Why?"

He had always been able to discuss anything with his wife, but looking at her right now, he couldn't find the words to tell her all that was in his heart, so he simply said, "It's all my fault, Nina."

She put her basket down and sat next to him. "What's your fault?"

"I got those men killed."

"Hush, Isaac. You did no such thing. Why would you even say something like that?"

"Because it's true. I didn't pull the trigger myself, but this psychopath picked them because of their involvement with me. I preach or reach out to lost souls and people come up dead."

Nina put her hand on his shoulder. "Baby, don't you see what this is? It's the enemy trying to get you to give up the call that God has placed on your life."

"I hate to admit it, but I'm just about ready to throw in the towel. I mean, maybe I should retire and let someone else take over the church. That way you and I can spend time traveling; seeing the world." He put his hand on her stomach and added softly, "Raising our baby."

She shook him. "You can't let the devil win."

"It would be different if the attack was against me only, but how can I keep going when people are dying because of me, Nina?"

She rubbed his arm. "I know this situation is not easy, but Isaac, you were called by God. And, I don't think He has re-called His assignment for your life just because some lunatic wants to reek havoc."

Isaac stood. "Well, maybe God should change His mind about me. What good am I if I can't even keep His people alive long enough so they can dedicate their lives to Him?"

"I believe that Dwight got saved the night before he died," Nina reminded him.

"Nina you're not listening to me. Something I'm doing is causing someone to kill people that I minister to. And since I don't know what I've done, I need to just back away from everything until I know what's going on."

Isaac was a whole foot taller than Nina, so she stood on top of the bed so that he had to look up at her, "And I say full speed ahead. Let the enemy know that you are not going to back down, but you are going to keep doing what the Lord has called you to do; bring souls into the Kingdom."

"What about the baby, Nina?"

She touched her stomach. "What does the baby have to do with this?"

"You asked me not to do anything that would put my life in jeopardy. Don't you think this lunatic is going to get tired of killing people that I minister to, and just decide to take me out of the picture and be done with it? So, if this guy is angry about my ministry, if I give it up, problem solved."

"I never asked you to turn your back on God, Isaac. Don't pin that on me," Nina jumped off the bed and headed for the door.

"You act like I want to stop preaching. Don't you know it would kill me inside to give my pulpit up—to stop ministering to the very people I know need me?"

Nina swung around. "Then don't stop following after God. Look, Isaac, all I know is, I married a fighter and I want him back." With that Nina stormed out of the room and left her husband to lick his wounds alone.

Donavan sat at the bar of one of Atlanta's hottest night-clubs with the same half full glass of beer that he'd ordered two hours ago in front of him. He'd been propositioned by two women and one cross dresser. To each one he said a manner able, "No, thank you." Truth be told, Donavan didn't want to be in a place like this, but the frat brothers he'd come down to party with turned out to be Bible toting and quoting choir boys. Donavan still couldn't believe what he'd walked into at his reunion.

There had been ten of them in the frat house. Two were dead, one in prison, two more were at home with their wives and sick children. But Charlie Brooks, the biggest woman hound in the frat house, Don Jenkins, the biggest drunk and Gordon Taylor, the atheist, had come to the re-union. The four of them left the reunion, and went to a local Applebees to catch up. Instead of talking about women and booze, they were talking about Bible study and church retreats they recently attended. The three of them took turns falling all over themselves thanking Donavan for praying for them when they were in college.

"Thanks, man, if you hadn't prayed for me, I'd probably

still be a cheater. I would have missed out on the wonderful woman I married and have been faithful to for everyday of our three year marriage," Charlie Brooks said.

On and on it went until Donavan couldn't take anymore. Yes, he prayed for these men. But, now he was the one in need of prayer. He couldn't just ask men who looked up to him to pray for his deliverance could he? Donavan stood up and told his old friends, "I'll see you guys tomorrow. I'm not feeling too good."

"But you can't go to your hotel room right now. We were getting ready to go over to Pete's house and pray with him."

Pete Jackson, the last of the accounted for frat brothers was not in attendance at the reunion. However, he lived in Atlanta in a 2.5 million dollar home. Pete's family had been wealthy beyond any of the other brothers' imagination when they were in college. But his family had recently lost everything because of bad investments, gambling and cocaine addictions. Pete's house was being foreclosed on and he was too ashamed to show his face at the reunion.

Donavan wanted to go with his frat brothers to pray for Pete, but how could he do that when he was all messed up himself. "You go ahead. I'll go to my room, take something for my upset stomach and try to meet you all over there later," Donavan said and then moved away from his friend as fast as he could. He'd caught a glimpse of the puzzlement on his friend's face, but was powerless to do anything about it. He didn't meet his friends at Pete's house, and he'd managed to avoid them for the rest of the reunion. Now, a week later he'd strolled into this bar wanting only to get drunk and forget his troubles. But he honestly couldn't stand the taste of beer.

"Why don't you go back home? Your dad needs you more than ever right now."

Donavan stared in the face of the bartender who'd just told him to go home and asked, "How do you know my father?"

The bartender shook himself. He appeared to be dazed and confused. But once he had regained he composure he told Donavan, "I didn't say anything about your father. I said you need to get off that stool if you're not going to buy another drink."

"Oh," Donavan said as he got off the stool and attempted to move away from the bar, but before he could move, the televisions that hung above the bar showing football games and music videos all seemed to change at once to a news station. Donavan's eyes were drawn to the television as he listened to a female news reporter say, "The infamous Ohioan preacher, Isaac Walker has just been arraigned on the charge of murder. Apparently the district attorney's office believe Pastor Walker murdered one of his church members. I'm also told that there may be more charges to come."

The woman turned away from the camera as the doors of the Dayton Municipal Court House opened and Isaac, Nina and Iona walked out. "Why did you murder that young man, Pastor Walker?" the eager young reporter asked.

Isaac stopped, turned toward the cameras and said, "I am not this monster you believe me to be. I love this city and the people in it. I have worked for decades to try and make it a better place for all of us. I could never harm Dwight or anyone else."

What's going on here? Donavan wondered. First, the bartender told him that his father needed him and now he was watching his father walk out of a police station being accused of murder. Donavan lowered his head; ashamed of the fact that his father now needed his prayers. But he was all prayed out; couldn't get a word to God if he rode on Elijah's coat tails as the Old Testament prophet guided his chariot all the way to heaven.

Chapter 20

Instead of being able to spend three weeks with her mother, Iona would have to break up her time between her mother and father. Her father's pre-trial hearing was next week, so she would go back to Dayton for that, and then come back to Chicago and finish her visit with her mother. Iona had asked Neil to find Larry Harris so they could try to find out who hired him to frame her father. So she would have to leave Chicago if Neil managed to locate Larry, the contract killer. There was one silver lining in all of this though; her mother was up and walking around. Another one of God's miracles?

Iona started unpacking her suitcase, putting her things away when her mother came into her room. "Are you ready to go?"

"Go? Go where?" Iona asked.

Cynda leaned against the door jam and smiled at her daughter. "You said that you would go to the Prayer Journey if I was able to go with you." Cynda spread her arms as if to say 'tada'. "I'm ready to go. The journey starts at ten this morning, so you've got about twenty minutes to get ready and then meet me downstairs."

Downstairs? That's right, her mother had climbed the stairs. "Are you supposed to be climbing stairs, Mother? Do you think you're well enough for all this?"

"Keith bought me a wheelchair, so I'm going to ride in it as we go through the Prayer Journey."

"Okay, I'll be down in fifteen minutes," Iona told her. She showered and threw on a sweat-shirt and pair of jeans just as her cell rang. She started not to answer it, but when she looked at the caller ID and saw that it was Donavan, she hurriedly pushed the talk button.

She plastered a smile on her face as she said, "Hey golden boy, is that you?"

Iona heard a quick intake of breath on the other line and then the line went dead.

"Oh no, what did I do?" Iona asked herself as she dialed her brother's number. He didn't answer, so she hung up and redialed. Still no answer so she left him a message. "Donavan, I didn't mean anything by the 'golden boy' comment. I was just joking with you. I love you, Donavan, okay? Please call me back. Daddy and Nina-Mama need you with them." She closed her flip phone and headed downstairs. As much as she would like to call and leave dozens of messages on Donavan's phone, she had to focus on her mother right now.

When she got downstairs, she walked into the family room to find her mother kneeling on the floor in prayer. Iona thought about the other day when she met Nina at the police station and how Nina told her that she never leaves her house without praying. Iona wondered if she should pray for Donavan before leaving the house, but she let that thought die an easy death.

Keith drove them to the church and took the wheelchair out of the trunk, carefully locked it in place and then helped Cynda climb aboard.

Cynda told him that they would be ready to go in about two hours, and Iona almost got back in the car and demanded to be taken home. But Cynda looked at her and said, "You'll enjoy it. I promise."

The prayer journey was made up of six different stages. There was a different room assigned for each stage of the journey. In the first room tubs of water with drying towels lined the floor and soft, soothing Christian music could be heard throughout the room. The water was for feet washing, like how Jesus washed the disciples' feet in the Bible. The instructor told them to grab a partner and wash that person's feet and then switch and allow the same to be done for them.

Iona washed her mother's feet, being careful to be gentle she asked, "Am I rubbing your feet too hard?"

"No baby, you're doing just fine," Cynda told her.

They switched spots and Cynda began washing Iona's feet. At the moment her mother sprinkled water atop her feet, Iona felt a type of cleansing; as if a breeze of fresh air had swept through her very being. She shivered.

"Are you okay?" Cynda asked.

"Yes, of course. I'm fine," Iona told her as Cynda wrapped her feet in a towel and dried them. They put their shoes back on and were escorted to the next room in the journey.

They went into the Who Am I room. In this room, tables and chairs lined the walls. On the table was a can of Play-Doh. Iona picked up the can, looked at Cynda and mouthed, "What are we supposed to do with this?"

Cynda hunched her shoulders.

The instructor closed the door as the last participant entered the room. "Hello everyone, and may you have a God blessed day!" the woman said in the most soothing voice Iona had ever heard. "Sometimes in life people try to mold us into what they want us to be," the woman began. "Sometimes we even create an image for the world to see, when inside we are something totally different. Today we are asking you to mold yourself. Take the clay out of the can and create the person you are behind closed doors; the person that you don't allow anyone to see. And don't worry, nobody will see your creation but you. So go on, get started."

Iona looked at the round blob of clay in her hands and could think of nothing to form this clay into. She sat it on the table, wanting desperately to get up and walk out of this room. But when she looked over at her mother and saw how earnestly she was working her clay into something, she decided that she wouldn't let Cynda down. She closed her eyes and began to earnestly search the secrets of her heart. Who was she? Not who she allowed others to see, like the self-assured woman in charge that she let everyone else see, but what did she think of herself when she was alone and no one was watching?

Iona picked the clay up and mashed it in her hands. All the while, asking herself again and again, who am I? Who am I? She put the clay on the table and stared at it. Within the flattened out blob of clay Iona saw lies, deceit and greed. In truth, she saw the monster that she had become and it sickened her. She began to form the clay into blobs of the hideous, lying, deceitful monster she knew herself to be. When she finished she stood up and walked out of the room. She went into the bathroom, locked herself in and allowed the tears to fall as she leaned against the door. She put her hand over her mouth to hold in the sobs that were threatening to seep out.

There was a knock on the bathroom door. Iona wiped the tears from her eyes, ran some cold water and splashed it on her face. Another knock on the door and then Iona heard her mother ask, "Are you in there, Iona?"

"Yes, ma'am. I'll be right out," Iona told her as she dried her face and opened the door. She grabbed hold of her mother's wheelchair and pushed her to the next room.

There were mounds and mounds of rocks piled around a fountain of living water in this room. At least that's what the sign called the water that flowed in the fountain. No tables were in this room, only chairs; and there were small baskets next to each chair.

The instructor told them, "The chairs you see are not for sitting, they are for you to kneel in front of and bow your head and pray. But what we want you to do when you pray in this room is to ask God to show you the different people that you may be angry with. Once you figure out who those people are, forgive them. If, however, you are unable to forgive, you need to pick up the basket next to your chair and put a rock in it for each person you just couldn't forgive."

Iona felt as if she might as well forget the prayer and just march right on over to the rock formation and pick up about ten or twelve rocks and go bust a few people in the head with them. She had one problem. There was one on her list she couldn't simply hit in the head and call it a day. Iona fell on her knees in front of her chair and confessed to the Lord that she was angry with Him. "You left me on my own and expected me to do the right thing. You didn't look out for my mother, father or my brother, but You still expect me to praise You." She was crying again as she continued to silently pray and tell God how much she hurt. She then felt a warmth she'd never known before cover her body. Iona couldn't explain it, but it felt like love; like compassion. And it made her cry all the more; made her sad for not wanting to draw nearer to God for so many of her adult years. And she found herself saying, "I'm sorry, Lord. I'm so sorry. I forgive You." And at that moment, she had finally allowed the Lord to love on her.

She lifted her head and noticed that Cynda was rolling her wheelchair out of the room and headed to the next room without her. Iona got up, and as she passed the rocks, she realized that she hadn't prayed about any of the people on earth that she had problems with. She'd gotten things right with God, but . . .

She walked back over to her chair, picked up her basket and then stood in front of the rocks. It hadn't escaped Iona's attention that her mother didn't need to pick up any rocks, but Iona sure needed the rocks. She put one in her basket for Johnny; three for her mother's sons, one for Diana Milner, the treacherous woman who caused Donavan to fall; and another one for the maniac that was trying to frame her father. She even put a rock in her basket for Donavan. She was angry at him for being a coward and running away when things got a little hard for him. *Some Golden Boy.*

By the time Iona reached the Cleansing Room, she had seven rocks in her basket. She sat down in the cleansing room and prayed for the people she hadn't been able to forgive. There was a basket in this room and one in every other room on the journey the instructor told them. Once the participant was able to forgive one of the members of their rock collection, that rock was to be tossed into the basket and they would, then move to the next room. Iona realized that the easiest rocks to deal with were the ones she put in her basket for her three younger brothers. They hadn't done anything to her. Their biggest crime to date was that of being born. Iona decided that she would no longer hold that against them. She put Junior's rock in the basket and then Joseph's and Caleb's. But those were the only rocks she was able to drop in the cleansing room.

The next stop was the deliverance room. This room was for things that ailed you. This room was treated like a doctor's office. Iona figured that she needed this room most since she still had four rocks in her basket. She sat in the waiting room with other people waiting to be seen. She was handed a clipboard with a piece of paper attached to it. On the paper, Iona was supposed to write down some of the issues she discovered she needed prayer to overcome. There was also a spot for her to write down the list of people she had not yet forgiven. She wrote all her information down, like the fact that she needed prayer for her deceitful, greedy ways. Iona also made sure to put down Johnny, Donavan and Diana as the three people she still had problems with. She didn't bother to put down the maniac that was trying to frame her father for murder, partly because she couldn't put a name with her anger and partly because she knew she'd never forgive that evil person until he was caught and prosecuted.

After about four other people had gone in, the receptionist walked over to her and said with a smile on her face, "The doctor will see you now."

Iona understood that the doctor she was about to see was more spiritual than natural, and that was just fine with her. She was in need of a lot of spiritual healing. The woman Iona sat down with introduced herself as Dr. Smith and then took the clipboard away from Iona and asked, "So why are you here today?"

Unashamed, Iona opened her mouth and told her doctor everything. She talked about her lack of spiritual balance, how her career has come to mean everything to her and how she'd willingly tossed God to the side to become successful in her field. She talked about being in love and being betrayed and how much that hurt. She told the doctor that she had come to believe that God had betrayed her family and on and on she went, until she had nothing left.

The doctor then took hold of her hands and began to pray for her and all her ailments. But this prayer was unlike any Iona had ever experienced. This woman touched the very core of Iona's being with the words she spoke to God. The prayer was electrifying, and before Iona knew it, she was on her knees crying and praying to God from her own heart. It was invigorating and unlike anything Iona had ever experienced. On her way out of the room, Iona was ready to forgive. She dropped the rocks she held for Donavan and Diana in the waste basket and kept moving toward her final stop.

In the Prayer room Iona was told that she must forget about herself and unselfishly pray for others.

Iona's mother was in this room, her head bowed in prayer as she faced the wall lined with chalk boards. Several sheets of art paper were taped to the chalk boards. On the paper were lists of people and organizations that needed prayer, such as, the pastor and his family, the President of the United States, congress, the senate, teachers and police officers. When Iona saw the word police officers, she immediately thought of Johnny and his betrayal. She looked down at her basket and noticed that she still had two rocks in her basket. One of them belonged to Johnny. She had loved him and wanted to build a future with him. To discover that he had just been playing her to get to her father stung, but she reminded herself that God had forgiven her for betraying Him, so she would have to do the same for Johnny. And just like that she was able to let go of another rock.

Iona sat down and began to pray for the lists of people she had been instructed to pray for. When she finished, she noticed that although her mother had obviously been in this room a lot longer than she, they both finished praying for all the people, organizations and communities at about the same time. But Iona wasn't going to let that get her down; her mother had been praying a lot longer than she had, so of course she would be able to speak with the Lord longer. Iona vowed that she would catch up with Cynda and Nina in the prayer department.

Smiling, Iona walked over to Cynda and told her, "This was an awesome experience. Thank you so much for bringing me."

"I knew you would enjoy it," Cynda told her with a smile

that equaled Iona's, then as the smile subsided she said, "Let's go on home, I'm getting a little tired."

"Oh, of course. I'm sorry I forced you to come with me."

"Don't worry about it. I truly enjoyed this experience."

Iona began pushing Cynda's wheelchair, but Cynda stopped her. She pointed to the basket that Iona brought with her into the prayer room. "You still have one rock left. Did you forget to put it in the waste basket?"

Iona turned toward her small basket on the floor next to the chair she sat in while she prayed. There was indeed one last rock left in it. She had been so caught up in praying for others that she forgot about the one thing that was still on her prayer list; her hatred for the person that was trying to frame her father for something he didn't do. She walked over to the basket, picked up the rock, bounced it in her hand a few times; felt the weight of it and desperately wanted to release it, but she couldn't. Iona slid the rock in her pocket and turned back to her mother. "Let's just say, God ain't finished with me yet. Okay?"

There was no judgment in Cynda's eyes or in her words as she said, "That's the way it is sometime. You keep that rock until you can throw it away without looking back, okay?"

Iona nodded and they left the church.

Keith was in the parking lot waiting on them. He got out of the car and helped Cynda out of the chair. "Ladies, how was your journey?"

Iona kissed Keith on his cheek and said, "Thanks for bringing us. This was an experience of a life time."

"So I see," Keith said. He opened the front passenger door for Cynda and waited as she slowly seated herself.

As Keith put the wheelchair in the trunk, Iona sat in the back and slid her hand around the rock that was in her pocket. It wasn't just a rock to Iona. She was holding unforgiveness in her hands and there was nothing she could do about it but pray that this situation would soon come to an end.

Iona's eyes grew wide as she realized that someone else was carrying a rock of un-forgiveness, and it was directed at her father. "Oh my God," she screamed. "I know what's going on."

Keith turned toward Iona. "What's wrong?"

Startled out of her own thoughts, Iona looked up. Realizing that it had been Keith talking to her she said, "Oh, I'm okay. I just figured something out." Then she took her cell phone out of her purse and called her father. When Isaac picked up the phone, she was so excited she could barely calm down long enough to tell him anything. "Daddy, I t-think I—"

"Calm down, Iona, what's going on?" Isaac asked.

She took a deep breath and said, "Okay, first off, you'll be glad to know that I rededicated my life to the Lord today."

"What!" Isaac exploded. "Ah, baby that's some wonderful news. I can't wait to tell Nina."

"That's not all, Daddy. I also figured out who is trying to frame you."

"Who?" Isaac asked quickly.

"Well, I don't exactly know who it is, but I think I know why he picked you."

Isaac said, "Go on."

"I went through this thing called a prayer journey today. During the journey I went into one room where we were told to put rocks in a basket for everyone that we had something against or were just angry with. I put seven rocks in my basket."

"Seven?" Isaac exclaimed.

Iona rolled her eyes. "Will you let me tell my story and stop judging me?"

Cynda laughed and said, "That's right, baby, you tell him."

"Mom thinks you should stop judging me also," Iona told Isaac.

"How's your mom doing?" Isaac asked.

"She's a little worn out after all that praying she did in the prayer room," Iona said with a chuckle.

Keith lifted a hand off the steering wheel and high fived Cynda. "My wife the prayer warrior."

Cynda turned back to Iona and reminded her, "Hey, you prayed too."

"Yeah, but your prayers were extra long. But it's cool, Mom. You just have a lot to talk to the Lord about," she told Cynda and then went back to her phone conversation. "Anyway, Dad, I had all these rocks, which represented people that I was angry with, and as I went into each room I was able to let go of a rock here and another there. But by the end of the journey, I still had one rock. It was my rock of un-forgiveness."

"Okay. But I don't understand how that relates to what's going on with me," Isaac said.

"Don't you see, Daddy? This is not some random guy out killing people just for the thrill of it. He is very specific with each victim. The people he killed were all thieves, and you tried to get them to accept God's forgiveness, and in some instances, you were successful. That's what I think this is about. There was someone in your life that you didn't forgive—someone that most likely stole something from you. And now this person sees you forgiving and ushering in God's forgiveness for others in the same predicament he was in and he sees you as a hypocrite."

"Iona, I have wiped my slate clean. I have forgiven everyone that has ever done anything to me," Isaac told her.

"Yeah, now you have. But I need you to go back. I know

you hate to do this, but I need you to meditate on your past and find the person that is holding you to your word."

"What word?" Isaac asked.

"Don't you remember the note, Daddy? It said 'No forgiveness for thieves, isn't that right, Pastor Walker?' The killer is throwing those words back in your face. There's someone you didn't forgive, Daddy, and I think that person is buried so deep in your past that you've forgotten. But, you need to remember if you want this to go away.

Part Two

Chapter 21

The Killing Years—Forty years ago

When the poor man's cocaine came on the scene, the world was not ready for how it would be rattled, shook and eventually robbed of once productive tax paying citizens. Crack was so affordable that small time hustlers could buy the product, flip it, and flip it until they became king pins and mafia dogs like the hustlers they had once worked for. That was how the killing started. Everyone wanted a piece of the pie, and all they had to do was gun down the crack king currently on top. But Isaac Walker didn't play that. He had built his organization by sweat, hard work and a bullet if need be. As far as Isaac could see, he wasn't going down, because winners went up.

However, Isaac did have a problem, and his name was Spoony Davidson. Spoony had groomed Isaac since he was eleven years old. He'd shown him the ropes: How to be a hustler 101 took place every day on the streets of Chicago, and Spoony was the teacher. Isaac was his prize pupil, or at least Isaac had been Spoony's pupil. These days, Isaac had his own instructor's license.

Spoony had given Isaac the money to make his first and second flip. After that, Isaac was using his own money; but he never forgot that Spoony had done him a good turn. So even though he could get his product a little cheaper if he found his own connection, Isaac believed that if you forgot the bridge that carried you over; when you need it again, the bridge just might explode on you. In short, loyalty was king with Isaac. So he sat in Spoony's basement waiting on him to arrive so they could get down to business and Isaac could get on with his day.

Linda, Spoony's wife and ex-call girl, had let Isaac in the house and told him to wait in the basement. She was sporting her monthly black eye and swollen jaw. Isaac had a feeling that the reason Linda no longer walked the streets had a lot more to do with how Spoony had rearranged her once pretty face than it had to do with the wedding ring she sported. Spoony would have put his own sister on the street if she owed him a nickel.

After waiting twenty minutes, Spoony came strutting down the stairs. He was midnight black with pearly white teeth that he coyly showed off as he smiled. "Hey, Ike-Man, what's going on?"

They called him Ike-Man because he beat men like Ike beat Tina Turner. "Nothing much," Isaac said as he remained seated.

"I hope I didn't keep you waiting too long. You know how it is. In our business you have to constantly put out fires."

Isaac smiled but said nothing. He knew how it was all right. When Isaac first went out on his own and Spoony was helping him set up his empire, their meetings were always held on time. That was the first thing Spoony taught him;

never waste another man's time. But as Isaac's empire began to grow, Spoony started coming to their meetings later and later. It was a power play, plain and simple.

Spoony stood behind the bar that was covered with red and black leather. The stools in front of the bar were also covered in black leather. He poured two drinks, both Remy Martin, and walked over to the black leather couch. He sat down, put Isaac's glass on the table and then leaned back. He propped his feet on the table and gulped down his drink. He saw that Isaac's drink was still on the table and asked, "You ain't thirsty?"

"You didn't hand me nothing. I thought both of those drinks belonged to you." Isaac hunched his shoulder. "The glass is still on your side of the table."

Spoony took his feet off the coffee table and sat up straight. "Oh, you too high and mighty to grab your drink from my side of the table?"

Isaac didn't respond. He wasn't the kind of man that was easily riled. He didn't make a habit of rising to bait that was thrown out for him to hang himself on. Even at twenty-three, he didn't play games. He took charge, handled his business and left the flexing to lesser men. In his rise to power he'd killed his share of hustlers without regret. In Isaac's mind, some scum needed killing. When they tried to kill you or muscle in on your turf, oh yeah, they were asking for a bullet to the head. But Isaac had never shot a man simply for disrespecting him. He figured that you earned your respect on the street one hustle at a time, and if you weren't getting respect, well then you needed to bring your game up.

"You ignoring me, nigga?" Spoony asked while drinking out of the glass he'd brought to the table for Isaac.

Isaac stood. Mentor or no mentor, he had earned his respect and he wasn't about to sit there and let Spoony strip him of it. "When you're ready to do business, you know where to find me. I'm out," Isaac said as he turned and headed for the basement stairs.

Spoony slammed the glass on the coffee table and stood. "You turning your back on me? You think you something now don't you? Big man, Isaac." When Spoony noticed that Isaac had not broken his stride to comment on any of his trash talking, and that Isaac was, in fact, about to leave, he said, "Come on, man, don't leave. You know I don't have good sense. I didn't mean nothing by what I said."

Isaac was half way up the stairs, but he turned and walked back down into the basement. No sense throwing away twelve years of friendship without at least finding out what was going on. Isaac sat down and asked, "What's with you?"

"Nothing," Spoony said while rubbing his forehead and his bushy eyebrows. "Some cats just been talking trash that's all."

"What kind of trash?" Isaac asked.

"You know how Marko and Brown are? They think you're trying to take over all of our territories, and they don't like it."

Marko Stevens and Calvin Brown were old school hustlers who ran the streets with Spoony when cocaine and heroine were the only games in town. But now that crack was on the scene, they were forced to move over and let former soldiers like Isaac take over their territory. But Isaac didn't much care what Marko and Brown thought. As far as he was concerned, if either of them got in his face about his business, their families would be doing some slow singing and flower bringing. "So what do you think, Spoony? Do you think I'm trying to take over your territory?"

Spoony sat down and slouched in his seat. "Naw, man, I don't think you're trying to take my territory. I know how you feel about loyalty. But people are talking."

Isaac knew they were talking. It was like that part in the

Bible when the women came out to greet King Saul and
David as they came home from a battle and the women
sang, "Saul has killed his thousands and David his ten thousand." The song didn't sit right with King Saul nor did the
fact that hustlers were saying that Isaac's hustle would soon
surpass Spoony's.

"Are we going to do business or not," Isaac asked.

"Oh, yeah-yeah." Spoony got up and went behind the bar
again. He pushed it out of its original spot, lifted a board
out of the floor and pulled out four bags of his stash. He sat
them in front of Isaac and Isaac handed him fifty thou.
"Nice doing business with you, home boy," Spoony said
while counting his money.

Isaac left Spoony's place and met up with his boys,
Leonard Styles and Keith Williams, so they could mix up
the dope and get it on the street. The three of them made
no excuses for being drug pushers, or their preferred term,
street entrepreneurs. They had met in juvee eight years
prior. Isaac and Leonard were fifteen and Keith was thirteen. They had each been through so much at their young
ages. Isaac's father had murdered his mother, Keith had
never known his father and his mother was a heroine addict
who'd traded down to crack and Leonard's people were
middle class and had divorced because neither could get
over blaming the other for their bad seed of a son. Now neither Leonard's father or mother wanted anything to do with
him. So the three of them banded together and became
their own family.

Leonard was bagging up some of the stuff when he asked,
"So how was our master, Spoony?"

"Paranoid as usual," Isaac said.

"That's from smoking up all the drugs he's supposed to
be selling," Leonard said.

Keith laughed. "You've got nerve. You get high on enough
of your own dope don't you?"

Leonard threw one of the crack rocks at Keith. "Shut up, fool! I just sample the product. Somebody has to make sure we're not putting bad dope on the street."

Keith laughed again, but Isaac didn't crack a smile.

"Seriously though, Leonard, you need to lay off the stuff. You're costing us money. Also, looking like a crack-head isn't pretty," Isaac said.

"I'm not a crack-head," Leonard retorted.

"Yet," Keith said.

"Whatever, y'all need to mind your own business, 'cause I got mine," Leonard told them.

Isaac shook his head as he and Keith exchanged glances. "All right man, you got it under control," Isaac said. "Just know that all your samples are now coming out of your cut."

Leonard pulled a wad of money out of his pocket and asked, "How much you need, nigga? I can pay for mine." He then turned to Keith and asked, "Where's your wad?"

"What are you talking about?" Keith asked Leonard.

"Boy, don't play with me. Your mother steals more dope from you than any amount I sample, so if I have to pay up, I know you gon' need to go deep in your pockets too," Leonard said.

Isaac knew how much it embarrassed Keith to discuss his mother's drug usage so he said, "Okay Leonard, we get your point, that's enough."

Leonard waved his money in the air. "Oh no, Ike-Man, it's time to pay up, remember? Let's *all* pay up."

"Shut up, Leonard, nobody needs to pay anything," Isaac said then looked toward Leonard. "Just remember to keep your sampling," he then turned to face Keith, "and your mother's stealing to a minimum. This is not a charity house—I lose money every time something goes out of here for free."

Leonard nodded and put his money back in his pocket.
"That's fine, I'll pay for whatever I sample from now on."

Keith rolled his eyes and mumbled, "crack-head."

Leonard threw another crack rock at him and said, "Your
mama."

Keith jumped up, ready to fight. He charged at Leonard,
but Isaac got in between them. "What's wrong with you?
Don't we have enough to worry about without fighting
against your own brother?" Isaac asked Keith as he held
him back.

"He's not my brother. He's a crack-head," Keith spat as
he spun around and grabbed his jacket. He headed toward
the front door, but just before he left, he turned back to
Leonard and said, "And don't you worry about my mother.
That's my business to handle."

"He's so sensitive," Leonard said as he watched Keith
walk out the door.

"Shut up, Leonard. Why do you always have to keep
mess going?" Isaac asked angrily.

"Don't even try to blame me for this." Leonard pointed
at the door Keith had exited and said, "That boy has been
keeping his stash at his mother's place all the while knowing
that she would steal from him; and you knew it too. He was
trying to keep her from turning tricks for her drugs, and I'm
not mad at him about that; but if the two of you want to
play Robin Hood and Little John, that's on y'all. But it's still
like I said, If I got to pay, so does he."

"Don't flex on me, Leonard," Isaac said while his cold,
dark eyes bore into him.

"I'm not flexing," Leonard said and then with a little less
bravado he added, "I'm just saying."

"Whatever."

Leonard reached into his jacket pocket and pulled out
three cigars. "Look, man, I not trying to argue with you

today. I brought these cigars with me so we could celebrate."

Isaac took one of the cigars out of Leonard's hand, sat back down at the table to continue bagging their dope and asked, "What are we celebrating?"

"What do you think? I'm a Dad and you're a godfather!"

"What!" Isaac jumped out of his seat and asked, "Did Clara have the baby?"

"Yeah dog." Leonard leaned back and lit his cigar. "I'm big daddy now."

"What are you doing here with us? When did she have the baby?" Isaac was so excited, one would have thought the woman had just birthed his baby.

"Relax, she had the baby last week. She called me from the hospital."

"Last week?" A puzzled expression was on Isaac's face as he asked, "Why are you just now telling me? Have you seen the baby yet?"

"Naw, man, I haven't seen him yet. I figured if I rushed over there, Clara would get the wrong impression and start telling her wacko family that we're back together and all that." Leonard had broken up with Clara as soon as she'd started showing. He'd told her to holler at him after she delivered his baby.

Isaac put on his coat and grabbed his keys.

"Where you going?" Leonard asked.

"To see my godson and tell him about his trifflin' daddy."

"See, there you go, trying to make me look bad," Leonard said while grabbing his coat. "I'm riding with you."

Tired of having to defend his mother's drug usage, Keith decided that he would confront her once and for all. He was still steaming mad about what big mouth Leonard had to say about him allowing his mother to steal drugs from him; but even though he was mad, Keith couldn't deny the truth in that statement. He hated knowing that his own mother turned tricks just to get high. So yes, he had allowed her to take a few rocks from his stash from time to time. But now that Keith thought about what he was doing, he realized that he had become an enabler to his mother. Because if he really wanted her to get off of drugs, he would lay down the law.

The rundown apartment his mother lived in made Keith sick, but she refused to let him move her to a better place. He knew she just wanted to be around her drug friends and continue to have easy access to all the pills and crack she could take in a day. Dirty diapers were strewn on the ground next to dirty needles, cans of baby formula and other trash. As he climbed the stairs to his mother's apartment he had to side step more trash and the drunks that paved the way. When he reached the third floor, he opened his mother's door with the key he had been given. She'd given him the key three years ago and said, "You might need to get in to revive me or identify my body."

Keith remembered that his mother had laughed after saying that to him. He hadn't found anything funny about it, nor did he find anything funny about the condition he found his mother in as he stepped into her small, one bedroom apartment.

Dorthea Williams was stretched out on her dirty couch. It had once been orange, but now it was brown with tints of orange. She was leaning over, vomiting on the carpeted floor. Between vomit and wipes of the mouth, she looked up at Keith and said, "Hey, son."

Keith didn't speak. He walked into his mother's bedroom opened her closet and took his bag loaded with his stash. And yes, it was indeed lighter than it had been the day before yesterday when he put it in her closet. He walked back into the living room, if you could call it that. It was more like the zombie room.

The zombie on the couch that used to be his mother saw the bag in Keith's hand and sat up. "Where are you going with that bag?" she asked.

"I'm not going to be your fix it man anymore, Mother."

"I-I'm gon' give this stuff up, son. You believe me don't you?" She heaved, laid back on the couch and turned back to the floor. Spilled out the rest of her guts, then told him, "This stuff don't mean me no good."

Keith stood at the door, his hand on the doorknob. He wanted to go to her, put her in the shower and clean up that mess. But he was tired of fixing everything for her.

"You're not getting another dime from me. Do you understand what I'm saying, Mama?" She didn't respond. "And I won't keep my stuff here anymore. You've stolen your last crack high from me."

Dorthea pulled herself back into a sitting position again and wiped her mouth. "Boy, why are you being so high and mighty? You're the dope man, remember? If you and your friends didn't supply the stuff, I couldn't use it."

His face was set. "And you won't blame me for your addictions ever again. At least not to my face. I'm not coming back here again. I refuse to see you until you get clean." He opened the door and walked out of his mother's life.

Chapter 22

The Killing Years Continued . . .

That night, Isaac, Leonard and Keith went to a night club on the south side of town where the liquor was good and the gold-diggers were fine. They sat at the bar tossing back shots and in general just enjoying their brotherhood. Isaac was on high about being a godfather. He told Keith, "You should have seen him, man. The most precious thing I ever saw in life."

Keith laughed. "You act like it's your baby."

Isaac got silent for a moment as he thought about that. He was only twenty-three, but he knew that he was missing something; a family. He told Keith, "I do want a child, but it has to be with the right woman."

Leonard lifted his drink and tapped Isaac's glass against his. "Amen, brother. 'Cause I have three problems with my baby's mama." He started listing the problems while holding up one, two and then the third finger. "My first problem with my baby's mama is that she wasn't somebody else—you know, somebody that I could really be all into; number two:

that chick has a psycho family. Her mom wants me to put a bullet in her mouth; and finally, she is a frigin bug." At that moment, his beeper went off. He let it testify of everything he'd just said as he let Keith and Isaac see the number on his phone. "See what I mean? Everything is a 911 call with that nut. I'm going to change my beeper number."

When Leonard sat down and gulped back his drink without making a beeline for the pay phone in front of the club, Keith asked, "You need me to give you a quarter so you can call ol' girl back?"

"Forget Clara, I am not about to call her and ruin my buzz," Leonard told them.

"What if something is wrong with the kid?" Isaac asked.

Leonard gave him a 'duh, are you stupid' look as his eyes bugged out of his head. "Do I look like a doctor? If something's wrong with the kid, they need to get him to the hospital rather than bugging me," Leonard said.

"Don't you worry," Keith said. "You'll get that father of the year plaque any day now."

"Forget you—I'm new at this. Clara knows what type of man I am. So she better pray that this whole Daddy thing grows on me."

A woman in a baby blue sequined dress, wearing her hair in a French roll, with long legs glimmering beneath shinny stockings came over to the side of the club where Isaac sat with his crew. She was dressed fine enough to be headed to an opera or a special night out for dinner and dancing with the one she loved; but there weren't many special occasions between hustlers and gold-diggers on the south side of town. It was Saturday night live at the night club; a chance to see and be seen.

Debbie McFearce set her sights on Isaac. She smiled as she reached him and squeezed in next to him at the bar. "What's up, baby? How've you been doing?" she asked.

"I'm doing. I see you're looking good as ever," Isaac commented as his eyes canvassed the lovely portrait of perfection in front of him.

She stepped back to show off her dress and her curves, she twirled around, then asked, "You like?"

"I like," he responded, then asked, "How much did Marko pay for that dress?"

Debbie shook her lovely head. "Naw, Marko didn't pay for this. I bought it myself. Anyway, I'm through with him."

"Is he through with you?" Isaac wanted to know.

"He kicked me and our son out. Didn't care what happened to his own son, he just wanted to move some other woman into my house; don't that sound like he's through with me?" Debbie asked.

"That's how it sounds to me," Leonard said with a laugh.

Debbie ignored Leonard and smiled back at Isaac. "You know what my mama used to tell me?"

Isaac had always loved and respected his mother. Up until the day she died, there was nothing she could ask that he wouldn't have done for her. He was slouched a bit in his chair. He swiveled around to give her his attention. "What did Mama say?"

Debbie raised her chest so Isaac could see the prize that was in front of him and then said, "Baby Girl, don't you fret. One man's trash is another man's treasure."

Isaac put his index finger and thumb to his lips and checked for drool, because his mouth was watering. Truth be told, he had wanted to get at Debbie for a long time. But, since she was with Marko, he let it go and settled for other women. "Your mama sounds like a wise woman," he told her as he stood, grabbed her arm and said, "Let's go find a place where we can talk about some things." They strolled across the dance floor over into a dark corner that held a few lounging chairs. Isaac and Debbie sat in one together.

Leonard and Keith watched Isaac as he worked.

Leonard shook his head. "Will you look at him? He's

about to take Marko's main squeeze, and he's doing it out in the open."

"Forget that. Marko let her go, and she's fair game," Keith said.

Leonard pointed to Marko Stevens as he leaned against the mirrored wall in front of the dance floor. Marko was the kind of hustler who dressed as if he was the CEO of a fortune 500 company responsible for paying taxes on legitimate businesses. In truth, Marko owned an auto dealership; two car washes and a drive thru; but he was still a pimp, drug dealer and numbers man.

"It don't look like he let her go," Leonard told Keith.

"What are you talking about?" Keith asked as he turned toward Marko, and then he saw what Leonard meant. Marko was leaned against the mirrored wall with his menacing eyes trained on Isaac and Debbie.

"You see how he's looking at them? He's going to make a move. I can feel it." Leonard began jumping around in his seat. He then got out of his chair and balled his fists. "That Negro don't even want that girl. But, I guarantee he'll put a bullet in Isaac just on GP." Leonard shook his head. "Naw, I'm not having it."

"Don't do nothing stupid," Keith said.

Leonard waved him off and strolled up to Marko as if they played on the same football team and were frat brothers. He gave him the Negro hand shake, then asked, "What's up, man? I know you're not thinking about trippin' in here, right?"

Leonard stood in front of Marko, blocking his view of Isaac and Debbie. Marko got agitated and lost his cool. He told Leonard, "Get out of my face, nigga."

Keith stepped to them and said, "You all right, Leonard?"

"You know me, Keith. I'm super fly," Leonard answered Keith while staring at Marko. "But this man's gon' have a problem if he talks crazy to me again."

"What?" Marko said as he pulled his nine hundred dollar Armani jacket off and let it fall to the floor. "Boy, I will crush you."

Two of Marko's soldiers came up on either side of him and grabbed his arms, holding him back. One of them whispered in his ear, "Not in here, man."

Marko shrugged them off and picked up his jacket. As he put it back on, he noticed Leonard staring him up and down. "What are you looking at?" His lip curled in disgust.

"Nothing," Leonard told him. "I'm just sizing you for your body bag. You look to be about six-one, two hundred and twenty pounds, A large bag will be good enough for you, right?"

The force of the blow Marko dealt to the left side of Leonard's square jaw caused him to stumble backward. Unable to hold his balance he fell on his backside while holding his jaw.

"You don't know me, boy. I will kill you," Marko spat. If not for the strict no guns, all-thugs-must-walk-through-the-medal-detector policy the club had, Leonard would have been shot instead of punched.

Keith stood in front of Leonard to give him time to get up off the floor and examine his teeth. "You ain't about to do that again. Not without going through me first," Keith told Marko.

Isaac saw the exchange from where he sat. He jumped out of his seat, almost knocking Debbie to the floor, and ran to where his boys were.

Marko turned to Isaac and said, "If you want to keep your crew in tact, you better keep them out of my face."

Before Isaac could respond, Leonard picked himself up off the floor and said, "No, you better stay out of our way. You ain't nobody."

"Shut up, Leonard," Keith whispered.

"Naw, naw," Leonard said while jumping around. "This

Negro thinks he's Al Capone or something. He hit me in the mouth and you think I'm just gon' let that go?" He was brave as long as he had back-up.

Isaac gave Leonard a stern look and then turned to Marko. "Look, as far as I'm concerned, we don't have a beef with you."

Debbie had walked up behind Isaac. Marko lifted his chin in her direction and asked, "If you don't have a beef with me, why you in here cozied up with my woman?"

Isaac glanced back at Debbie. She was still looking good to him and he still wanted to get with her so he said, "She told me she was a free agent. So the way I see it, if you don't want her, I'm willing to try her out."

Marko glared at Debbie and asked, "Is that what you told him? You're a free agent now?"

"You put me out, Marko," Debbie reminded him.

Marko pointed toward the exit and told Debbie, "Get your butt outside and wait for me by my car."

Debbie pulled on Isaac's arm and moved him a few inches away from the group. She asked him, "Are you really interested in seeing if we can make something happen?"

Isaac nodded. "I'm interested."

Debbie let his arm go and turned back to Marko. "I'm not leaving with you. Go on home to your new woman and leave me alone."

As Marko smiled, he showed his predator like pointy teeth. "All right then." Marko turned to his boys on either side of him and said, "Let's go."

After Marko left, Isaac and his crew tried to enjoy the night as best they could. Leonard was still fuming about almost getting himself knocked out. He thought Marko and his henchmen shouldn't have been allowed to walk out on their own two steady feet. They should have been dealt with, taken out on stretchers, and rushed to the hospital. Isaac re-

fused to go there with him and told Leonard to, "Shut up."
He looked around the night club and then back to Leonard.

Isaac said, "We'll discuss this at my house when we leave
this joint."

Isaac played his hand close to his vest. He didn't believe
in letting outsiders know his plans, unlike Leonard who
spilled his guts every chance he got.

When they left the club, Isaac took Debbie home with
him as Keith and Leonard followed in their own cars. Debbie
grabbed herself a sandwich out of Isaac's fridge and went into
his bedroom to give him time to speak with his boys. Leonard
and Keith sat down with Isaac around his kitchen table.

"Okay," Isaac said, "How did all that mess get started?"

Keith rolled his eyes in Leonard's direction and said,
"Genius here got mad, because Marko was staring at you
and Debbie."

"He looked like he was about to do something," Leonard
said.

"How many times have I told you looks don't mean a
thing?" Isaac asked Leonard.

"Look, you handle your business the way you handle it and
let me handle mine," Leonard said with his chest stuck out.

"Yeah, we all saw how you handled your business while you
were picking yourself up off the floor," Keith responded.

Leonard jumped out of his seat, angry. "You think I can't
handle that sucka? I was ready to do it. But y'all were busy
screaming peace, peace like scared little punks."

"You're a fool," Keith said as he stood and got in
Leonard's face. "You're going to get us all killed someday.
You never think before you open your big mouth and I'm
tired of picking up after you."

"What did I do that was so wrong?" Leonard asked, the
picture of innocence.

"You told the man that you were sizing him for a body
bag, you idiot," Keith yelled.

Isaac stood now and paced the room. He ran his hands through his wavy hair and looked at Leonard.

"What?" Leonard asked.

The education of Leonard was a never ending endeavor, but none-the-less, Isaac felt compelled to try, try, try again. "How many times have I told you to never threaten a man unless you are prepared to carry out your threat at that very moment?"

"If I'd had my gun, I would have shot that fool," Leonard said.

"Do you have any idea who Marko Stevens is and how connected he is?" Isaac asked.

"You scared?" Leonard taunted Isaac.

"Naw, stupid, I'm not scared; I'm wise, and I don't start trouble I can't finish," Isaac spat.

Leonard stepped back, holding his hands in the air. "So are you saying that I can't handle Marko?"

Isaac wasn't listening. He was looking out his kitchen window as he noticed the lights of a car being turned off, but the car kept moving slowly down his driveway. "Get down!" Isaac screamed just as the window shattered and bullets splattered through the apartment. Keith fell down as a bullet sped past his forehead. Leonard coward underneath the kitchen table, shaking and bug eyed.

The door to Isaac's bedroom opened and Debbie walked out asking, "What's with all the noise out here?"

Several more bullets rang out through the apartment and Isaac heard a thud. He crawled through the kitchen and into the living room. Debbie was stretched out on the floor. Isaac crawled over to her. Blood was seeping through the top part of her dress on the right side. *At least the bullet hadn't gone in near her heart,* Isaac thought as he tore her dress, pulled off his shirt and pressed it against the wound. "Debbie, can you hear me?"

"W-what's g-going on?" she asked, visibly dazed.

"You've been shot. Hold still and I'll get you out of here in a minute."

Keith pulled his gun out of his holster, got off the floor and sent bullets flying out of the window. Pop-pop-pop. Screeching tires backed out of Isaac's drive and sped down the street. Isaac picked up his telephone, and dialed 911. He gave them the address and then hung up. The gun fire had stopped, so he walked back into the kitchen to make sure Keith and Leonard were okay. Keith was reholstering his gun and leaning against the wall. Leonard was still shaking and cowering underneath the table. Isaac kicked the table and asked him, "So are you scared yet?"

Isaac went back to Debbie without waiting on a response. "He didn't have to do this. He doesn't even want me anymore," she said as Isaac held his shirt against the wound.

"Just hold on, okay Debbie? An ambulance is on the way," Isaac said.

Debbie put her hand on top of Isaac's and weakly declared, "I'm not going to die. I wouldn't give him the satisfaction."

"Keep thinking like that, Debbie. Just keep thinking like that." Isaac heard the sirens outside his door and hollered for Keith to let the paramedics in.

The paramedics came in and carted Debbie out of the house. She held onto Isaac's hand until she reached the front door. "I'll see you at the hospital," he told her.

Leonard finally came from underneath the table as the door closed behind the paramedics and said, "Man, that fool is crazy. We got to do something about him now."

"We will." Then Isaac said in a calm voice just like he was asking his friend to go pick up a pizza, "Go get that body bag you sized Marko for. He's going to need it."

They didn't actually break into a morgue to get a body bag. They brought a suit bag out of Isaac's closet with them and threw it on top of Marko after breaking into his house. When Marko opened his eyes and saw Isaac in front of him with his Glock trained on his head, his eyes widened as he heard Isaac say, "The next time you open your eyes, you'll be begging Satan to turn the heat down." And with that, Isaac shot him in the head.

On the nightstand, Marko had five bundles of green backs. Each bundle was ten thousand. Isaac took the bundles.

Leonard was giddy as he said, "Let's loot this place."

"No," Isaac said. "I don't want anything from him." He lifted the cash. "He owes this to Debbie."

"Ah man, do you know how much money we could make selling off this fool's stuff?" Leonard asked.

"Do you ever quit?" Keith asked as he headed toward the door.

"He don't know how to quit," Isaac said with a laugh as they all walked out of Marko's house as if they had done nothing more than visit a friend in the wee hours of the morning and shared a cup of coffee with him.

The next morning, Isaac visited Debbie in the hospital. She was bandaged up, but all in all she looked pretty good as she sat up in the bed.

"Hey you," Isaac said as he walked over to her bed.

"Hey yourself," she said smiling.

"You're looking good."

"I told you I wasn't going to let him kill me."

Isaac took the package out of his coat pocket and laid it in her bed.

"What's that?" Debbie asked.

"A little something to help you get on your feet."

Debbie opened the bag and stared at the contents. "Where'd this money come from?"

All Isaac said was, "It's yours."

Debbie asked matter of factly, "I don't need to worry about Marko anymore, do I?"

"I don't think he'll ever bother you again," Isaac told her.

Her eyes watered. She looked away from Isaac for a moment and then turned back to him and said, "Thank you."

Chapter 23

Present Day

Pastor Walker was in the front of the sanctuary, bowed down at the altar in prayer. His deep chocolate face was pensive, as his mind kept reeling into the past. Iona had asked too much of him. For decades Isaac had tried to forget what manner of man he had once been. So much death happened around him back then—now he only wanted to bring life and that more abundantly to people who believed on Jesus. He wasn't that man anymore, and remembering the destruction that had been caused by that former man made his heart sick. "How much more, Lord? How much more?"

Remember it all, Isaac. There's something you left undone, came the gentle instruction from God.

Isaac didn't want to remember anymore of those maddening times. Because even as his mind's eye pictured himself in the hospital giving Debbie McFearce that packet of money, he knew he would have to remember what she did with that money, and that Marko turned Debbie into a junkie while she lived with him. The moment she was released from the hospital, she went and blew that money on so much dope that her heart exploded and she died.

Johnny walked into the sanctuary and Isaac stood to greet him. "Son," Isaac said.

With eyes downcast, Johnny asked, "How can you still call me that?"

"Because you have become a son to me; just like Donavan doesn't stop being my son because he messed up, neither will I stop thinking of you as my son in the Gospel."

"Pastor, I came to see you today because I wanted you to know that I don't believe that you are a crook or that you are doing anything to harm your congregation. Yes, I started my investigation with that premise in mind, but after sitting in this church and listening to the Word you preach, and yes I will admit, after checking the church's financial records, I came to believe not just in you, but in God."

"I know you did, son."

"And I had already told JL that I had closed my investigation on you. So some of the things he told Iona were false. Not that she'll ever believe me."

Isaac sat down on the front pew and asked Johnny, "Why do you think this JL person would be interested in having me investigated?"

"JL Tyler, he's a prosecutor, sir," Johnny answered. "I really don't know why he was so interested, but I'd like to tell you a little more about me so you can understand why I even considered investigating you." Johnny sat down next to Isaac and told him all about his preacher father and his suicide committing mother. He told him about his visits to the church that his father still resided over.

When Johnny finished his story and left to go back to work, Isaac's heart was heavy. He looked up at the pulpit and thought about Johnny saying that he wasn't doing anything to harm his congregation. Funny thing was, Isaac hadn't only harmed people in the past, he was now harming his own congregation every time he stood behind that pulpit and preached.

Tomorrow was Sunday, and the man who was never scared even when bullets flew over his head was now terrified that a sermon he preached would cause another man to lose his life. And, he just couldn't have that. For almost thirty years, Isaac's life had been about his pulpit. Could he really separate himself from it? What would that separation do to his relationship with God? Isaac bowed his head and put his hands over his face. The enemy was wearing him down, and Isaac didn't know which way to turn.

Brogan stood in the back of the sanctuary watching over his charge. Angels were lined against the walls. They had been called to this town, and this particular sanctuary because of the continual prayers of Isaac, Nina and other faithful saints. Now, they were standing off to the side waiting on word from the captain of the host. The battle would be deadly, they already knew that. The evil one had been gritting his teeth over Isaac's many victories for far too long; he would surely send his mightiest warriors to finish the job.

Miguel, who was one of the newly recruited angels, walked over to him and said, "He is weakening."

"Isaac is a mighty warrior for the Lord, but the enemy has been intensely focused on him for much too long without us being able to intervene," Brogan said. Then with a reassured nod of his head he added, "The captain will give us orders soon."

Donavan broke down and went to see his frat brother, Charlie Brooks. He told him everything that was going on in his life; how he'd messed up and how his dad needed him, but he was too ashamed to go to him. When Donavan finished his story he admitted, "For years, all I did was walk up right before God and pray for others, now I'm the one in need of prayer."

Charlie patted Donavan on the back as he said, "I don't have any stones to throw at you, brother. We've all been at this crossroad. Isn't that what the Bible says, all have sinned and come short of the glory of God."

"I know that in theory, Charlie. I just don't know how to get past what I did in order to get back to the place I had been with God."

Charlie held out his hands to Donavan. "Well then, let's pray and ask God to show us what to do."

Chapter 24

In the wee hours of the night, pain exploded throughout Cynda's body. Keith tried to hold and comfort her, but his touch only made the pain worse. He got off the sofa bed and knelt down beside the bed to pray. Cynda began crying out to the Lord. Every inch of her body ached, and shooting pains were rocking her very existence. Sweat beaded down her face as ever increasing pain ravaged her body. Cynda had gone through childbirth four times and still could not relate the pain she was now enduring to that of childbirth. She knew with every fiber of her being that she was dying.

She looked to heaven and said, "Not now, Father, not now." She turned her face toward the posters on her wall and began reciting, "Healing is the children's bread; It is by your stripes that I am healed . . ."

As Cynda was sweating and going through her third round of scripture reciting, another pain shot through her and caused her eyes to roll back and her head to bob. She was delirious now as she heard Keith cry out, "Don't take her from me, Lord. Help us God, please!"

Where was Keith? She couldn't see him, but she wanted

to comfort him; let him know that it would be all right. She tried to open her eyes and lift her head, but this bright light was in the room blinding her. A smile crossed Cynda's face as the light subsided and Arnoth, the angel that had been with her from the time she was nine years old, stood before her. She knew her lips weren't moving because she couldn't speak, but her mind said to him, "Nice to see you again, old friend."

He had a sad expression on his angelic face as he said, "Nice to see you as well."

"Don't be sad," Cynda told him. "I'm going to live."

He lowered his head, but did not answer her.

"No, no. Don't be like that. I know you came here tonight to see me safely to heaven, but I need you to do something for me."

Arnoth lifted his head and told her, "The time has already been set."

"I believe in miracles, old friend. So I need you to go tell my Father that I haven't finished my race down here. Tell Him that I'll be happy to come home once I've completed the assignments He gave me." She lifted her hand to shew Arnoth back to heaven. "Go tell Him; He knows what He called me to do."

Arnoth smiled as he appeared to be hearing another voice, one way up high, and then he left just as quickly as he had come. Before Cynda could rejoice over her angel delivering a message to God, the pains came back. She realized that while her angel stood in the room, she felt no pain, but once he left, she again felt as if she was being ripped apart. She wanted to call him back. She had changed her mind. She would go home now, if God would take this awful pain away.

Cynda heard Keith singing "There's no God like Jehovah." He got on the bed and rubbed her back like he had done during childbirth. He was a good man, and she wasn't about to leave him either. Keith was her love, her friend. *Lord, I'm only forty-six.*

"How does that feel?" Keith asked after rubbing her back for a while.

She wanted to tell him it felt wonderful; just what the doctor ordered, but she was drifting.

Chapter 25

Back To The Killing Years

After Marko's death, Isaac's empire grew larger. Isaac took over a third of what belonged to Marko, Spoony took another third, and Brown took the remaining piece. But, according to rumors on the street, Brown wasn't happy with his cut of the action and Isaac and Keith had to meet with some of the other hustler's in Chicago on tomorrow.

Leonard's sampling of the product had exploded into full-blown drug addiction. Leonard had started stealing from the operation, so Isaac finally had to cut him from the payroll. Having no place to go, Leonard moved in with Clara, the mother of his son. Isaac would drop by from time to time bringing food and pampers. He would also put a little money in Clara's hand, hoping that she wouldn't let Leonard talk her out of it.

Keith had his own sorrows as well. He kept receiving reports from their runners that his mother was out tricking. Isaac knew Keith wanted to go to her, but he was tired of fixing everything for her. It seemed that even though they were on top, too much had gone wrong and the game was getting old. So as they counted their stacks of money, neither Keith nor Isaac could find anything to smile about.

Keith blew out hot air and then threw a stack of fifties against the wall. "Man, I'm tired of this. We have worked hard to get to where we are, and these guys just keep trying to push us back."

"You know how it goes," Isaac said. "They were in the game before we were, and they don't think we deserve to have as much of the take as we're getting."

"I really don't care what they think. I'm not pulling back for them," Keith said with determination.

Isaac's face was set in calm resolve as he told his friend, "I'm glad you feel that way, 'cause we just may have to kill a few more of them before this is all over."

Keith put his gun on the table and said, "Bring it on."

Isaac stood, took some of the money off the table and put it in the safe. Keith brought the rest of the money to the safe. Isaac turned to Keith and said, "Look man, we have been way too focused on people who don't want us around; let's finish up our business and go find some women to hang out with for the night. All right?"

"Sounds like a plan," Keith agreed.

They jumped into Isaac's brand new Lincoln Navigator and headed to each of their spots, dropping off bags of happy rocks. They usually left the stuff in one of their crack houses and gave one of the runners the job of distribution, but they needed a release; a thrill rush. And nothing was more thrilling than riding the Dan Ryan with a cop tailing you why you carried enough drugs to get life in prison. When they finished their thrill ride, they went in search of female companionship.

Isaac was dating about five women at that point in time, but the only one he really cared about was Valerie Middle. She was down for him and willing to help him build his empire and he liked that about her. He also knew that Valerie was not a drug-head so he didn't have to worry about having another Debbie incident on his hands if he gave her a bundle of money to take care of things.

Keith was only seeing one woman. That was how Keith was. He didn't like spreading his love around. He was always looking for a woman he would be interested in marrying. The girl he was currently seeing was Lydia. So they picked up their women and headed out for a night on the town. It was lobster, steak, Remy Martin and bubbly for everyone.

In the midst of one of Isaac's drinks, he looked at Valerie and decided he wanted her for his woman. "So when are you going to move in with me?" he asked.

Valerie didn't hesitate. "Tonight," she told him.

With a self-assured smile on his face, Isaac nodded his head and replied, "That's what I thought."

Lydia asked Keith, "What about you? When are we going to take the next step?"

Keith shook his head. "Oh no, I'm not in this mess. The last woman I lived with was my mama and I didn't like the way she kept house. It's going to take me a long time to get over that."

The group laughed, but Isaac knew the truth. Keith didn't want to live with just any woman. He wanted to live with his wife. The boy should have never become a hustler as far as Isaac was concerned. He should have been a professor or a minister; some occupation where people followed the rules and lived honorable lives.

"Don't listen to him," Isaac slurred. "My boy don't believe in shacking up. He believes in marriage and picket fences; three kids and two car garages."

"Shut up, Isaac," Keith said while squirming in his seat.

Valerie told Keith, "There's nothing wrong with wanting all that. I think it's beautiful." She hit Isaac in the arm and said, "I just happen to be with a man who doesn't care about love and commitment."

Isaac rubbed his arm. "Didn't I just commit to you? How many other women do you think I've moved into my house?"

Valerie didn't answer.

"None, that's how many," Isaac answered for her.

"I'm sorry," Valerie said sarcastically. "I didn't realize how blessed I was."

"What are you talking that blessed stuff for? That sounds like church and I'm too drunk to hear about church stuff," Isaac told her.

"Well, you're going to hear about church stuff around me, Isaac Walker. I grew up in the church, and I'm not about to forget that just to please you," Valerie told him.

She was feisty. Isaac liked that. He thought they would do nicely together until something better came along anyway. "Let's go home," Isaac said.

"All right, but I'm driving. You and Keith are too drunk to get behind the wheel of a car that I'm in," Valerie told them. Isaac handed over the keys and got in on the passenger side. Keith and Lydia got in the back and Valerie drove them to Keith's place.

When Keith and Lydia got out, Isaac told Valerie, "You drive good. What kind of car do you want me to buy you?"

"Are you serious?" Valerie asked.

Isaac leaned his head against the window, and with a drunken goofy expression on his face that he had mistaken for cool, he asked, "Do I look like I'm joking?"

Valerie laughed. "You don't want me to tell you what you look like right now. But I'll take a red BMW."

"Done!" Isaac shouted. "We'll pick it up tomorrow." And they did, right before Isaac and Keith's meeting with the rest of the top street hustlers. So Isaac drove Valerie's BMW to the meeting, and she drove his Navigator to her apartment and loaded it with her clothes.

At their meeting, however, things did not go as smoothly for Isaac, as moving a woman into his house and buying her a car to put a smile on her face did. No one smiled as Isaac and Keith glanced around the table. Spoony was at the head, Brown was on his right. To Spoony's left was Stevie Johnson, a carrier turned top-dog once Marko's organization had been destroyed. Two other cats were at the table. On Brown's left was another old school hustler named Shinny Watson and next to Stevie was Pete Jones, a guy who came up alongside Isaac. He just wasn't closing as many deals as Isaac of late, but whose fault was that?

"Isaac, your take has doubled in the last year, and some of the brothers here think that you are trying to take over," Spoony told him.

"Have I ever taken anything from you, Spoony?" Isaac asked. Spoony didn't answer so Isaac asked another question. "And don't I still bring all my business to you? So why haven't you already told these cats to lay off?"

Brown said, "Look here sonny-"

Isaac turned his cold black eyes on Brown and said, "You ain't my daddy, and I'm not your son. I'm a man, and if I speak to you respectfully, I expect the same in return. Understand?"

Brown stood up and exploded. "Boy, I will slit your throat. How's that for respect?"

Spoony touched Brown's arm and said, "Brown, man, we came here to discuss this like reasonable men. Sit down, please."

Brown flopped back into his seat as he told Spoony, "You just better tell your boy to check his self, before I do it for him."

Stevie put his elbows on the table and tried his hand at intimidation. "Isaac, people are concerned."

Brown added, "And we are all a little worried about your family's safety. People are getting uptight, thinking that you and Keith are earning money that should have been theirs. Anything could happen."

Isaac wanted to laugh in Brown's face. The only family he had left was his usually-wrong daddy and he would gladly give up the address to Usually-wrong's house if they wanted to do him a favor and kill that maggot. Thank God and good riddance was how Isaac saw it.

Keith was another matter. He stood up and told them, "If you think I'm going to sit here and listen to you threaten my family, you've got another thought coming. Bring it on," Keith said as he strutted to the door and waited on Isaac to join him.

Isaac slowly rose out of his chair, understanding he had now entered a game of winner take all—loser eat six feet of dirt. He nodded at Spoony and said, "I'll see you around."

Spoony nodded back with a look on his face that said, "I sure hope so."

Over the next three months, Isaac and Keith's cars were bombed. Their homes were riddled with bullets, so they started moving from hotel to hotel. Their runners were gunned down in the street. Isaac and Keith went to war and hit them harder than they were hit. By the end of that three month period, Stevie, Shinny and Pete were no longer of this world. The only two that were at that round table meeting left alive besides Isaac and Keith were Spoony and Brown. Spoony had arranged a meeting with Isaac and Brown and had them both agree to end the war. Isaac willingly agreed to stay on his side of town and leave Brown to his side. And with that, it was over. But, just when Isaac and Keith thought they could breathe easy again, two things happened.

Leonard came home, when Isaac was at Clara's bringing some money to help with the bills. He stole her bill money the past few months, and they were getting ready to be evicted. Leonard walked over to Isaac as he sat at the kitchen table playing with his godson and said, "I miss you, man. How you just gon' drop me like this when we supposed to be boys."

Isaac handed the baby back to Clara and told Leonard, "There's no place in my organization for crack-heads."

Leonard started jumping around the kitchen like a man without hope, flailing his long arms and kicking in the air. He turned back to Isaac and pulled at his worn and tattered clothes and asked, "Do you think I want to be like this?"

"We warned you more times than I can count about sampling the product. Is it my fault that you wouldn't listen?"

Leonard walked over to Isaac and got on his knees. "Help me, man. Don't you see me? Look at me, Isaac. I need help!"

Isaac was saddened by the man that knelt before him. Leonard's cheeks were sunken, and he had the ashened look that crack-heads get. His boy had sunken low, and Isaac sat on the sidelines while it happened. "I'll tell you what," Isaac began. "If you agree to go to rehab, then I'll have your back all the way."

Leonard stood up and stepped away from Isaac. "Man, rehabs don't work. Why do you want to make me waste time like that when I could be back on the block helping you?"

"If you're serious about getting clean, it'll work. Take it or leave it."

Leonard tried to reason with Isaac but he grabbed his keys and walked out of the house with one last parting remark to Leonard. "Have Clara call me when you check into rehab. I'll send you some roses."

Isaac received a call from Joey, one of his runners. Joey told him that Keith needed to get over to his mother's apartment a-sap. Isaac got Keith on the phone and told him, "Man, you need to get over to your mom's place. Something has happened."

"I told you I don't want to be bothered by her drama anymore," Keith said.

"You need to get over there, Keith. One of my runners just called and told me that the ambulance and police are at her place."

When they hung up, Isaac sped toward Ms. Doretha's apartment on the lower South Side. He pulled up at the same time Keith did. He watched as Keith jumped out of his car and ran up to one of the police officers. Then Keith turned and watched the paramedics bringing the bed out of the apartment with a body bag on top of it. He ran over to them. The police officer followed, trying to hold him back.

"Get off me, man. That's my mama," Keith yelled as he trodded forward.

The paramedics set the ambulatory bed down and stood in front of it, waving Keith away. "You don't want to see her now, sir," one of them told him.

Isaac ran over to Keith and tried to pull him away also. But Keith jerked away. "I have a right to know if that is my mother." Keith pointed at the body bag.

"She's been cut up, man. Don't do this to yourself," the other police officer said.

Keith grabbed the bag and quickly unzipped it before he could be stopped by anyone. A thin arm fell out, but Keith wasn't looking at the arm. He was looking into the slashed and bloody face of Doretha Williams. He put his arms around her and became covered in blood because her chest was cut-up as well. Keith didn't notice how bloody he was becoming. He just wanted to hold his mother one last time. "I'm sorry. You hear me?" he asked her. "I'm sorry."

Isaac pulled Keith off of his mother so the paramedics could close the bag back up. Keith tried to fall back on the body, but Isaac grabbed him. Tears were streaming down Keith's face as Isaac hugged him. Isaac's own mother had been carried out by the paramedics covered in blood. As they hugged, Isaac and Keith became forever bonded in blood.

"Come on, man. Let me take you home," Isaac said.

"No. I can't leave her like this, Isaac. She needs me, man."

"You need to get out of here. Let these people do their job." Isaac pulled Keith away again, and this time Keith allowed him. He took Keith over to his car and opened the passenger side door for him. "Get in, Keith. I'll have Valerie come pick up your car."

Keith was numb as Isaac drove off. He clenched his fist and smashed it against the dashboard. "Brown did this. I know it in my gut."

Isaac didn't say anything, but he thought Brown might not have anything to do with Doretha's death. Ms. Doretha was prostituting to get her drugs. Anyone could have done this as far as Isaac was concerned.

"We should have killed him right along with the rest of them."

"I'll tell you what," Isaac said. "Let's check into it. If Brown had something to do with this, then his family will cash in his insurance policy."

As it turned out, the killer just about begged the police to come and get him. He'd left his fingerprints all over Doretha's apartment and body and bragged to numerous friends about the murder. Michael Hopkins was arrested in a coffee shop that was owned by Brown. And, it was no wonder that the murderer was arrested at Brown's coffee shop, since he was one of Brown's top soldiers.

Keith and Isaac were watching the news while Valerie fixed steaks for them. The arrest was televised, so after watching Michael Hopkins get carted out of Brown's coffee shop, Isaac and Keith looked at each other and nodded. That night they went out in search of Brown and whoever might try to get in their way. They found him at Fat Al's juke joint. It was ten at night so there was only four people in the joint; Fat Al, Brown and two of Brown's henchmen. Brown was sitting at a back table sucking on a barbecue rib bone. His men were at the bar. Isaac and Keith sat at Brown's table and trained their guns on him from underneath the table.

Isaac told Brown, "You shouldn't have done it."

Brown put his barbecue down and asked, "What are you talking about?"

"We didn't move in on your operation. We didn't touch anything of yours, but how you had Doretha killed was foul." Isaac shook his head and then finished with, "We can't let that go."

Brown turned to Keith. "I didn't do anything to your mother. Don't act crazy and get yourself killed in here."

"Brave talk for a dead man," Isaac said.

Brown laughed in Isaac's face. "Man, get out of here before you get hurt."

"We never forgot how you warned us about our family, Brown," Keith said.

"And now we've got a warning for you," Isaac said, and then pulled the trigger and shot Brown in the gut.

Brown began lifting out of his chair. "You can't shoot me," he said.

But, Isaac didn't understand him, because he lifted his gun and shot him again; this time in the head. As Brown fell face forward on top of his barbecue, Keith shot two of Brown's henchmen as they tried to pull out their guns.

"What's up, Fat Al," Isaac asked as he pointed his gun at him.

Fat Al raised his hands. "I'm not taking sides, Ike-Man. I

have a family and I just want to get out of here and see them again."

"You remember your family when the police ask you about this. Okay?" Isaac said as he and Keith backed out the door.

Chapter 26

Present Day

Cynda had gone back into the hospital late Saturday night after she passed out. Keith didn't know what else to do but dial 911. By Sunday morning, Cynda had been pumped full of morphine and feeling no pain. Iona sat next to her mother's bed watching and praying. Keith and the boys were there as well. The hospital staff kept giving them that understanding mournful look that they give to family members who don't have much time left with their loved one. Iona ignored them. Her mother and her father's God was now her God and she believed He could do anything but fail. She leaned in close to Cynda and asked, "Do you want us to get your posters and put them on the walls of your hospital room?"

Cynda shook her head. "I want to go home. I'll wait on the rapture," she said in a whisper.

Iona knew her mother was a little loopy from all the pain medication being pumped into her body, but she was still of a mind to declare her faith in a God who could do the impossible. Iona admired this woman more than she ever had; and hoped to grow up to be just like her.

Iona moved over to Keith and asked in a low voice, "Do you think we can get her out of here?"

Keith continued looking down at his wife as he answered, "Not until her pain subsides."

Iona nodded, walked back on the other side of her mother's bed, grabbed her Bible off the night table and sat down to read and pray.

By Tuesday morning, Cynda was released from the hospital. On Thursday morning as Iona sat next to her mother's bed making calls and getting ready for her father's pre-trial, Cynda said, "You should be with your father so you can give this case your full attention."

Iona very much wanted to be by her father's side in his time of need. But, this was also Cynda's time of need. How could she choose? There was no way that she could abandon one for the other, so she split her time between the two people she loved most on this earth. Somehow she would make it work.

"It'll be fine, Mama. I'm going to go back in the morning for the pre-trial hearing. I'll catch a flight right back here the same night and then I'll continue to work on the case from here," Iona told her mother.

Cynda adjusted herself in bed as she told Iona, "I'd like to go to Dayton for the weekend."

Iona laughed. "Don't be ridiculous, Mama. You need to stay here and regain your strength."

"Since when do you tell me what I can and can't do?"

"Oh, you want to play it like that?" Iona put down her note pad and left the room. When she returned, Keith was with her. "Now tell him what you want to do," Iona told Cynda.

Cynda smiled at her husband and patted an empty spot on the bed. He sat next to her. She lifted his hand and began to lightly rub it back and forth. "Baby, I know you're worried about Isaac and want to be there for him right now."

"My place is here with you. Isaac understands that," Keith told her.

"I want to go, Keith. I haven't seen Nina in years. It'll be nice," Cynda said.

"Talk some sense into her, Keith," Iona said. "She's in no condition to go anywhere."

Cynda became agitated. She thrashed back and forth on the bed. "What's the difference if I die in Dayton or Chicago," she angrily demanded. A look of horror set on Iona's and Keith's faces and Cynda softened her tone. "Look, I don't plan to die today or even this year for that matter. I just want to go to Dayton so Iona can be with her father and you can be with your best friend; or really when you think about it, he's more like your brother." Cynda touched Keith's hand again. "Remember what you told me? The two of you were bonded by blood. Remember that?"

Keith nodded and then said, "Let me see if I can get a nurse to come with us."

"Who needs a nurse? I've got an angel talking to God on my behalf," Cynda told them.

"Be that as it may," Keith said. "You're not leaving Chicago without a licensed professional by your side."

"O ye of little faith," Cynda quipped playfully.

"O me of great love," Keith corrected and left the room to contact the hospital.

Iona sat back down next to her mother, shaking her head.

"What?" Cynda asked.

"You may be able to sweet talk Keith, but I'm still mad at you. I think you should stay here and rest," Iona told her as she picked up her note pad and got back to work on her father's case. She was determined not to let her mother's inability to realize the gravity of her condition put her in a bad mood—or any worse of a mood than a woman who discovers that her mother is dying of cancer and her father is being indicted on a murder charge could be in.

Iona's flight left at six a.m. Keith drove her to the airport, hugged her and said, "We'll see you sometime this evening over at Isaac's house."

"Are you sure this is the right thing to do?"

"No, but I'm sure it will make Cynda happy. And right now that's all I have left, so I'm doing it."

Later that evening, Iona sat in her father's kitchen going over the pre-trial information with him and Nina. Isaac wasn't allowed at the pre-trial hearing, so Iona let him know that the prosecutor didn't seem to have any new information. She told Isaac, "The scheduling conference is next week. You'll need to be present for that."

"Let me check my calendar and make sure I don't have a prior commitment," Isaac said.

"It's not funny, Daddy," Iona said while shoving his shoulder. "This is serious business, and I need my client to understand that."

"I know, Baby Girl. But, if I don't find something to laugh about, I'm going to go insane," Isaac told her.

Nina chimed in. "Okay, I'll find a comedy for us to watch when you and Iona get finished, but right now you need to focus."

Isaac patted Nina's hand. "Okay, baby, I'm focused." He turned back to Iona, "What else do you need from me?"

"I need to pull your telephone records from the house, your cell, and the church. The victim's mother claims you called and asked the victim to come out to your car that morning, so we need to prove that you didn't make that call."

"Do me a favor, Baby Girl."

"Sure Dad, what do you need?" Iona asked.

"Call him Dwight. I want to keep it personal. Someone

murdered Dwight with no other motive than to punish me—and I don't know why. So keep saying his name, Clarence's, and Vinny's names to me so that I never forget to ask why them and not me."

"Don't say it like that, Daddy."

"It's true. Whoever killed those men probably didn't even know them. Had no beef with them. The killer had me on his mind with each kill." Isaac shook his head and added, "I just can't move past the thought that even though I have given my life to Christ, I have killed again."

Nina stood up and put her hands on Isaac's shoulder. "That is not who you are, Isaac. You are a man of peace; a man of love. You are more Christ-like than anyone I know." She hugged him from behind and Isaac clung to her hands as they wrapped around his chest. "You're not responsible for the deaths of those men, baby. The killer is."

"Amen to that," Iona said.

Isaac asked, "Has your investigator come up with anything on that contract killer yet?"

"No, but he will. Neil is a pain, but he's good at what he does," Iona answered and then changed the subject. "Are you two okay with Mom and Keith coming down this weekend?"

"More than okay," Nina said and then turned toward her stove. "As a matter of fact, I need to get my pasta boiling. Your mother loves my pasta salad."

"I don't know how much of it she'll be able to eat. She hasn't had much of an appetite lately." Iona lowered her head and then told Isaac and Nina, "She's not doing so well."

Nina nudged Iona and said, "Lift your head, Iona. My God is a miracle worker."

"That's right," Isaac said while palming Nina's belly.

Iona looked embarrassed as she asked, "Do you two know how old you are?"

"Hey, don't blame me. Your Nina-Mama can't keep her hands off of me." Isaac stood and flexed. "Can you blame her?"

Nina swatted him on the butt and said, "Get out of here and let me get this dinner finished. If you stay in the kitchen, I might be too overcome by your sex appeal to pay attention to what I'm doing."

Iona laughed as Isaac strutted out of the kitchen. She stayed behind and helped Nina fix dinner as she had done for so many years while growing up in this house. But, she looked around the expansive kitchen with its marble counters and expensive ceramic tiled floors and realized that she and Donavan hadn't grown up in this house. Although both Iona and Donavan had a room reserved for them in this big, beautiful home, they had never lived here full-time. Nina and Isaac had only moved into their newly built luxury home seven years ago. Iona and Donavan grew up in a much smaller home in the Dayton View area of town. It was the house that a preacher and a struggling novelist could afford, but as God continued to bless them year after year, they expanded.

As Nina sliced the roast she had just taken out of the oven, she looked to Iona and said, "Your father and I have been meaning to talk to you about something."

Iona was cutting onions and green peppers for the pasta salad. "What's up?"

"Your father and I have been saving money for you and Donavan. We know how hard it is to start your own business, so we wanted to provide assistance if you or Donavan decided to do something like that. But when Donavan left, we gave him a portion of his money and we wanted to know if you wanted yours now as well."

Iona stopped chopping and asked, "How much money are we talking about?"

"Right now you've got twenty-five thousand. But, we add about five thousand a year to each account."

"Sounds good to me. Keep holding mine until I need it," Iona told Nina right before the doorbell rang.

"They're here," Nina said excitedly, then wiped her hands and ran for the door. She swung it wide open and smiled as the boys ran through the door trying to get out of the early March chill. Cynda stepped in with Keith close to her side. She stretched out her hand and touched Nina's belly and said, "Hello, miracle child."

Nina smiled and said, "Hello, miracle woman."

"I like the sound of that," Keith said as he kissed Nina on the cheek. "And congratulations to you and the old man."

"I heard that," Isaac said as he walked toward them. The four hugged. Cynda's nurse walked in and Keith introduced her. "This is Cathy. She's here for Cynda."

Nina and Isaac shook hands with Cathy and introduced themselves. Then they all went into the dining room to eat dinner and catch up.

Once dinner was finished, the kids went into Donavan's old room to play video games while the grown-ups went into the family room to talk about the things they didn't want to say in front of the kids. Once they had fully covered the storms they were facing, they formed a circle, joined hands and prayed. Iona clasped hands with Isaac and Cynda, ready to pray like never before.

Saturday, Nina, Cynda, and the boys relaxed in the house with a movie marathon. Cynda's nurse preferred to lounge in her room with a book. Iona, Isaac, and Keith went driving around checking out the locations where each body had been found, hoping to stumble onto something the police overlooked.

Nina brought a tray of popcorn, turkey sandwiches, and leftover pasta into the family room for the kids and Cynda. They sat together laughing over comedies and crying through dramas. The two were as comfortable together as best friends; but that had not always been the case.

Thirty years ago, Nina and Cynda had been rivals for Isaac's affection. He had strung both of them along, because he couldn't make up his mind what he wanted. When Isaac finally decided that he wanted Nina, Cynda began to hate both Isaac and Nina. She did things to them that threatened to tear them apart. But, the love of God kept Isaac and Nina together and helped them to forgive Cynda her many transgressions.

Nina turned to Cynda while the kids were glued to the TV and asked, "How are you holding up?"

"I'm going to make it," Cynda said, then smiled and added, "Don't think I'm going to leave you here with your man and mine too."

Nina laughed. "You better stick around. I told you before, I've got all I can handle with that husband of mine."

On Sunday morning, the whole crew went off to the House of God Christian Fellowship. "I can't wait to hear you preach, buddy," Keith said as he patted Isaac on the shoulder and walked out the door.

Isaac didn't respond, but he had already asked Elder Rhiner to minister to the congregation this morning. The way Isaac saw it, he hadn't preached last Sunday and no one got killed, so if he stayed out of the pulpit this Sunday as well, maybe he could save another life. But, when they got to church and the Spirit of the Lord began to move throughout the church, Isaac became convicted about his cowardice. He wasn't saving a life by not preaching, he was stepping out of the will of God. It was the first Sunday of the month and the deacons were passing out the grape juice and crackers for communion. The praise singers were singing, "It's the blood that gives me strength—from day to day." Isaac was weak. He didn't have the strength to go through the storm that was raging in front of him. Sitting in his pastor's chair, he bowed his head and broke down as a torrent of tears cascaded down his face.

Brogan and Miguel walked down the aisle in the midst of the church members as they walked to and from their seat to get their communion juice and cracker. They were over seven feet tall, but no one could see them. However, their presence along with the multitude of other angels in the room was definitely felt by all. They walked into the pulpit area. Brogan stood on the right side of Isaac and Miguel stood on the left and put their hands on Isaac's shoulders and ministered peace to the weakened soldier.

As the praise team was still singing about the blood reaching from the highest mountain to the lowest valley, Isaac heard the voice of the Lord whisper in his ear, *When you are weak, I am strong*, and he got on his knees and raised his hands in praise and total surrender to the will of God. Once Isaac lifted his hands to the Lord, Brogan and Miguel retreated to the back of the sanctuary once again and waited on further orders.

Elder Rhiner was seated next to Isaac. When Isaac was able to get up from his praise spot on the floor, he sat back down in his seat and leaned toward Elder Rhiner and said, "If you don't mind, I think I should preach today."

Elder Rhiner patted him on the shoulder and said, "You do the Lord's will, pastor."

Isaac smiled. That was exactly what he intended to do from this moment on. Nothing would stop him from doing just what God had called him to do; bring wayward souls to the kingdom.

Isaac stood before the congregation and declared the goodness of God as he had done for several decades now. When Isaac finished with his sermon, he made his altar call and stood back to see the increase of God. Ten people came to the altar, and Isaac was thankful for every one of them, but he was most thankful to see Diana Milner, the woman who was caught fornicating with Donavan, walk down the aisle, and stand before one of the altar workers with her head bowed and hands raised to God.

Iona came down the aisle, sat down on the front pew, and waited for Diana to finish lifting holy hands unto the Lord. Iona waited for the altar worker to hand Diana some tissues to wipe her tears and blow her nose. Then Iona stood next to Diana and said, "Would you please follow me? I need to speak with you."

Looking down from the pulpit, Isaac said a silent prayer for his daughter's continued growth in the Lord. He hoped that his daughter had really learned to forgive that day she went through the prayer journey with her mother. He wasted a lot of time with hatred in his heart, and brought a lot of heartache to many families. Isaac's rampages resulted in slow singing and flower bringing. His daughter wasn't as deadly as he had once been, so he had no fear that Iona was going to kill Diana as they walked off to the prayer room. He just hoped his daughter would not let unforgiveness grip her heart again.

And, that's when Isaac remembered. Standing there with his hands on his pulpit, watching his daughter walk toward the prayer room, Isaac remember the unforgiveness that had been in his heart toward thieves; Or at least, one thief in particular.

Chapter 27

The Killing Years Once Again

Isaac and Keith had worked their way to the top of the Chicago drug trade, but they weren't celebrating. They had lost so much to this city; mothers, Isaac's brother, friends and girlfriends, that they were ready to pack their bags and go. Spoony knew about a hustler in Dayton, Ohio by the name of Ton-Ton who needed help establishing his market. Eager to get away, Isaac and Keith volunteered for the job.

Of course, they didn't leave Chicago empty-handed. They had made millions and spent bundles on houses, cars, clothes, jewelry and women; lots of women. Besides the money, Isaac also brought Valerie to Dayton with him. At first, he moved her into his home. But, he soon found her a place of her own. Things were going good for Isaac and Keith in this new city. Then Leonard showed up. He was fresh out of rehab, looking as dapper as ever with a woman that wasn't Clara on his arm, and no idea how his son was doing. Isaac didn't pretend to be a one woman man, but he believed a man should take care of his responsibilities. You lay down with a woman and create a baby; you stay there and take care of that child. But Leonard was his boy, so he ignored his behavior and took him back into the fold.

The hustler they came to Dayton to help build up his territory, got himself arrested on a triple homicide, so Isaac took over Ton-Ton's territory without much hassle at all. Keith and Leonard became Isaac's enforcers, and they split the territory. Within six months time, Keith's territory was flourishing while Leonard's was losing more and more money every month. During one of their meetings, Isaac asked Leonard, "What's going on?"

"Nothing much. I'm just working hard to keep you on the throne." He bowed and dramatically waved his arm in the air. "All hail King Isaac."

Isaac got right to the point. "I'm losing money, Leonard."

Leonard shrugged. "People do get off drugs you know. We're competing with rehabs, crime stoppers, and Christmas for goodness sakes. What do you want me to do, go tell every crack-head in Dayton that they can't go to rehab or buy their children presents at Christmas time?"

"Shut up, Leonard. When have you ever known a crack-head to care about Christmas presents?"

"Clara cares. She's blown up my cell every day this week, begging me to take her Christmas shopping for the kids."

Clara had left Chicago to follow Leonard to Dayton, but Leonard had ignored her and his son once she got here. She ended up moving into the Desota Bass project homes and getting on crack after waiting one lonely night after the next for Leonard to come see about her. She had another baby, which Leonard claimed was not his, so now he had an excuse not to do the right thing. As each day passed, Isaac became more and more disgusted by his friend. His lip curled as he told Leonard, "I need my money."

Leonard stuck his chest out and spread his arms out wide.

He took a step forward. "You accusing me?" He took another step and asked, "You think I'm stealing? Is that it?"

"I've told you before, don't flex on me," Isaac warned Leonard and then continued. "Now I don't know if it has gone up your nose, in a pipe, on a woman-."

Leonard laughed. "I know you not talking about nobody spending money on women? Man, you've got nerve."

Currently, Isaac was dealing with about five women. He was really into about three of them. Valerie, Cynda and Nina. He was paying for Valerie and Cynda's apartment, and making sure they had everything they needed. After all, they were running his drugs from state to state. He moved Nina into his house and that was causing a lot of friction with Valerie and Cynda. He needed them in his business, so he spoiled them to keep their mouths shut about Nina. But, that was his money he was spending. "Let me put it to you like this, Leonard, I give you drugs to distribute and sell, but after you've sold the stuff, the money you bring back ain't matching; so get me my money by tonight or you're out."

"Just like that, huh? You gon' put me out again?" Leonard put his fist in the palm of his hand and rubbed it. He blew out hot air through his nostrils and then said, "Nigga, we built this business together." Leonard banged on his chest with his fist. "You forgot that didn't you, King Isaac? It was me in them streets, blowing fools away so you could be on top."

"I told you before, Leonard, I don't have room for a crack-head in my organization. If you're back on the pipe, you got to go."

"And that's another thing," Leonard said indignantly. "Why you always gotta rush to call somebody a crack-head? And, why I gotta be the one stealing? Why wouldn't you suspect one of my runners before accusing me, huh? I'm your boy. Doesn't that count for something?"

"Tonight, Leonard—get me my money, tonight."

Leonard flailed his arms in agitation. "Oh, so it's like that, huh? You gon' talk to me like I'm nothing after all the stuff we've been through?" When Isaac didn't respond, Leonard asked, "So what if I can't get the money by tonight, what you gon' do? You gon' kill ya' boy?"

When Isaac didn't respond, Leonard threw up his hands and said, "Forget it, I don't need this. Count me out now— do what you want with my territory, I'm out!" Leonard turned and stormed out of the crack-house Isaac owned on Grand Avenue.

Isaac called Keith and informed him that Leonard was no longer a part of their organization, and that he would be taking over Leonard's territory himself. Then, he left the house on Grand and went home. But, instead of finding peace, he found Nina packing her clothes, screaming and crying. Isaac lifted his hands and asked, "Would you calm down and tell me what happened?"

"The same thing that always happens around here," Nina retorted. "One of your women slashed my tires and another one—might be the same one for all I know, called here today, and informed me that you and she have a date to go to Chicago."

"Nina, I don't know who keeps doing things to your car, but believe me, when I find out, I will deal with that person. As far as Chicago, I go there on business trips all the time, you know that."

Nina threw a pair of jeans in her suitcase and then turned to face Isaac with tears in her eyes. "I can't deal with this anymore, Isaac. I'm pregnant and I have to worry about me and my baby."

For a moment everything went still for Isaac. Had he heard her right? Did she just say that she was pregnant? Was he going to be a daddy after all these years? A thousand questions roamed through his mind as he imagined Nina's belly growing with his child. When he was finally able to move from the spot that held him captive, he went to Nina, picked her up and swung her around.

The expression on her face was that of surprise as he put her back on her feet. "You're happy about this?" she asked.

"Are you kidding? I would love to have a son, and to have him with you. That makes it all good." Isaac wasn't going to wait a week after the birth of his son to go out and buy cigars to celebrate like Leonard had done. He was going to go get them now. He couldn't wait to call Keith, and truth be told, he wanted to call Leonard too; but they were in different places now and he had to let that go. He moved Nina toward the bed and made her sit down. "Why would you even be thinking about leaving me now of all times?"

Nina wiped away the wetness on her face and told him, "I didn't think you would want the baby for one thing."

He looked at her as if she had suddenly grown an extra head. "Why wouldn't I want my baby?" Isaac was young and successful as a street hustler. He had also gained a notorious reputation for handling his business; but he was no fool. He knew that one day, someone smarter, faster, and more notorious than he would come along. That would be the day he would be required to pay for all his transgressions. This certainty had caused him to yearn for a son since he clipped his first hustler in the back alleys of Chicago.

He knew with certainty that one day he would lay in the spot he'd left many victims. In Isaac's mind, even if an executioner's bullet did take him out of the game, he would live on—through his son.

"I want him more than you know, Nina. And you and my son will live with me. I don't want to be a part-time father. I want to be here—not like how my scum of a father was."

"I don't even know who my father is," Nina said. "I don't think my mother ever knew either. Maybe that's why she

gave me up for adoption, so she wouldn't have to keep looking into my face and not know."

Isaac hugged her. "My son will never have to wonder
about who his father is, okay, Nina? Don't talk about leaving me anymore. We're together for life now."

Nina broke free from Isaac's grasp and asked, "Are you
going to stop cheating on me?"

"Nina, I don't want nobody but you. I've told you that
time and time again."

"Tell Valerie, and tell Cynda."

"There are things about my business that you don't understand. Valerie and Cynda work for me from time to time.
But, you're the one I'm living with, so that ought to tell you
something."

"So you're not going to get rid of them?"

"No," Isaac answered point blank. "And, I'm not letting
you go either. So, you might as well unpack your bags and
adjust to life with me."

Three of Isaac's crack houses got robbed within four
weeks of him dismissing Leonard. Workers at two of Isaac's
houses swore that Leonard was the man behind the mask.
The take had been a little over a hundred thousand from all
three houses and Isaac was fuming. He had two houses that
still hadn't been hit and it was Isaac's bet that Leonard was
stupid enough to go after them also. So, he armed his last
two houses with enough men and ammunition to guard
Fort Knox; and he waited.

He was at home in bed with Valerie when he got the call.
Nina had left him, and Isaac had been trying to take his
mind off that when Leonard started robbing him. Needless
to say, Isaac was not a happy man.

He went to his location on Blueberry Drive and saw the
outwitted gunman tied to a chair with his mask still on.

Isaac had told his workers not to take the gunman's mask off; just tie him up and then call. His instructions had been followed, and Isaac was happy about that. He didn't need anyone knowing who was truly behind that mask; that way, they wouldn't be able to say for sure that Isaac must have murdered the guy because he was the last one with him.

"You all did good," Isaac told them as he leaned next to the gunman and said, "Don't say a word. I'm going to have you out of here in a second, okay?"

The burglar nodded.

Isaac loosed him from the chair and then retied his arms behind his back and walked him out of the house and placed him in the back seat of his car. Isaac sped off and, after about a minute, he heard the burglar say, "Thanks, man. I thought those guys were going to kill me."

Isaac was silent.

"Did you see their faces when you walked me out of there? You spoiled their fun." The burglar laughed.

Isaac's heart sank as he thought of the first time he'd heard that laugh. They had only been thirteen; both sentenced to two years in juvee, and nowhere to go once they were released.

They were in the lunch line and Leonard nudged him as Mark Spellman, a fourteen year old convicted murderer, tripped over his own big feet, fell and bumped his head on the concrete floor. "That's gotta hurt," Leonard had said as he doubled over laughing.

Mark was so embarrassed that he got off the floor, grabbed Leonard by the collar and swung on him. But something made Isaac grab Mark's fist before it connected with Leonard's face.

Isaac pushed Mark and told him to back off.

They were both over thirty now, and Isaac had run out of memories; run out of excuses for his friend's bad behavior. He couldn't even hear the laughter anymore. He drove to a wooded area on the outside of town and turned off his car.

Isaac pulled Leonard out of the back seat and walked him down a tree lined path.

"Where are you taking me?" Leonard asked.

"Where do you think I'm taking you?"

Leonard started squirming. He tried to pull away, but Isaac's grip was to strong. Leonard could do nothing but go where he was led. When they reached a spot that Isaac was comfortable with, he snatched off Leonard's mask, untied him and shoved him to the ground.

Leonard said, "I'm sorry, okay, man? Is that what you want to hear? I needed the money for my family."

Isaac pulled out his gun. "You don't take care of your family. Remember?"

Leonard was on his knees now. "Isaac, man, please don't do this." Isaac stood over him, gun in hand. "Come on, man. We been through too much together."

"Guess you should have thought about that before you kept stealing my money."

Leonard closed his eyes. Sweat ran down his forehead. His hands were shaking like a newborn crack baby. "You're my son's godfather. Come on, man. Lenny Jr. needs me."

Isaac thought about that for a second. Leonard hadn't been a true daddy to that boy a day in his life. But, Isaac was godfather to this man's son. He promised to look after the little tyke. And, that was serious business. "Tell me where my money is, and I'll put it in a trust fund for my godson."

"I spent it, man. I spent it." Leonard started crying. Seriously, he was crying like a little girl with a sprained ankle. He was always a punk.

"What could you have spent a hundred thousand dollars on in a month's time?"

Leonard wiped some of the sweat and tears off his face and bent his head and cried some more.

Isaac cold cocked him with the handle of the gun. "Stop all that crying!" Leonard may be a no good thief, but he and

Isaac had been friends. He could at least help this man go out with some dignity. "What did you do with my money?"

"I bought Tanya a house."

"You did what?" Isaac couldn't believe it. He just absolutely couldn't believe that he was godfather to the Lollypop Man's son. "You bought a house for Tanya, that trick who is right now, laid up with Keith in her new house?"

Leonard shook his head back and forth. "I didn't know, man. I thought she loved me."

"You had a girl that loved you, but you chose to be the Lollypop Man to one who's not even true." If Isaac kept this fool around, Lord knows how much of his hard earned grip would come up missing. "Good night, old friend. This is where we part company." Isaac squeezed the trigger and snuffed out a life-long friendship.

Chapter 28

Iona sat across from Diana in the prayer room. Her first instinct when she saw Diana at the altar was to lay into her. But, as they walked together toward the prayer room, Iona's mind drifted back to the prayer journey she'd gone through with her mother and how she felt after rededicating her life to the Lord. She didn't want to take that feeling away from Diana, but she needed to have something answered. "I'm not going to keep you long, Diana, I'm sure you have things to do."

Diana put her hand on Iona's shoulder and said, "Let's be straight with each other. I know that you don't like me. And, I understand. So, I don't want you to feel as if you have to be nice to me. Just go ahead and ask me whatever you want to know."

The calm and humble way Diana addressed her, made Iona realize that a change had taken place in Diana's life. She was not the same conniving woman Iona had once pegged her for. Iona began to feel comfortable with this woman.

"Diana, there's something I've wanted to know since you and Donavan were caught together."

Diana lowered her head.

Iona held up her hands. "I'm not trying to throw that in your face. My question is about the email my father received. Daddy thinks that Donavan emailed him, but I say that Donavan wouldn't have wanted my father to catch him in a position like that in a million years." She hesitated for a second, then asked, "Did you email my father from Donavan's computer?"

"Yes."

"Why did you do it?"

Diana tried to turn away, but Iona put her index finger on Diana's cheek and said, "Stay with me, Diana. I need to know why you did it."

Diana's eyes watered as she admitted, "I was being black mailed." She wiped her eyes. "Before I worked at the church, I had been arrested for prostitution."

"Let me guess," Iona said, "The prosecutor offered you a deal if you did a number on my brother?" Diana nodded. "And, would that prosecutor happen to be JL Tyler?"

Diana nodded again.

"My God." Iona stood up and paced. "What does that man have against my family?"

"I honestly don't know, Iona. But, he was adamant about bringing your father down and was willing to use me, Donavan, and anyone else to do the trick. He thought that once Pastor Walker caught us together, he would fire me, and protect his son. But, it didn't happen that way. I told him that I would not file suit against a man that had done nothing wrong, he never called me again."

"Why is he so fixated on my family?" Iona wanted to know, and was determined to get to the bottom of this before nightfall. She thanked Diana for her honesty and headed toward the door.

Diana said, "Wait. There's something else."

Iona turned and looked at Diana quizzically.

"Someone was emailing me, giving me details about Donavan; like what he was interested in and the things he didn't like in a woman. I would receive those emails about once a week. Always in the evening, and always on a Thursday."

"How do you know JL wasn't sending the information to you?"

"Because I mentioned it to him once, and he didn't have a clue what I was talking about."

But why? Why? And who? Iona continued asking herself as she walked from the prayer room to her father's office.

Isaac, Nina, Keith, Cynda and Johnny were in Isaac's office. Johnny was behind Isaac's desk working the computer. Isaac and Keith had just told Johnny about their past history with Leonard and the fact that Isaac now believes that Leonard's son was behind the killings. "After each murder, the killer sent me an email that reminded me that I don't like thieves."

"You do know that I am a police officer," Johnny reminded Isaac. "And that I have to investigate any crime you tell me about, right?"

"Johnny, I'm not afraid of paying for the things I've done in the past, but I would be a coward to allow one more person to get killed if I didn't try to stop this. And I think I know why these things are happening."

"Okay, now the way I understand this situation is, this guy named Leonard got murdered, and now you think his son is after you because he believes you did it?" Johnny asked.

Actually, Isaac had told Johnny that he had killed Leonard, but Johnny was having selective hearing so Isaac played along and asked, "Do you think you can find out what happened to Lenny Jr.? Leonard was never much of a father to him, but you never know. Lenny might still feel that it's his duty to avenge his father."

"Like I told you Pastor, you can google anybody. What was his last name?" Johnny asked.

Isaac looked to Keith for help. Keith said, "As I remember it, Clara's last name was Jones. And you and I both know that Leonard didn't sign the birth certificate, so I'm sure the boy's name would have been Jones also."

Johnny typed a few words into the search engine. *Leonard Jones, Dayton, Ohio, Criminal record.* Several entries appeared. He clicked on the one that said Criminal Records, then typed in Lenny's name, city and state. There were about seventy-five criminals with the name Leonard Jones, but only one with a relative named Clara Jones. Johnny clicked on that entry and Isaac's expression became very somber.

"I never even tried to help him," Isaac said as he viewed robbery, armed robbery and kidnapping convictions. One after the next.

Iona opened the door to her father's office and saw her mother and Keith seated on the couch. Nina was in front of the open refrigerator grabbing bottles of juice and water. Her father was standing behind his desk, in conference with the traitor, the deceiver—Johnny the heartbreaker.

"What are you doing in here?" Iona demanded as she closed the door behind her.

"Hello, Iona," Johnny said as he turned his attention away from the computer. "Your father told me that you rededicated your life to God last week. Congratulations!" he said the words in such a warm, jovial tone that Iona almost believed he was truly happy for her.

But, Iona came back to her right mind and decided his remark was meant to remind her that Christians were forgiving people. But, as far as Iona was concerned, forgiving ain't forgetting. She said, "Yes, it was a wonderful experience. You should try it."

"Iona!" Isaac admonished.

Iona's hand went to her hips. "Daddy, Johnny is trying to have you arrested for embezzling the church's money. He probably even believes you had something to do with those murders, and you let this Judas back into your office, and give him access to your computer after I warned you to have nothing to do with him."

"Johnny explained everything to me, Iona. We can trust him," Isaac said.

She folded her arms across her chest and said, "I'm your lawyer, and I say we can't trust him."

Johnny put his hands on her father's desk and raised himself into a standing position. "We can go over this later, Pastor. Just give me a call when—"

"No. I need to know about this now. Iona needs this information as well, so let's just all try to get along." He looked at his daughter and said, "Okay?"

Iona glared at her father, and stormed out of his office, slamming the door.

Nina ran after her. "Iona, wait." But, Iona started running so Nina yelled, "Your father remembered something from his past. He just wants Johnny to check into it."

Iona heard Nina, but couldn't bring herself to turn back around. The sanctuary was almost empty now, so she was able to get through without bumping into anyone. She went straight to her car and got behind the wheel, banged her head on the steering wheel and let the tears flow. She was angry with herself for acting such a fool, and she knew it was only because her heart still ached over being played by Johnny Dunford.

"Lord, please help me forget about Johnny." She didn't want her heart hung up on a deceiver.

There was a knock on the driver side window. Iona wiped the tears from her face and looked up.

"Roll down the window, Iona," Johnny said.

"No!" she screamed at him and then noticed that she hadn't locked the car door when she got in. She reached for the lock at the same time Johnny reached for the handle. She hit the button a millisecond after he opened the door. "Leave me and my family alone, Johnny. Haven't you done enough to us yet?"

He knelt down. As his knees touched the ground, he took her hand off the steering wheel and held it. "You were right about me, Iona. I did start seeing you just to get closer to your father; but it was part of my investigation."

She pulled her hand from his grasp.

He went on. "But you're wrong about the reason I stopped seeing you." He reached for her hand again, but Iona held it clenched. He gave up and told her, "I fell in love with you, Iona."

Another tear trickled down her face, but it was not from joy. She was angry. She put her key in the ignition and turned it as she hollered, "How dare you. You dumped me. Do you remember that? People in love don't just walk away."

Johnny lowered his head and told her, "I stopped seeing you because I was ashamed of what I had done. I didn't think I deserved you, but I didn't stop loving you."

"You don't know how to love and you don't deserve me, Johnny. You will never throw me out like useless thrash ever again." She sped off with her door open as Johnny tried to lean in closer to her. She stopped to close her door when she reached the end of the driveway. She looked back and saw Johnny falling head first to the ground. A smile creased her lips as she thought about the concussion he would suffer.

Iona put Johnny out of her mind. She looked into her

glove compartment to ensure that her Glock was in there, then she turned out of the parking lot and headed for interstate 75. She needed to get to the suburban side of town because she needed to visit a certain prosecutor.

When Iona first asked Isaac to go back into his past, he hadn't wanted to do it. There was too much hurt, too much destruction in his past. But, the Lord gently reminded him that he had left something undone in his past, Isaac eagerly excavated the crevices of his mind, trying to dig up the thing he'd left undone. And, he found it. And right now he stood in his back yard with his hands in his pockets, thinking about Leonard Michael Styles. His old friend's body had never been discovered. To this day, Isaac still didn't know what happened to Leonard's body.

Since Isaac knew that Leonard would never come home again, he went to see Clara right after he killed his friend. Lenny Jr. and Clara's daughter sat in the living room watching cartoons when Isaac walked in. Clara sat down on the couch and looked up at Isaac.

"Have you heard anything from Leonard?" Isaac asked her.

Clara didn't respond, she just stared at him.

Isaac pulled a bundle of money out of his jacket pocket and handed it to Clara. "Take this for you and the kids. I'll make sure you get more as you need it," Isaac assured her.

Clara didn't reach for the money. She continued to stare through Isaac as she told him, "I don't want anything from you."

Isaac started to protest, to tell her that she needed this money to take care of her children, but then he saw what had been in her eyes since he walked into her house—a knowing. Her eyes told him that she knew he killed Leonard. Isaac would bet his life on the fact that Clara knew that Leonard had been robbing Isaac's dope houses, and since Leonard had turned up missing for the past three weeks, she'd rightly deduced that Isaac did something about it. At the time, he'd felt justified in putting a bullet in Leonard. Now, as he looked at Clara, saw the grief and hatred in her eyes, he couldn't justify his actions; guilt assaulted the core of his being and he turned to walk away.

As Isaac opened the door to leave, Clara told her children, "Wave bye-bye to your father's best friend. We won't be seeing him ever again."

Isaac knew without a doubt that Clara had spoken prophetically. He would never again try to contact her. The guilt in his heart wouldn't allow it. He promised Leonard he would take care of his son, but in the end, he turned his back on his best friend's family. Until today, Isaac had no idea what had become of Clara and her children. But, he would soon know the full truth of what his neglect had done to his old friend's family. Johnny was running their names through the police database to see where they were now.

Isaac lowered his head and dug his hands deeper in his pockets. Keith stood in the backyard with Isaac as they both held onto old memories. "I hated Leonard for so many years," Keith admitted.

Isaac looked to his life long friend. "I knew you were angry with him, so was I, but I didn't think you hated him."

"I blamed him for my mother's death. If he hadn't put me on the spot about my mother stealing drugs from us, I wouldn't have put a stop to it, and maybe she wouldn't have died like that."

"It wasn't your fault, Keith."

Keith raised his hands. "Yeah, I know. But she was my mother. And I was selling the very dope she died trying to get. It just doesn't seem right now—looking back."

"Nothing we did back in the day was right. But we were a product of our environment," Isaac told his friend.

"Yeah," Keith agreed. "The best thing we can do now is

raise our children in a different environment and pray that they never run into a Spoony or Marko or any of the rest of them guys."

"People think they can get in the game, make a little money and then walk out with their souls in tact. But it never happens." Isaac extended his arms, pointing out toward the city. "How many people were taken away from this world because of drugs or hustling? Look at you and me. We may have survived the game, but we still got wounded."

Keith put his arm around Isaac's shoulder as they turned and headed back into the house. Their movements were slower than when they were young punks making their way in life. They were more cautious, more wise, and a great deal more humbled.

"Yeah, old friend, we certainly did get wounded," Keith agreed.

Chapter 29

"**O**pen up this door, JL!" Iona screamed as she pounded on the door. "You better get yourself to this door within five seconds or I'm going to let all your neighbors know what you've been up to."

The front door swung open and JL stood in front of Iona in a multi-colored bathrobe, boxers, a wife beater and knee high white socks. "What are you out here screaming about?" he demanded.

Iona glared at him. "Did you murder those three men?"

"What?"

She pushed him out of her way and stepped into his house and said, "Don't play innocent, JL. You wanted my father in jail, so when your two stoolies stopped rolling over for you, you got desperate and started killing people."

JL laughed. "That's very entertaining, Iona. Did you make that up all on your own?"

Iona had indeed given her life back to God, but she was still Daddy's little girl. She wasn't much of a talker when it came to situations like this. She much preferred to get the violence started and may the best rumbler win. She would put that on her prayer list tomorrow. Today, she lifted her arm and struck JL, then kicked up her legs, swung them around and connected with his gut. JL fell backward and Iona kicked him one more time. The kick sent him reeling back toward the floor.

"What's wrong with you?" JL screamed as Iona pulled a gun out of her pocket while standing over him.

"I don't like you," Iona said as she pointed the gun at him.

"Wait! Wait!" JL put his hands over his face. "Okay, what do you want? Just tell me?"

Yeah, her men always aimed to please—after she slapped them around a bit. "Did you kill those men and try to frame my father?"

"No! I'm a prosecutor. I put killers in prison," JL screamed at her.

"Then why are you coming after my father?"

"Because he's a murderer," JL spat the words at her.

"You've got the wrong man," Iona told him.

"Go ask him."

Iona stared at JL in the same way she looked at her clients when trying to determine guilt or innocence. At that moment, Iona knew that JL really did believe her father was a murderer. But, that didn't explain his behavior before the murders occurred. "Explain yourself," Iona told him.

"I have my reasons."

"Why did you force Diana to chase after Donavan and why did you encourage Johnny to spy on my father."

"Okay, maybe I wanted to catch him doing something wrong. But, I wasn't going to plant anything on him."

Iona hit JL in the head with the butt of the gun. She leaned in close to him. "Let me explain something to you. If you think my father is a murderer, you better know that I'm every bit Daddy's little girl and I will blow you away before I let you harm him. Now, tell me why you're doing this to my father."

JL's eyes bugged out as he looked into Iona's cold dark eyes. He started to sweat and then raised his hand. "I'll tell you—just move that gun away from me."

Iona took two steps back and lowered the gun. "Speak."

JL sat up and scooted against the wall while holding his head. "Your father destroyed my mother."

Iona opened her mouth ready to denounce JL for the liar he was, but then she remembered that many years ago, before her mother married Keith, Cynda had claimed that Isaac had ruined her life also.

"If my father did anything to your mother, it was over thirty years ago. Why are you after the man now, when he is nothing like the man he once was?"

"People don't change," JL assured her.

"That absurd statement proves that you don't know my father at all." She shoved the gun back in her pocket and headed for the door as she said, "I'm going to speak with Judge Landis tomorrow, and have you removed from prosecuting my father's case. And, if you say anything about my visit, I'll report you to the bar association for what you did to Diana."

"You're crazy! You're not going to get away with this."

"Shut up, JL. Just be glad I didn't shoot you," she said as she walked out the door.

"I got that information you asked me to check on, Detective."

"Hold on a second. Let me pull over," Johnny said while holding his cell phone to his ear. He pulled into the Church's Chicken parking lot on Gettysburg and pulled out a note pad and pen from his glove compartment. After Iona left him on the ground, Johnny was too humiliated to go back into the church. He called the precinct and asked Fred, the computer specialist, to run Clara and Lenny's names through their database as Isaac had asked him to do. Fred was always quick, so Johnny knew he wouldn't have long to wait before knowing something. "Okay, Fred. I'm ready. What did you find out?"

"Let's start with the woman, Clara Jones," Fred said. "She died in prison nineteen years ago. And the son, Leonard Michael Jones, died in a failed bank robbery five years ago."

If both of them are dead, then who is stalking Pastor Walker? Was Pastor Walker even thinking about this the right way? Maybe there was someone else out there with an ax to grind—there had to be.

"Thanks for getting back to me so quickly, Fred. I just wish you had some better news."

Johnny closed his flip phone, and left his parking spot to get back onto Gettysburg. Heading north, he passed the street his father's church was on. Then he thought about Iona saying that he didn't know how to love and got angry. Maybe he'd know how to treat a woman right if his father had treated his mother the way she deserved. Even if the man didn't want anything to do with the woman he'd impregnated, how could he so easily forget that he had a son? Johnny turned his car around and drove to his father's church. He was tired of being on the outside looking in. So this time he got out of his car and sauntered up the walkway. He stood in front, looking at the massive wooden double doors. When he was a child, those doors had been so intimidating and heavy that he couldn't open them. His mother always had to open it for him.

But Johnny was a man now, capable of opening his own doors and solving his own problems. He pulled the door open and headed for his father's office. Service had ended more than an hour ago, but the old man always stayed long after everyone else had gone. Lord only knows what he was doing. Maybe he was trying to make another baby that he wouldn't do a thing for.

Johnny knocked on the office door and heard, "Come in."

He opened the door. His father was standing in front of the big picture window in his office. It faced the parking lot. He was looking down as if in a trance. He didn't turn around to see who had walked into his office. All he said was, "Hello, son."

Iona got back in her car, put the gun into her glove compartment and headed back to her father's house. Her mind was racing trying to figure out what was going on. Her father was a man after God's own heart just like King David had been. But, just as King David's life had been turned upside down by sins he committed earlier in life, so too was Isaac Walker's.

Iona was trying to put everything together, but nothing was making sense. What did she know? Her father had done something to JL's mother, and JL wanted him to pay for it. But, he said he wasn't willing to frame Isaac. He preferred to wait until he had something on him, because JL didn't believe that people could change.

If JL was telling the truth, there had to be someone else out there with an ax to grind over something Isaac Walker had done to them. Iona was convinced that whatever it was, it was a past offense. Since she came to stay with Isaac and Nina, the only Isaac Iona had ever known was the one who lived to minister and help bring wayward souls to the kingdom.

Half way home, Iona checked her voice mail. Vivian and Neil had left messages. Neil's message said that he hadn't located Larry Harris yet, but he knew who had bailed Larry out of jail a couple weeks ago. Iona deleted Vivian's message before listening to it so she could hurry up and call Neil back.

She tried Neil three times and didn't get an answer. Iona left him a message and then dialed Vivian. She hadn't talked to Vivian since she left town last week and was feeling a little guilty about not checking on her.

When Vivian answered, Iona asked, "Hey, girl, how are you doing?"

"I'm okay. I was calling to check on your mom. How is she doing?" Vivian asked.

"It was touch and go there for a minute, but she's actually on the road to recovery now. God is good."

"That's what they tell me."

"Hey," Iona said. "I'm only going to be in town tonight, I'm heading back out tomorrow so why don't you come hang out with me at my dad's house."

"I really don't feel like going anywhere tonight. I just moved back into my apartment, but I'm still not comfortable here."

"Ah, hon, I hate to hear that." Iona had a thought. "Why don't I come hang out with you for a little while?"

Chapter 30

Johnny closed the door and walked into Bishop Thomas Tewiliger's office. It wasn't a huge space; just enough room for a desk, chair, credenza and file cabinet. There was no couch or fridge that held bottles of water and juice for guest. Just this small room with a man standing at the window, looking down toward the parking lot.

"Have a seat, son," Bishop Tewiliger told him.

There was that word again, 'son'. He'd never heard those words when he was a child and needed so desperately to have this man call him son. It would have been nice if his father had stood in his pulpit and announced to the congregation, "I have a son and he attends this church." Bishop Tewiliger had seven whole years to announce to the congregation that his son was a member of his church. After his mother took her life, Johnny would have been so grateful if his father would have come to the hearing the day he was made a ward of the court and announced, "He is my son, I'll take him home." But, he hadn't been a son to Tewiliger then, and he certainly wasn't going to stand for the man calling him son now.

"My name is Johnny," he said, then put his hand on the chair in front of his father's desk, refusing to sit like an obedient dog. "Call me Johnny."

Still looking out the window, Tewiliger said, "I've watched you from this window on so many occasions. You looked so lost as you sat out there in your car just staring at this building. I wanted to go to you, hug you and make amends for what I did to you and your mother."

Johnny felt a cold wetness stream down his face. He wiped the unwanted tears away as he said, "I came in here today to let you know that I discovered that I am no better than you. A woman loved me, and I deceived her too. All my life I blamed you for what happened to my mother. I said that I would never be like you, but now I see that you and I are cut from the same cloth. We don't deserve to be loved by a dog, let alone a good woman."

Tewiliger turned to face Johnny. His eyes were hollow and full of pain as if he had paid a lifetime for the sins he'd committed. "If you've wronged some woman, please go to her, son. Make it right. If something happens to her, you won't be able to live with yourself."

"Looks like you're doing okay."

"No, son. You don't want to end up like me. Even though I rejected you and your mother, I still lost my wife, and I'm about to lose this church. The deacons are having a board meeting tomorrow to have me thrown out."

Johnny wished he could muster enough sympathy to feel sorry for his father, but he didn't have it in him, not just yet. He turned away from Tewiliger hoping that this meeting had been enough and that he would never need to see this man again in life. That's when he noticed the eight by eleven inch framed photo on Tewiliger's credenza. Actually, there were several photos on the credenza, but the one that caught his eye was of a woman that he was acquainted with. He pointed at the picture and asked, "How do you know her?"

Tewiliger walked over to the credenza and picked up the frame. There was a sad expression on his face as he said, "She's my wife's niece. She used to attend church here."

"I didn't think she was into spirituality."

"She tried," Tewiliger said, "But after her mother and brother died, she had so much hatred in her heart that she couldn't stay with the Lord."

In a way, Johnny could understand that. When his mother died and his father didn't come for him, he no longer wanted anything to do with God either. Then he met Pastor Isaac Walker. Thinking of Pastor Walker got his mind back on the right track. He asked Tewiliger, "Did you say that her mother and brother are dead?"

Tewiliger nodded.

"Do you know how they died?" Johnny asked.

"Her mother had a drug problem, so she was in and out of prison because of it. The last time she went to prison, she died in a riot. Her brother died trying to burglarize a home."

Johnny opened the office door, and started walking out of the church without saying another word to his father. He opened his flip phone and called Isaac.

Isaac answered on the first ring and said, "Hey Johnny, did you find out where Lenny Jr. is?"

"Where are you, sir?" Johnny asked.

"I'm at home," Isaac answered then asked again, "Did you find out anything about Lenny?"

"There's no easy way to tell you this, so I'm just going to come right out with it." Johnny took a deep breath before saying, "Lenny got killed in a failed burglary attempt several years ago."

Isaac was silent for a moment then he said, "I should have stayed in contact with him. I just deserted the boy."

"Look, Pastor Walker, I've seen kids that grew up in the best of homes and still ended up in the prison system. Lenny made his choices. You had nothing to do with them."

"I know that in theory, but I still could have tried."

"You know what, Pastor? You've been there for a lot of people. I'm one of the people who benefited from the way you've unselfishly given of your time and wisdom. So the way I see it, you've more than made up for your neglect of Lenny."

"Thanks for saying that, Johnny."

"There's something else you should know. Clara, Lenny's mother is also dead. She was killed during a prison riot."

"You're kidding, right?" Isaac asked.

"I wish I was. But it's true. I'm sorry to have to deliver such news."

"You know what this means, Johnny? We're back to square one on trying to discover who murdered the people I ministered to."

"Not exactly," Johnny said and then asked, "Did Clara have a daughter?"

After a thoughtful pause Isaac answered, "Yes. Yes, she did. I forgot all about her, but I remember Leonard swearing up and down that the girl wasn't his. But, I'm sure she was his."

"What's the daughter's name?'

Isaac turned to Keith and asked. "Do you remember what Clara's little girl's name was?"

"No," Johnny heard Keith answer.

"Sorry, we don't remember," Isaac told Johnny.

"Okay, let me make a call and I'll get back with you." Johnny hung up with Isaac and dialed Iona's cell. It rang five times and then he heard Iona's voicemail. He hung up and tried again. Same thing happened. Johnny hung up and threw his cell in the passenger seat. "I'll go find out myself," he said as he started his car and backed away from his father's church.

Nina and Cynda were playing scrabble with Cynda's boys when Nina looked at her friend and said, "We need to pray."

Cynda looked at Nina for a moment, nodded and then turned to Keith Jr. "I need to go pray with Mrs. Nina, can you make sure the boys get their things together? We will be leaving for home when Iona and your father get back."

"All right," Keith Jr. said.

Cynda smiled at her son and patted his shoulder as she walked into the living room with Nina. "What's up," Cynda asked.

"I'm sensing danger. We need to pray for God's protective hand to be over our loved ones."

They bowed and began to pray.

As their prayers went up to heaven, Brogan, Davison, Arnoth, Miguel and a host of other angels unsheathed their swords and lifted them high. Brogan looked at the angels he was about to lead into battle and said, "The time is near. We will soon do battle with the enemy and his demonic forces."

Davison said, "We will fight; for all that is holy and all that is right!"

Chapter 31

Iona kicked her feet up on top of Vivian's coffee table as she leaned back on her friend's sofa sipping hot cocoa. She knew she couldn't stay long, because she wanted to get back to her father's house before Cynda and Keith got on the road. But, Vivian was still having a hard time dealing with her near brush with death, and Iona wanted to spend a little time with her friend. They were both laughing as Iona confessed her attack on JL.

"Man, I wish I had been there," Vivian said. "Did he really just lay on the floor like a spineless wimp?"

"Well, I did have a gun on him," Iona admitted.

Vivian roared with laughter. She held her stomach as she just about doubled over.

"It's not funny, Vivian, I could be disbarred for this."

Vivian waved her off. "Girl, quit worrying. You're not going to be disbarred. With all the stuff JL was doing, there's no way he'll turn you in."

Iona took another sip of her hot chocolate and said, "I can't believe I lost it like that."

"I can. Whenever anyone crosses you, you always lose it like that," Vivian said.

"Yes, but I rededicated my life to God last week, and I don't want to continue taking care of things the way I normally would. I want to do what pleases God, but I'm failing miserably."

Vivian rolled her eyes at the mention of doing what pleases God and then asked, "Okay, if you wanted to please God, then why did you act like that when you went over to JL's house?"

Iona looked at her friend and answered honestly. "I was just so angry, I don't know if you've ever been that angry. But when I had the gun to his head I think I could have killed him."

Vivian nodded and then said, "I've been that angry."

All of a sudden Iona was beginning to feel drowsy. She put her cup down and said, "I still don't understand why he thinks my father destroyed his mother."

"Your father didn't destroy JL's mother. She was a junkie long before Isaac met her."

Iona turned to Vivian. She was having a hard time focusing, and when she looked at her friend, there were three, no four people that looked just like Vivian floating all around the room. "Huh?" Iona asked.

"I said," Vivian began again, "JL's mother's name was Debbie. She was a junkie and she OD'd true enough, but your father had nothing to do with it."

"H-how d-do you know anything about it?"

"My mother told me," Vivian said.

"But your mother doesn't know my father. The first time they met was a couple weeks ago at the hospital," Iona reminded Vivian.

Vivian said, "That was my aunt. She adopted me when my mother went to prison."

Iona thought she heard Vivian say something about an

aunt and an adoption, but she couldn't be sure. She wasn't thinking straight. All she wanted to do was sleep. So she closed her eyes and let her head fall back against Vivian's sofa.

Johnny was banging on Vivian's door when the apartment manager came out of his apartment and asked him to quiet down. Johnny flashed his badge and said, "I need you to open this door for me."

"You got a warrant?" the manager asked.

"No. It's an emergency. I just need to make sure that Vivian is okay."

"Ain't nobody in there," the manager told him. "They left about five minutes ago."

Johnny grabbed the man by the shoulders and demanded, "Who did Vivian leave with?"

"That lawyer friend of hers." The man scratched his head trying to pull out a name.

Johnny said, "Iona Walker?"

"Yeah that's her. Prettiest lawyer I've ever seen. But she sure can't hold her liquor."

"What are you talking about?" Johnny asked, practically shaking the man.

"She was real wobbly as they left; had to lean on Vivian. Then Vivian laid her in the back seat of her car and drove her home."

"They took Iona's car?"

"That's what I said."

"Thanks, man." Johnny let him go and ran to his car. He put out an APB on an off white Lexus and gave the dispatcher Iona's license plate number, then hung up and called Pastor Walker. When Isaac picked up he asked, "Are you still at home?"

"Yeah," Isaac said. "What's up?"

"Were those emails about the victims sent to your home email address or your church email address?"

Isaac told him, "They were sent to me at church, why?"

No time to mix words. Johnny jumped into his car, started the ignition and said, "I think Iona has been kidnapped. Can you meet me at the church so we can see if another email has been sent to you?"

"What?"

"Sir, I know this is upsetting, but can you meet me at the church?"

"I can access the church email from my home computer. I'll go check it right now," Isaac told him.

"Great, I'm on my way, sir," Johnny said then hung up the phone and sped up the street.

He would not let this happen. Iona would not die without knowing how much he truly cared about her. He would not end up an old man with haunted, hollow eyes like his father. Iona would live and he would make amends for how he had deceived her. But the more he thought about it, Johnny wondered if he had deceived Iona or himself. Were the words of love and adoration he spoke to her true, and he had just been too dumb and blind to know it? "I'm coming, Iona. This is not over," he promised as his speed increased.

He made it to Isaac's house in ten minutes flat. Yeah, he had to turn on the siren in his unmarked car. This was an emergency situation, and he didn't care who had a problem with it. He pulled into the driveway of Isaac's house and jumped out of the car. "Did you find a note on your email?" Johnny asked Isaac the moment the door was opened to him.

"Nothing," Isaac told him.

"It's Vivian, Pastor. Iona's secretary was Lenny's sister and she blames you for what happened to Leonard, her mother and her brother."

Isaac closed his eyes and then said, "And now she wants to destroy me?"

Johnny nodded. "She's got Iona, Pastor. I just left her

place, and the manager verified that Iona left with her, but he thought Iona was drunk—I think Vivian might have drugged her with something."

Isaac pulled at the hair on top of his head as he let out a war cry that vibrated against every wall in his large house. "Not my baby, Lord! Not my baby!"

Nina ran into the room. "What's wrong?" She watched her husband go into meltdown. Isaac couldn't answer her as he fell on the ground and continued moaning out to the Lord. Nina looked to Johnny as Cynda joined her in the foyer. "What did you tell him? What's wrong?"

Johnny looked at the two women who'd filled the role of mother in Iona's life. How could he tell them that a murderer had just kidnapped their child? He hoped they were as strong in the Lord as they appeared to be, because this wasn't going to be easy. "The person that murdered those three men and tried to frame Pastor Walker has just abducted Iona."

Cynda put her hand to her mouth as tears ran down her face.

Nina said, "Oh my God. Who? Do you know who took her?"

Keith came into the foyer with their bags, "What are you screaming about? Are you that upset about us leaving?" Keith jokingly asked Isaac.

"Put the bags down, baby. We're not going anywhere," Cynda told him.

Keith's eyes took in the tears on his wife's face, Isaac stretched out on the floor calling out to God. Keith turned to Johnny and asked, "What's going on here?"

"Iona's secretary is Leonard and Clara's daughter," Johnny began.

"The one Leonard always said didn't belong to him?" Keith asked.

"I don't know whether she belonged to him or not. But, I believe she is the person responsible for the recent murders that are being pinned on Pastor Walker, and she just kidnapped Iona."

"What? Ah, don't say that," Keith said with his hands on his head.

Nina took action. She told the group, "We need to pray. We need to get God in on this before we go doing anything on our own." She looked at Keith and pointed at Isaac. "Bring him into the prayer room and let's all go before God."

There was a lot of moaning and groaning going on in the prayer room. Everyone in the room was devastated by this last turn of the hand. They called out to God and prayed that He would guide them, point them in the right direction, and show them how to bring Iona home safely.

When they were finished praying, Isaac wiped the tears from his eyes, and went into his home office right across from the prayer room and checked his email. The same email address that had appeared in his inbox after Vinny and Dwight were murdered was once again in his inbox. The subject line simply read, "Iona."

Nina pointed at it and jumped up and down. "There! That email is about Iona."

Isaac clicked on the email and read it with his prayer warriors standing behind him.

Isaac,

Do you now understand how it feels to have something stolen from you? Because that's what you did to me. You, who could not tolerate a thief, stole from me when you took my father from my mother and left me and my brother with a broken woman.

You can run from your sins, but one day they will come back to bite you—today is your day. I will now take from you, just as you took from me. That is, unless you are willing to trade your life for Iona's.

If you are that brave, then meet me at the spot where you last saw Leonard Styles. You won't miss it. There is a big X in the spot where you left his body. Be there at 6:00 p.m. to take Iona's place, or you can pick her body up from that spot one minute later. Think I'm playing with you? Be late and see.

Nina backed away from the computer. Her hand was against her mouth as she cried out, "No!"

Isaac got up and held his wife. "I have to do this, baby," he said against her ear.

"I know," she said through tears.

Isaac released her and rubbed her growing belly. "Iona is coming back home alive, and I will too, Nina. I won't leave you alone to raise our baby."

She nodded but said nothing.

Isaac walked out of the room, grabbed his coat and headed toward the door. Keith and Johnny grabbed their coats and said, "I'm coming."

Cynda gently touched Keith's face and said, "Go get my baby."

He nodded.

Nina told the group, "Don't worry, we will be here praying." She and Cynda clasped hands and held onto the faith that is able to move mountains. "God will come through for us." Nina placed a call to Louise Jordan, the intercessory prayer warrior at the church. She told her the situation and asked her to begin calling the saints to get a prayer chain going. Then she and Cynda went back into the prayer room.

Chapter 32

Even though her head was pounding when she woke, Iona noticed two things right away. Her hands were tied tightly in front of her, and her legs were criss-crossed and bound together at her ankles. Actually, she noticed three things; Larry the contract killer was standing over her pointing a gun at her head. Iona tried to think. Where was she? Some place cold and dirty and full of trees. This lunatic had her outside in the woods in snowy March weather.

How did she get here with him? And where had she been? *Vivian*, Iona thought. She had been at Vivian's house. She frantically looked around, searching for any sight of her friend. Larry noticed and asked, "What are you looking for? A way out? There is none."

"What did you do with Vivian?" Her voice raised. "I swear, if you hurt her I'll kill you. Do you hear me? You will regret what you did."

Larry laughed.

"What's so funny?" Iona demanded to know.

"You," he told her as he pointed to the ropes that held

her bound. "You're all bound up, and you still act like you're Rambo or somebody."

"Where is she, Larry? Please tell me you didn't harm Vivian."

"Why would I harm her? She's the one who paid me to kill you."

Disbelief crossed Iona's face. "You're a liar. I knew you were behind all this mess. Only a sick, twisted person like you would murder people you don't even know just to pin it on my father."

Larry kicked her in the chest. "Shut your mouth. When I need you to speak, I'll let you know."

The pain of his kick went through Iona's body like the blade of a fisherman cutting through his bounty. She wanted to hold her chest but her hands were bound.

"Keep your smart mouth shut and you'll just get this bullet in your head when it's time. Say something else out the way to me and I'll torture you before I kill you."

Iona was breathing hard. Inhale-exhale, trying to relieve the pain in her chest. Finally she said, "I just want to know where Vivian is."

"Here I am, Iona," Vivian said as she walked up behind her.

Iona swiveled around on the ground, getting more dirt on her pants and shirt, but she didn't care. She just needed to make sure her friend was all right. "Thank God," she said when she first caught sight of Vivian. But then she noticed the gun in her friend's hand and wondered aloud, "You did this to me?"

"Of course I did this to you. I bailed Larry here out of jail, and put him on my payroll. And, before you get all teary about our friendship, I did give you fair warning."

"What are you talking about?" Iona asked, confused by her friend's bazaar behavior and that weird psychotic look in her eyes.

"Are you going to tell me that you don't remember me telling you that you couldn't trust your own strength to save you from an attacker? That you weren't as invincible as you think you are."

Iona remembered the conversation a little differently. Vivian had come back to work on a Thursday after just getting attacked on Tuesday—Iona told her to go back home, and Vivian claimed to be afraid of being at home.

"I watched the news last night, Iona. So, I know that Clarence is dead. All night long I kept imagining that psycho sneaking into my apartment and finishing the job. I had to get out of there." Vivian had told her.

"You're a martial arts expert, Vivian. If someone breaks into your house, break his arm."

Pure terror swept across Vivian's face at the mention of someone breaking in on her. "That's just it, Iona. I know how to defend myself, but this guy was still able to sneak in my house and knock me out. Things like that just make you realize that you're not invincible after all."

"You weren't pretending," Iona said as the idea struck her. "You really were hurt. My father prayed for you—I saw the whole thing with my own eyes."

"Yeah, I handed Larry my inhaler and he hit me much harder than I had instructed before he left the house to go kill Donavan."

Iona blinked once and then again. Her voice caught in her throat as she asked, "You murdered my brother?"

"Naw, Larry here can hit a girl and knock her unconscious, but he claims some supernatural being scared him off of Donavan. Do you believe that mess?" Vivian asked with a sneer.

Yes, Iona did believe it. Her family always talked of how angels helped God's people in their time of need. She looked to heaven, hoping that the Lord could see that she was in need.

"Didn't I tell you that all that martial arts stuff wouldn't be able to help you? Didn't I tell you?" Vivian cackled.

"Why are you doing this? We were friends," Iona said.

"We were never friends, Iona. Get that straight here and now. I pretended to be your friend, just to keep tabs on your family."

Another deceiver, Iona thought then asked, "But why?"

"Your father pretended to be my father's friend. Then he murdered him."

"You're a liar!" Iona spat.

"My father's name was Leonard Styles. He was your father's best friend, and co-conspirator in the drug game. My father ended up using more drugs than he was selling, and he even robbed a few of Isaac's dope houses. So, your wonderful father decided to murder his best friend."

Now Joey McDaniels made sense to Iona. She remembered how her father's eyes lit up, when that particular hustler gave his life to Christ. Joey committed the same crimes as this Leonard had. And, all these years later, Joey must be her father's atonement for Leonard, the one he didn't help.

"But, my father saved your life," Iona reminded Vivian. "That's got to count for something."

"I'm going to kill him, Iona," Vivian told her with no remorse. "He's on his way out here to trade places with you. Isn't that sweet, that a father would give His life for his child?"

Iona knew of another man who gave his life for not just her, but the world. And, she was silently praying to Him now. Vivian thought she had taken all her strength away, when she bound her legs and arms. But, she allowed Iona to unleash another strength that Iona wanted so desperately to rule in her life. *Heavenly father, I'm leaning on your strong arm now. I need your help like never before.*

With all the prayer that was going on in the small city of Dayton, God loosed another platoon of angels to assist Brogan and his team. But, their victory was in no way secure. Satan increased his army of destroyers, and they were more than ready for the fight ahead.

Demons were on the highway, trying to cause other cars to run into Isaac, so he would not make it to his destination on time. Brogan sent a troop of angels, with swords drawn, to deal with those menacing spirits on the highway. He sent another troop to guard Isaac and Nina's house, and the other people that were taking part in the prayer chain. He wanted to ensure that no menacing spirits stopped those prayers from reaching heaven. Many humans weren't aware just how important their prayers are to the angels that fight battles for them. If a human stopped believing and gave up praying, an angel could very well be killed in the midst of battle.

There were a mountain load of demons in the woods on the outskirts of Dayton. That's where Brogan and the rest of his team headed.

Davison walked next to him as they entered the woods. He scrunched his nose and asked Brogan, "Do you smell that?"

Brogan nodded. "Death. It's all around us."

Jaundiced green eyes cast menacing glances from their spot on tree branches, as they watched the army of the Lord boldly walk into their encampment. One of the small monkey like imps flapped its black wings, as it flew from the trees into the heart of the woods to tell his leader what he had seen. It touched down behind gargoyles with knots on their tar-like bodies that were the size of rocks. Their beady eyes were close together as if they didn't possess a bridge to their small noses. The imp nudged his way through the demonic monsters. They were getting rowdy, raising their fists and swords and talking about crushing some heads and doing damage.

"Don't touch me, monkey-boy," one of the guerilla monsters said.

"I'm just trying to get to the general. I have something to tell him."

"What makes you think he wants to hear anything from a tiny imp like you?" Guerilla monster picked up the imp, and flung him toward the trees he came from. "Get back to your post."

The monkey-like imp flew away, and did not return. They would find out soon enough, that warrior angels were here to send them back to the abyss. The imp cackled with glee, as he perched back on the tree limb and positioned himself so he would have a good view of the slaughter.

Brogan looked at the sea of angels that had entered the encampment with him and said, "We came here together, I'm praying that each of us live to fight another day. So let's get in and get out while we still have prayer support." Brogan lifted his sword and the other angels did the same as he yelled, "For all that is holy and all that is right!"

And with that, the angels charged through the woods in search of their enemies.

Back in Dayton, a group of women had convened at Louise Jordan's house to pray. They were gung-ho when they first arrived, but an hour into the prayer, a few of the women wondered how long, how long. One of them flat out asked Louise, "Do you think we can stop praying now?"

The angel of the Lord stood behind Louise. He put his fingers on her temples and allowed her to hear from heaven. *My soldiers need your prayers, daughter.*

Louise turned to the group and told them, "We must continue."

Chapter 33

As Isaac took the exit he'd taken thirty years ago, and headed down the dark and lonely road toward the woods that he'd left Leonard's body in, he drifted back in time. There were no flecks of gray in his hair. He didn't have aches in his knees or back pain, and Leonard was in the back of his car tied up. As Isaac, Keith and Johnny stepped out of the car, Isaac felt as if he were making a guest appearance on *Cold Case* and that he was walking this path with Leonard by his side. He looked to his left, and saw Leonard, his old friend from juvee. Leonard's hands were tied and the ski mask he used for his burglaries was still on his face. Isaac wanted to help him; untie those ropes around his arms, take that ridiculous mask off his face and beg him to do the right thing. Get off drugs, get a straight job, and most of all, give his life to the Lord.

Isaac didn't do any of that. He gave Leonard chance after chance. Back then, Isaac felt that friendship only got you so far. Now, Leonard was in hell. Isaac ran his hand through his hair wishing he could go back. If he could, he would never have picked up a gun and would never have ended anyone's life. It hadn't been worth the life sentence of regret he earned with each murder he committed. God had indeed forgiven Isaac's sins, but Isaac had never forgiven himself for all the pain and destruction he'd dealt to the innocent and not so innocent.

"This must be the spot," Isaac said when he spotted the red X on the ground. He then glanced at his watch. It was five forty-five.

Johnny said, "We've got a few extra minutes, so I'm going to look around this place to see if I can find Iona."

Johnny walked off and Isaac and Keith stood looking at the huge X that had been spray painted in the ground. Isaac wondered how Vivian knew where to place the X. Leonard's body had never been found, so how would this girl know where he'd left the body?

Keith and Isaac looked at each other. They heard a rustling in the trees and just about jumped out of their skin. This wasn't the old days when they would have brought a gun to a gun fight. In the world they now lived, the only weapons they had were prayer and the Word of God; and they had to trust that their heavenly weapons would be enough to see them safely through.

"I really don't want to be here," Isaac said.

"Tell me about it," Keith responded as he looked around. "Feels evil out here; like something is watching us."

Brogan was the first to slice through the crowd of demons. His mighty sword gutted two demons at once. And then a mighty battle cry soared through the sea of angels that pierced the very core of heaven as the angels attacked.

The leader of the demons stalked toward Brogan and demanded. "Why are you here? What have we to do with you?"

"We are sent by the Lord. You will not prevail against the man of God," Brogan told him as he lifted his sword and positioned himself to fight.

"He dies today, Brogan, leader of the troop of angel weaklings."

Brogan raised an eyebrow.

"Yes, I know you, Brogan. You and Isaac brought many evil doers to the Lord, but it stops today," he said as he pulled out his sword, "because you will die today also, Brogan."

Davison swooped down on a group of demons. The surprise of seeing this eight foot warrior angel left the guerrilla monster-like demons in mouth dropping, slime oozing surprise. Davison wasted no time in slicing them from gullet to gut.

Miguel wasn't being shy about his either. In no time flat he backed three demons into a corner and dealt with them like he caught them stealing his angel wings.

Iona pulled at the ropes that were wrapped around her arms. They were so tight that she couldn't get her fingers between the ropes, and her arm in order to wiggle out of them. She closed her eyes and prayed, "Lord, please don't forget about me."

Vivian kicked her in the side. "That is so like you; Praying to God when you need Him, but not giving Him the time of day when you don't."

Iona didn't respond.

Vivian told Larry, "Go check to see if papa bear has come to get his daughter yet."

Larry left and Vivian sat down on a tree trunk next to Iona and asked, "How's your brother?"

Iona rolled her eyes and ignored the question.

"He called you at the office a couple weeks ago." Iona turned back to Vivian, interest in her eyes. Vivian picked at the dirt in her nails as she continued. "Yeah, but I let him know how ashamed of him you were for sleeping around when he was supposed to be a man of God."

"You're evil," Iona said, and then as pieces of the puzzle fell into place, Iona's eyes bore into her former friend. "It was you! You're the one that emailed Diana on Thursday evenings, giving her information on how to get at Donavan." If Iona's hands were free, she would have hit her own self upside the head. "And, I was the one giving you the information after our kickboxing classes. All this time I thought you had a thing for Donavan; asking me all those questions. But, you were just setting him up. You were my best friend, Vivian. Doesn't that mean anything to you?"

"Oh boo hoo. If you weren't going to be dead, I would let you ask your father about best friends betraying one another. He'd have a humdinger of a story to tell you."

Larry came back with news. "Her father's down there, and he's got another man with him."

"I didn't tell him to bring anyone," Vivian said as she kicked Iona again. "Who do you think he has with him?"

Iona took a couple of deep breaths to combat the pain she felt from Vivian's vicious kicks to her stomach and chest. When she was able to speak she asked Larry, "Does the man look to be about my father's age or younger?"

"Your father's age for sure," Larry said.

A shadow of disappointment briefly crossed Iona's eyes as she said, "It's Keith, my father's best friend and my mother's husband."

"Oh yeah," Vivian said. "Good o' faithful Keith." Then Vivian snapped her fingers and taunted Iona, "I know you didn't expect Johnny to be with your father."

Iona said nothing, but her eyes gave her away.

"You did, didn't you? Poor stupid, Iona. You made such a fool of yourself over that man and he never even cared about you at all."

Iona turned away from them and began to pray silently again. Man may have disappointed her, but God was on her side. No one would ever convince her that God didn't truly love her and want the best for her.

Vivian stood up, and patted Iona on the head as she said to Larry, "You come with me since it's two of them."

Larry pointed at Iona. "You want me to put a bullet in her before we go?"

Vivian turned back to Iona. Tapped her finger against her lip and then said, "No. I think I'd like for her to see her father's dead body before she dies."

"I don't know, Vivian. I don't think that's such a good idea."

"Good thing I don't pay you to think. Now bring your muscles with me so we can go take care of the good pastor and his sidekick." She walked away from Iona as she and Larry walked through a jungle of trees to get to the other side of the woods.

Johnny had been searching the wooded area for at least fifteen minutes. He looked at his watch and saw that it was exactly six p.m. He knew that time was running out for Iona. What was he going to do if Iona died up here? How would he go on? He had to find her; had to let her know how much he loved her. *Lord, don't let her die without knowing that I truly do care.* Over and over Johnny kept praying those exact same words to the Lord as he walked through a band of trees.

A branch that he hadn't touched swung back and swiped him across the face. Johnny looked up and could almost swear that he saw wind and motion colliding together in the air like a tornado. He picked up speed and began to run, hoping to get as far away from the trees before the whirlwind touched down and uprooted one of the trees. In high school, Johnny had been a track star. He'd jumped hurdles and ran all the way to the finish line to collect his first place trophy more times than he could count, so he easily jumped over the thick branches that lined the ground of this wooded area. He turned back to see the whirlwind touch down in the midst of the woods. One of the huge oaks broke and tumbled his way.

The opening was right in front of Johnny. There was a little bit of valley land just past the trees, there was also a brook where water had probably flowed through at one time. It was now dried up and could be called nothing more than a ditch. Johnny ran through the valley and flung himself into the ditch. He turned his face toward the wooded area and saw three trees tumble down. One of them was at the edge, between the trees and the valley. As it tumbled, Johnny saw that it was headed straight for the ditch he'd just thrown himself into. He opened his mouth and prayed, "Sweet Jesus, help me! Don't let me die without finding Iona."

Chapter 34

Back in Dayton, Nina and Cynda were still in the prayer room with heads bowed calling out to the Lord. Keith Jr., Joseph and Caleb walked in. The spokesman of the group, Keith Jr. said, "The boys and I have been talking, and we think we're old enough to pray."

Cynda lifted her arms so she could embrace her oldest son. Keith Jr. fell into her arms. Joseph and Caleb went to Nina and hugged her.

Tears fell from Keith Jr.'s eyes as he said, "We know Iona is in trouble, Mama. She's our sister and we want to pray for her too."

"Grab a spot and bow down before the Lord," Cynda said. "We can use all the prayers we can get on this one."

"And make sure you pray for Keith, Isaac and Johnny's safe return while you are praying for Iona. We don't want to lose anyone," Nina told them.

As the boys bowed down to pray, Nina thought of how many times she had come into her prayer room and had not asked Iona or Donavan if they wanted to join her. She knew now that that had been a mistake. She touched her belly and swore silently that she would share the experience of prayer with the child that was growing inside of her. But even as she was thinking on the baby growing inside her, something wondrous happened.

The front door opened. Nina got off her knees and ran down the stairs in time to see Donavan standing in the foyer putting the house key Nina had given him back in his pocket. She silently thanked God for answering another of her prayers as she ran down the stairs and hugged her son.

"Donavan, I'm so glad you came back home. Some lunatic kidnapped Iona. Your father went to get her back. I need you to help us pray for your father and Iona." Nina knew in her heart that Donavan coming home at this particular moment was a sign from God that her other loved ones would soon be walking through that door also.

Donavan pulled back. "God doesn't want to hear from me, Mama. Maybe I can help by calling the saints at our church and asking them to pray."

"We've already done that, Donavan," Nina told him and then she gently put her hand on his shoulder and asked, "Donavan, do you believe that sex outside of marriage is wrong?"

He didn't put up a fight on the issue, he simply nodded.

"Do you believe that what you did with Diana was wrong?"

He nodded again, but this time the nod was accompanied by tears of regret.

"Then son, why don't you ask God for forgiveness and then help us pray through this storm?"

It sounded so simple when his mom put it that way, and Donavan did just that. He joined his mother and Cynda and her children in the prayer room, got on his knees, asked God for forgiveness and then began to bombard heaven on his father's and Iona's behalf. Because the saints of God may fall down, but with God's grace and mercy, they can always get back up again.

"Where is my daughter?" Isaac asked when Vivian and Mr. Clean came into view.

Vivian walked toward Isaac with the gun swinging from her right hand. She had a self-satisfied smirk on her face as she continued to approach. Once they stood in front of one another and Larry had his gun trained on Isaac, Vivian said, "X marks the spot."

"Where's my daughter?" Isaac asked again.

Ignoring the question, Vivian said, "I knew you would be able to find it even without my artwork. It's not every day that you shoot your best friend, and leave him in the woods to die, is it, Pastor?"

Isaac mournfully looked at the spot then answered, "No, it isn't."

"You murdered my father, and never once thought of what it would do to me and my brother," Vivian screamed.

Isaac continued looking at the red spot on the ground. She was right. He would have found this spot without her artwork. He left a piece of himself here all those years ago. In the first few years after he'd killed his friend, he had nightmares about what he did and sorely wished he could take it back.

Keith put his hands on Isaac's shoulder and whispered in his ear, "You've been forgiven, man. Remember that."

"Look at me!" Vivian screamed. Isaac was jolted from his shoulda, woulda, coulda wishes and dreams. As he brought his eyes back to Vivian she said, "You were my brother's godfather and yet you never even bothered to see how he was doing, and I sure didn't see you at my brother's funeral."

"I was wrong for that, I admit it," Isaac said. "But Iona has nothing to do with any of this. Please," he begged. "Release my daughter and do whatever you want to me."

"You didn't even ask how I knew the exact spot where you left my father," Vivian said.

Isaac looked down again, but he didn't ask.

Vivian told him, "My mother followed you out here. She watched you kill my father. You left his body for wild animals to tear it apart. But she buried him right in the spot you're standing on. She used to bring me and Lenny Jr. out here once a year. During that time she would retell the story of three friends."

Isaac couldn't take hearing anymore. He shouted at her, "Let my daughter go, Vivian!"

"Maybe I'll kill both of you," Vivian said.

Thinking and talking fast, Isaac said, "That wasn't our deal. Remember your email? You said if I came out here, you would take me in place of Iona. Surely you are a woman of your word. Come on, Vivian, give me some proof that my daughter is alive."

Vivian turned to Larry and said, "Go get her."

"What?" Larry said as he shook his head. "No, Vivian. This is a bad idea. Let's just do them and then go do his daughter."

"I hired you, remember? Go get her. I want Iona to watch as her precious father and stepfather die in front of her."

The limbs of the tree knocked the wind out of Johnny as it fell on top of him. He laid there unable to move, panting for air. As he wondered how he would get out from under the tree, a flash of blinding light appeared before him. Johnny put his arm in front of his eyes until the bright light subsided. When he uncovered his eyes, a man as tall as the trees stood in front of him. He wore a radiant white robe and had a bloody sword in his right hand. Golden wings flapped behind him. "What in the world?" Johnny said.

"Not of this world, my friend. I am of the army of the Lord." He sheathed his sword and said, "We don't have much time, so let me get this tree off of you and show you where they have hidden Iona."

The angel lifted the tree as though it were nothing more than a heavy bat a kid had left in the yard and tossed it to the other side of the valley. Johnny was still laying in the ditch unable to move because of the pain in his chest. The angel reached down and laid his hand on Johnny's chest.

Hot lava soared through Johnny's body. He convulsed and lifted his hand to stop the pain the angel was causing, and all at once, the pain was gone. Johnny felt no pain, and was able to get out of the ditch on his own. "Thanks," Johnny said as he touched his chest and found that the pain from the tree falling on him was indeed gone.

"Hurry," the angel told him as he cut through the valley and around another wooded area. They walked up rock laden steps and then he saw Iona stretched out on the ground, hands and feet bound; mouth wide, singing a praise song to God.

Johnny had heard nothing so wonderful as Iona singing, "You are great, You do miracles so great."

He ran to her side and held her tight. "Thank You, God. Thank you." He leaned over and kissed her and then said, "I didn't know if I would ever see you alive again. Oh, baby, I'm so sorry for everything I've done."

Tears streamed down Iona's face as she looked to heaven and then back to Johnny. "God sent help?"

"Yes, baby. I am the answer to more than one of your prayers. You need to have faith in me. Okay? I love you, Iona. Do you hear me? I love you."

Iona nodded, but then said, "Untie me. They will be back soon."

Johnny kissed her one more time, and Iona kissed him right back. He untied the ropes around her arm. Iona rubbed the reddened parts of her arm where the rope had dug deep, then Johnny released the ropes from her ankles. "Can you stand up?" he asked.

"Give me a minute," Iona said as she continued to rub her arms and ankles.

"Let me do that," Johnny said, then he began massages her ankles while Iona worked on her arms.

Iona said, "Okay, that's enough. We have to find my father. Vivian is going to kill him."

As Johnny gave Iona his hand to help her lift up, Larry came around the bend.

"Not so fast," Larry said as he aimed his gun at Iona.

Johnny jumped in front of her just as Larry pulled the trigger. The bullet hit Johnny in the chest, ricocheted off him and struck Larry in the upper shoulder. Larry dropped his gun and clung to his shoulder screaming, "You shot me, you shot me."

Johnny dived on top of Larry while he was whining about his shoulder wound and knocked him to the ground. He then flipped him over, took the cuffs out of his back pocket and cuffed him.

Iona was too stunned to move. She screamed, "Johnny are you shot? Are you shot?"

Johnny lifted himself off the ground and brought Larry up with him. There was no blood or wound of any kind on Johnny, but there was a great deal of blood drizzling down Larry's right shoulder.

"I'm okay," Johnny told her.

"B-but how could that be? I saw him shoot you."

Johnny smiled and looked off toward someplace in the air

as far as Iona could see. "I'll tell you all about it later." He pointed to Larry's discarded gun and said, "Pick that up and let's go get your father."

Iona bent down, grabbed Larry's gun, and then followed Johnny and Larry down the rock laden steps and through a sea of trees to get to her father.

"You are right about me, Vivian. I failed you and your brother. I didn't think about the consequences of my actions or who I might hurt with my acts of vengeance. I know now that killing a man doesn't solve my problems; it creates a whole heap of problems for the families that are left behind. I ask you to forgive me, Vivian. I'm truly sorry for what I did to you."

Vivian listened to Isaac as he admitted his guilt. This was the moment she'd waited on for so long. But he was taking the joy of this moment away from her. She had imagined that he would admit what he'd done and then grovel and beg for his life; not ask for her forgiveness. "Don't ask that of me," she said. "Just as I will never be forgiven for the people I murdered, you will never be forgiven for what you did either."

"That's not true, Vivian," Keith said quickly. "God forgives sins. Allow God to show you mercy and to wrap you in His arms of grace. He loves you more than you know."

"Shut-up," Vivian said.

Vivian's refusal to forgive him and Keith's words about mercy and God's arm of grace brought thoughts of Donavan to Isaac's mind. His son was wrong in sleeping with the church secretary, but now Isaac wished he hadn't treated his son so harshly when he dismissed him. He wished he hadn't just closed Donavan's door and walked away after finding him in such a compromising position. If he had it to do over again, he would have walked into Donavan's living room and wrapped his arms around his son and showed him mercy. He would have remembered the words of Jesus when the Pharisees brought the woman caught in adultery to him. "He who is without sin, cast the first stone.

Give me another chance Lord. Don't let me die out here in this desolate place and bring my son home so I can make this right, Isaac prayed.

"Don't preach to me." Vivian continued screaming at Keith. "God doesn't care one bit about me. He has never cared!"

"He does care, Vivian," Iona said as she, Johnny and a handcuffed Larry approached them.

Vivian swung around to face them. "Don't come any closer." She swung back to Isaac. "I'll shoot him. I swear I will."

Iona trained Larry's gun on Vivian with her right hand, but she let the other drop to her side. As it did, she felt the bulge in her pocket. Then she remembered that ugly, hateful rock she'd been carrying around in her pocket. She'd carried it around with her since the prayer journey. It was the rock of unforgiveness she carried for the person who skillfully framed her father for murder. She now had a name for the rock. Iona lowered Larry's gun and then reached into her pocket and pulled the rock out. She looked at the rock in her hand, and found it distasteful. She had carried it everywhere with her, but she no longer wanted this heavy burden. She let go of the anger and bitterness she felt toward the woman she'd called her best friend. As the rock fell to the ground, Iona said, "I forgive you, Vivian."

"How can you say that?" Vivian screamed. "I'm about to kill your father."

Tears streamed down Iona's face as she looked from her father to Vivian. She told her, "I still forgive you. I refuse to live my life bitter and hateful because of what others have done to me. I choose to forgive you—I choose to be free."

Vivian began to cry and the hand that held the gun

shook. "I don't know how to forgive, Iona. I never had a family like yours to teach me things like that."

"Let God teach you," Johnny said as he walked toward her. "I didn't have a mother or father around either. I had hatred in my heart just like you, but once I gave my life to the Lord, I began to see things differently."

Vivian turned to Johnny and said weakly, "Stop, don't come any closer."

"I want to help you, Vivian. I know how it feels to blame someone for everything that went wrong in your life. But you can't live like that," Johnny said.

"How else am I supposed to live then?" Vivian asked Johnny.

"You're supposed to live through God. Let Him heal the wounds others have caused." Johnny reached out his hand as he moved closer. "Give me the gun, Vivian. Don't take another life. Your vengeance will become your own torture—you'll never forget it."

"That's the problem," Vivian said as she turned back to Isaac with tears in her eyes. "I can't forget, and I'll never forgive." She then lifted the gun and shot Isaac.

Brogan was in the midst of the woods slaying the enemy's soldiers when he sensed that Isaac's life was in jeopardy. He gutted the warrior demon in front of him and attempted to get out of the fray of the battle when another hulking, menacing figure stepped to him.

"Where do you think you're going?" The monstrous demon asked as he unsheathed his battle worn sword. "You ain't leaving here alive and neither is that preacher man."

"Pray, saints, pray," Brogan mumbled as he let his sword do his boasting.

Isaac grabbed his chest and fell on the X that marked the spot where he'd left Leonard all those years ago.

"No!" Iona screamed as she watched her father fall. Keith knelt down beside Isaac and began to cry out to God. Iona took off running toward him.

Vivian told Iona, "Stop or I'll shoot you too."

Johnny raised his gun. "Drop it, or I will kill you. I mean it, Vivian." Johnny's gun was pointed at Vivian's back.

"Shoot me in the back, policeman. See how that goes down on your record," Vivian said as she raised her gun in Iona's direction.

"I'll do it, Vivian. Don't be foolish." Johnny didn't care if he lost his job for shooting a woman in the back. He could live with that; he just couldn't live without Iona.

Iona made it to Isaac and fell down on her knees in front of him. Suddenly Vivian started shooting wildly in Isaac's direction.

Brogan slashed his last demon and sent him back to the darkness he came from, then sprinted toward his charge. Isaac was on the ground with a bullet in his chest by the time Brogan got there. A woman was standing some yards away shooting at his charge. Brogan moved like the matrix in front of Isaac, Iona and Keith and blocked the bullets that Vivian sent their way.

Johnny's mind was frantic with fear. All he could imagine was that Vivian had not only shot Isaac again but was about to put a bullet in Iona and Keith. He trained his gun on Vivian and pulled the trigger. Vivian kept shooting, so he shot her again, and again until she was down and the gun fell out of her lifeless hand.

"Daddy, Daddy! Can you hear me, Daddy?" Iona cried over her father's body.

Isaac's eyes fluttered as he tried to focus on his daughter. "Tell Nina that I'm s-sorry. Tell her, I really wanted to be there to see the baby."

Tears flowed like a river from Iona's eyes. Her father had

always been so strong, always been such a force in her life, but he now looked frail and weak. She held him in her arms and cried out to God. "Help us, Lord. Don't let him die like this."

Keith was praying and sobbing. Johnny came over to them. Larry was still in cuffs and Johnny was pushing him forward. He told Larry to sit down and stay down as he bent down next to Isaac and said, "The ambulance is on the way. Hold on, Pastor."

Keith was applying pressure to Isaac's wound. "You gon' make it, man. Just hold on."

Isaac looked at Keith. Pain was etched on his face but his eyes filled with memories. "W-we made it through." He coughed and then continued, "D-didn't we, old friend?"

"You're no friend of mine," Keith said through sobs. "We're brothers; always been family."

Isaac nodded with a smile as he closed his eyes.

Iona shook him. "No, Daddy! Don't go to sleep. Wake up!"

Johnny pulled Iona in his arms. "Baby, it's going to be all right. Trust God on this one."

Iona turned to Johnny a look of helplessness was on her face. "He's giving up, Johnny."

"Then we need to pray," Johnny told her.

Pray, that's right. Iona had a thought and then said to Johnny, "Let me see your cell phone." She hurriedly dialed Nina's number. When Donavan answered she started crying again. "Donavan, oh thank God that you're home."

Isaac's breathing was heavy, but he managed to open his eyes and turn toward Iona.

Iona said, "Dad's been shot, Donavan. Tell everyone to pray like never before."

Isaac lifted a weary hand toward the cell phone. "Let me speak . . . need to say sorry."

Iona hung up the phone and turned determined eyes on

her father. "No! I'm not letting you say sorry or goodbye to Donavan, Daddy. I'm also not giving Nina-Mama any messages from a dead man. So if you want them to know how you feel; then live. Do you hear me, preacher man? Live!"

The paramedics raced down the dirt and gravel path in the midst of the wooded area. Iona's screams guided them in the right direction as she continued to command Isaac to "live." Johnny pulled Iona away from Isaac so the paramedics could put him in the ambulance.

Iona rode in the ambulance with her father. She prayed the entire drive. When they reached the hospital, Iona thought of Nina and Cynda and knew that they were praying with her. Iona finally realized how they had learned to pray such long prayers. They had developed a relationship with God, because they continuously turned to Him in their times of trouble.

As Iona stepped out of the ambulance her hair was tousled, her silk blouse was covered in blood and tears stained her beautiful face. She looked nothing like her normal self-assured persona. She was weak. Cynda had shown Iona that the prayer of faith could save the sick. So, with her last ounce of strength, before she passed out and was put on a hospital bed and taken into the emergency room for observation, Iona prayed and believed that God would raise her father up and see her family safely through this storm.

Epilogue

The church was packed. It was the fifth Sunday of the month of November. It was also baby dedication Sunday. Nina sat in the front row of the sanctuary with her new born baby. She smiled down at her precious gift from the Lord and exhaled. It was a long journey, but she now held the promise of God in her hand. Nina had named him Isaac. Yes, he was a junior, but the name meant so much more than that. For Sarah and Abraham had named their long awaited gift from God Isaac, so it seemed fitting that since God had blessed Nina, a barren woman just like Sarah, that she should give her baby a name that meant laughter as well, because he had brought a special joy to her life that she hadn't known was possible at her age.

The day Iona had been kidnapped and her husband had been shot, it was the baby that was growing inside of her that brought her peace as she prayed for them. Nina was thankful that God heard her prayers and had brought both Iona and Isaac back home. Isaac had come home after getting a bullet pulled out of him and having a lengthy hospital stay, but she wasn't complaining. Her man was alive and that's all that mattered.

Isaac stood behind the pulpit and smiled down at Nina. He then turned his attention back to the congregation and said, "This is a very special fifth Sunday for me. One of the things I love to do as pastor of this church is dedicate babies back to the Lord. And there have been a lot of babies needing to be dedicated in this church." He looked at Nina again with pure joy etched on his face. "But today I get to dedicate my own baby to the Lord. At one time, I didn't think I would live to see this day. But God was merciful to me."

He stretched out his hand toward Nina and said, "Can you bring our son to the altar so that we can give him back to the Lord?"

Nina stood at the altar before her husband. Isaac Jr. was wearing all white, the traditional color for a christening. That was because, a baby dedication was like a christening, except instead of using water, the baby was anointed with a dab of oil on his or her forehead.

"Would the godparents please come and stand with us at this time?" Isaac asked.

Keith and Cynda stood and made their way down to the altar.

Nina turned and watched them walk toward her. It was during the weekend that Iona had been kidnapped, and she and Cynda spent the day in fervent prayer that Nina assured Cynda that she would live to become godmother to her unborn child. Cynda took the challenge, and as each month passed, she kept living. The doctors looked at her in wonder and amazement as she began to regain the weight cancer had eaten away. But Cynda had taken everything in stride. "Prayer changes things," she told her doctors when they couldn't find a trace of cancer in her body and couldn't explain what happened to it.

When Cynda reached Nina, she leaned close to her ear

and said, "I told you I would be at my godson's dedication, didn't I?"

With a broad smile Nina said, "Cynda, I've got a feeling that you'll be at his wedding, and then at the dedication service for his children as well."

"You better know it," Cynda agreed.

Isaac instructed the congregation to stand as he dedicated baby Isaac back to the Lord with the sprinkling of oil.

Donavan was seated in the pew directly behind Nina. Iona sat next to him. She had a monster size engagement ring on her finger and Johnny Dunford was on her other side. As the oil was sprinkled on her little brother's head, Iona left her seat and went to stand with her family. She stood between Nina and Cynda and put her arms around both of them. She kissed Cynda on the cheek and then turned to Nina and said, "I'm so glad Daddy is here to see this."

"God is good all the time, my sweet Baby Girl. Remember that always, okay?" Nina lovingly told Iona.

Brogan, Davison, Arnoth and Miguel stood in the back of the church unseen by human eye, but very much a part of the service. They had fought a good fight the day Isaac and Iona's lives were threatened by the evil one. The two Walker warriors had laid down their carnal weapons and wholly depended on God to fight their battle. They had prayed and believed, even when they couldn't see God working on their behalf; and that is why the angels still stood guard over their charges right now. The prayers of the saints allowed them to live to fight another day.

The four angels unsheathed their swords, lifted them high in the air and said in unison, "For all that is holy, and all that is right!"

A Note to my Readers

When I started *Through The Storm* I wanted the book to be fast paced and suspenseful. Then an unexpected thing happened. I attended a Prayer Journey at my church and I knew that I had to share that experience with my readers. When I arrived at my church for this journey, I didn't realize that I had unforgiveness in my heart. I decided to be honest with myself during every stage of the journey—and yes, I had to put several rocks in my basket, but by the end of the journey, with the help of God, I was able to get rid of each rock. Hallelujah! When I left my church that day my plans for *Through The Storm* changed. I now wanted to get one pertinent thing across to my readers. PRAYER IS POWERFUL!

I truly believe that Christians (me included) get so caught up in our day to day problems, that we forget to pray about our situations. Instead, we rush in and try to fix our problems without even bothering to ask God for a solution. But, what if God is in heaven just waiting to send His angels to fight our battles, if only we would take the time to ask Him? It's a wonderful thought isn't it? I believe it's true. I believe that God wants to see us safely through our storms.

This entire book was built on James 5:15: *The prayer of faith shall save the sick, and the Lord shall raise him up; and if he have committed sins, they shall be forgiven him.*

I hope, if nothing else, *Through The Storm* encouraged you to pray about the things in life that concern you-because God is concerned about you and wants to raise you up.

Until the Next book,

Vanessa

Reader's Discussion Questions

1. Do you believe that angels exist and are assigned to God's people in order to protect us?

   Daniel 8:15-19   Psalm 34:7-8 Luke 22:43
   Hebrews 13:2   Revelations 5:8-11

2. Most of the characters in this book believe that prayer changes things. How important do you believe prayer is in our daily lives?

   I Samuel 12-22-23 Psalm 5:2   Psalm 55:17-19
   Luke 18:1-8   James 5:15-16 I Thessalonians 5:17

3. Iona didn't hide her flaws. She was in need of deliverance and didn't care who knew it. During the prayer journey, everything became much clearer and she was able to repent and rededicate her life to God. Are you in need of a prayer journey? Or better yet, why not design your own prayer journey at your church and invite others to attend. It is a life changing experience that you will never forget.

4. Isaac found joy in ministering to criminal minded individuals. This was actually the ministry that God had given him before the foundation of the world. Therefore, his ministry was birthed from his past. Is there anything in your past that currently fuels the ministry that God has given you?

5. Nina received an answer to a twenty year old prayer when she conceived another child? How about you? Is there something you've been praying for that hasn't

manifested yet? Do you still believe that God can answer that prayer?

6. Iona and Johnny's relationship began in deception. Would you forgive a man that deceived you if he had since turned his life over to God?

7. Donavan loved God but made a mistake when he fornicated with Diana. He then was so ashamed that he turned away from God instead of falling on his knees and asking for forgiveness. Have you ever been so ashamed that you tried to run away from the presence of God only to find that you couldn't run far enough to get away from God?

8. As a Christian, do you believe it is wrong to fornicate (sex before marriage)? Do you understand that the Bible speaks against fornication and to be Christ-like we are supposed to follow the lead of Jesus Christ?

    Romans 1:18-32   1 Corinthians 6:15-20

9. The Bible tells us that the prayer of faith will save the sick. When Cynda was diagnosed with a deadly illness, she was tenacious in her belief that God could heal her. Were you inspired by this character? Did Cynda make you believe that God could do the impossible if you just had a little bit of faith?

10. As you were reading *Through The Storm*, hopefully you could see how unhealthy unforgiveness can be. Therefore, take a moment to search your heart and determine if you need to forgive someone—do it and just let it go.